Tea
and Spices

Tea and Spices

an erotic novel

Nina Roy

CARROLL & GRAF PUBLISHERS, INC.
NEW YORK

Copyright © 2000 by Nina Roy

First Carroll & Graf edition 2000

Carroll & Graf Publishers, Inc.
19 West 21st Street
New York, NY 10010-6805

Library of Congress Cataloging-in-Publication Data is available.
ISBN: 0-7394-0830-5

Manufactured in the United States of America

prologue

The woman opened the tattered scrapbook. The pages, as thin and dry as autumn leaves, contrasted sharply with the photographs of fresh, succulent youth. The black-and-white photographs, some yellowing at the edges, depicted an array of characters who had formed the core of the woman's younger days. Not even the faded quality of the photos could lessen the healthy aura exuded by the subjects.

Men and women, dressed in the crisp suits and dresses of the British Raj, sat within sprawling bungalows, either smiling with the promise of their new positions or assuming a more regal stance. Indians often stood stoically in the background, bearing tea trays and bamboo fans. Some of the scenes were set in the outdoors—the varied plains of Uttar Pradesh, a man perched precariously atop an elephant, a cricket game held in green gardens amidst gazebos and potted flowers. A scenario intended to be a slice of England within the vast, incomprehensible land of India.

The woman smiled as she turned the pages. What life she had felt in those days, what zeal radiated in her veins. As far as she had been concerned, convention and propriety were rules made to be broken. And even though time had returned her to London, her desires continued to burn like a candle flame. Desires that had been kindled in the dust and scorching heat of India. She would not have changed her decisions for anything.

chapter one

India, 1925

Eight servants stood on the steps of the bungalow, lined up like a row of tin soldiers. From behind the protective glass window, Devora Hawthorne looked at them and realized that they were in her charge. She glanced at her husband, who sat beside her in the stifling interior of the car.

"Are they all ours?" she asked.

Gerald Hawthorne nodded. "Yes, darling, you'll have to learn how to address them. Some of them speak English, but the dishwashers and the *dhobis* all live in nearby villages. They know only the most rudimentary English phrases."

Devora sat back as the driver guided the car up the dusty road to the plant-filled driveway in front of the bungalow. A trickle of perspiration dripped between Devora's shoulder blades. She longed for a cool bath. She'd been warned of India's oppressive heat, but after what seemed like days of traveling, she also felt grimy and exhausted. She brushed dust off her dress, hoping that she looked authoritative and presentable for the servants. The last thing she wanted was to get started on the wrong foot with them.

The car jerked to a halt at the base of the steps. Gerald helped Devora descend from the vehicle. The flatness of Uttar Pradesh seemed to stretch around them endlessly, but a number of trees lined the area around the enclave of British bungalows, providing welcome relief from the sun. Three horses were tied to a post in the driveway, snorting and kicking up dust with their hooves.

Devora approached the servants, painfully conscious of eight pairs of eyes staring at her curiously. She tightened her grip on Gerald's hand. He had been in India long enough to attain some degree of comfort with customs and propriety, but everything was totally new to Devora. She felt both out of place and overwhelmed by the multitude of differences: the wide, dusty hills, the broken shacks by the sides of the road, the women balancing water pots on their heads, the cows and goats meandering the streets so freely. "Bizarre" was the word that came to the mind of a woman who had been picking rain-dampened English roses from her garden just last week.

Glad that her wide-brimmed hat concealed her face somewhat, Devora nodded in greeting as Gerald introduced each servant by name. Their names flew past like lilting, exotic music—Rohan, Kalindi, Sanjit. The one name Devora remembered was Rohan, the head servant. He was a tall man with a thicket of black hair and strong, sculpted features that appeared completely expressionless. He wore a crisp, white knee-length jacket and trousers with a wide black sash around his waist. He greeted Devora deferentially, murmuring the words, "Welcome, *memsahib*." Devora nodded in response, aware of an apprehensive feeling in the pit of her stomach.

Trying to ignore her feelings, she followed Gerald into the bungalow. Her unease slipped away like water off polished marble as she took in the surroundings. The bungalow was small, but imported English furniture decorated the rooms, along with framed watercolors on the walls and even a mahogany sideboard. Fans rotated slowly overhead, stirring the heavy air scented with Indian spices. Bamboo plants and flowerpots stood in strategic locations and gave the place an atmosphere of elegance. There was even a small grand piano near a doorway leading to the veranda. The windows all stood open, allowing for cooling cross-ventilation.

"Like it, darling?" Gerald asked, looking rather eager for her response.

Devora smiled and nodded. "I love it. It's just beautiful."

"It used to belong to the Calipore district's doctor, but he and his wife returned to England a few months ago. His wife did have a very English touch."

"And such a tasteful one."

"The Thompsons just down the road are having a garden party tomorrow night so that you can meet the neighbors," Gerald went on. "Mrs. Thompson is delighted to have another Englishwoman to show around. She's been here for nine years, so she'll take good care of you."

"Aren't you going to be around?" Devora asked.

"Of course, but I have to work, darling." Gerald leaned over and gave her a kiss on the cheek. "I can't always be around to entertain you. However, you'll find plenty to do, I'm sure. And when summer arrives, you can go with the other women up to Simla, where it's much cooler. All of the British officers' wives go there during the hot season."

Devora bit her bottom lip. She and Gerald had been married for more than a year, but he'd been in India for the second half of their married life. She had been hoping that her arrival here would mean spending more time with her husband. Ah, well, plenty of time to worry about that later.

"Do you think I could have a bath?" Devora asked. Her scalp was beginning to tighten with the approach of a headache. "I'm terribly hot."

"Of course. All you have to do is ring for one of the servants and they'll provide you with whatever you need." He picked up a silver bell and rang it.

Within seconds, Rohan appeared at the door. "Yes, *sahib*?"

His voice was deep and rich, calibrated by his melodic Indian accent. Devora looked at him for a moment, rather intrigued by the regal, self-possessed way he carried himself in spite of his status as a servant.

"Mrs. Hawthorne would like a bath, please."

"I'll have Kalindi draw one for her." Rohan turned and went to delegate his orders.

"We'll have some tea after you have your bath," Gerald told Devora. He sat down in one of the cushioned wicker chairs and propped his feet on a stool. "If there's anything the Indians know how to do correctly, it's making tea."

"Are they bringing my valises in?" Devora asked.

Gerald flicked open his cigarette case. "Yes, they've brought them round the back. The bedroom's just over there, and we also have one guest room."

"*Memsahib,* your bath is ready." Kalindi padded quietly into the room, her petite figure clad gracefully in a cotton sari. Her skin was the color of mocha, her large eyes as dark as a pool of ink. She gave Gerald a quick glance from beneath her eyelashes. "*Sahib,* you wish something?"

"Yes, go make us some tea."

Devora found the bathroom and closed the door behind her. She stripped off her clothes and placed them on a stool to be washed later. A cracked mirror hung above the sink, and Devora winced when she caught sight of her fatigued expression. *Nothing a bath and a nap won't cure,* she thought.

The instant she stepped into the cool water of the clawfooted bathtub, her limbs went weak with sheer pleasure. With a groan, she sank back against the side of the tub and closed her eyes, letting the water wash away the weariness and stress of being in such a foreign country.

Neither she nor Gerald had expected him to be posted to India so soon after their marriage, but they couldn't deny that it was a step forward in his career. They had agreed that he would get settled in India for six months and then apply for her to join him. In the letters he'd sent during those months, Gerald had said that he was settling well into his new life in India, finding it to be a complicated and often difficult country, but an intriguing one nonetheless. Even having been in the country for less than two days, Devora could well understand what he had meant.

She sighed and wriggled her bare toes in the water. The damp greenness of England seemed very far away, almost as if it were part of another lifetime. Closing her fingers around a thick bar of soap, Devora began scrubbing away the grime of travel, working up a rich lather as she stroked her hands over her abdomen and legs. The scent of sandalwood filled the air. She slid the soap underneath her breasts and arms until her skin shone a clean, pinkish hue.

A sudden knock at the door made her look up in surprise. "Who is it?"

"It's me, darling. Are you all right?"

"Yes, of course. I'm fine."

The doorknob turned. Gerald stuck his head in the bathroom, his eyes glinting as he took in the sight of Devora's submerged, naked body. Devora couldn't help blushing; after all, she and Gerald hadn't seen each other in six months. Before that, they'd only just started getting to know each other physically.

"Gerald, I'm awfully tired . . ."

"I know. Here, let me wash your hair." He stepped into the room, closing the door behind him.

Devora watched her husband as he scrounged around in a drawer for a hairbrush. She had been attracted to Gerald from the moment she first set eyes on him at a friend's dinner party. He wasn't particularly tall, but he had nice, broad shoulders and long legs. The Indian sun had streaked his blond hair with bleached highlights and colored his skin a deep tan. *He looks good,* Devora thought, *healthy and strong.*

She leaned against the side of the tub again as Gerald moved the stool behind her. He removed the pins from her hair, then began brushing the dust away with long, sweeping strokes. Devora murmured a sound of approval, her body reacting instinctively to the once-familiar touch of her husband's hands. The hairbrush tugged gently at her scalp like a bristly, delicious massage.

"Mmm, I've missed you," Devora said.

"Me too, darling." Gerald picked up a small pitcher and poured water over Devora's hair before lathering soap into the light-brown strands. His fingers worked firmly at her head, easing away the remnants of Devora's headache. "You must be careful when I'm not here, though. Don't walk about in your dressing gown or anything revealing, and above all don't tell the servants anything that you don't want repeated. Indian women are notorious gossips."

A smile played around Devora's lips as she rubbed her head against Gerald's massaging fingers. "So are British women."

"Devora, I'm serious."

"I know. I'll be careful."

"And you can always go to the Thompsons' if you have any trouble."

"What kind of trouble could I possibly have?"

"Oh, you know. If the servants become disobedient or if you suspect them of stealing. It might take some time before they get used to taking orders from you."

"Well, I'll just have to be extremely authoritative then."

"Yes, stand your ground with them. If you show them who's boss, they'll obey you."

Devora frowned. "Really, Gerald. They're not dogs."

"Trust me, Devora. I know Indians much better than you do."

Devora was in no mood to argue, so she merely gave another little moan of pleasure as Gerald rinsed her hair. Soapy water trickled in rivulets over her body. Then, Gerald's hands slipped down to the back of her neck, rubbing the tight tendons until they became pliable under his touch. Slowly, his stroking hands moved over her shoulders and down to her small breasts. He cupped them in his palms, flicking his thumbs over her rigid nipples.

Devora let her eyes drift closed. She hadn't been touched by a man since Gerald left for India, although that wasn't to say that she hadn't had any opportunities. She had even considered being unfaithful, but something always stopped her in the end.

Probably the stiff, British propriety that had been instilled in her since childhood. Thank heavens she might have the opportunity to scrape some of that away in India and let her natural inclinations spill forth.

Gerald continued massaging her breasts, creating a most delicious river of sensations through her body. He smoothed the crevice underneath the pale globes before his hands slid lower, over the slick, wet surface of her belly. His finger dipped into the indentation of her navel and through the soaked curls of her mons. Devora parted her lips to draw in a breath of air.

"Spread them, darling," Gerald whispered, his tongue lightly teasing the shell of her ear.

Her heart thudding, Devora spread her legs to allow Gerald free access to her swelling sex. Her blood surged when he pushed his forefinger into the moist valley of her labia, coating his finger with the viscous fluids of her arousal. His breathing rasped hot against her ear as he began to slide his finger up and down the crevices and into the tight hole. Devora gasped, curling her hand around the edge of the tub. Gerald thrust his finger back and forth as if foreshadowing a far more intimate kind of intercourse. His thumb circled her clit, urging it out from beneath its protective hood. Devora whimpered, abandoning herself to the sensations of cool, refreshing water and Gerald's hands on her body. Dust and fatigue became subsumed by arousal, flowing through her veins with increasing force. Gerald's left hand continued fondling her breasts and teasing the hard peaks while his right hand worked steadily at her cunt.

Devora had been left to her own devices for so long that the feeling of someone else touching her affected her like an electric shock. A strong orgasm rippled through her body with such suddenness and strength that she cried out in pleasure, trembling with a suffusion of vibrations. Gerald's fingers pressed hard on her clit and milked every last sensation from her body.

"Good?" he murmured, pressing a kiss against her neck.

"Oh, yes," Devora sighed. "Very good."

"I'm so glad you're here, darling. India is difficult to get used to at first, but I'm sure you'll love it in no time."

"I hope so."

"Finish your bath, then come and have some tea." Gerald stood and dried his hands on a towel. He dropped another kiss on her head before leaving.

Feeling sated and very loose, Devora rinsed the remaining lather off her body. She wrapped herself in a cotton robe and went into the bedroom. Her clothing and belongings had all been unpacked and neatly arranged in the chiffarobe and chest of drawers. *Not a bad way to live, having people do all the mundane chores for you,* Devora thought as she sat down at the dressing table and began to brush her hair. She might get very used to this kind of lifestyle.

After slipping into a very modest and concealing housecoat, she went into the sitting room. Kalindi was busy pouring tea, her movements both light and graceful. Devora didn't fail to notice how Gerald's gaze was fixed on the young woman, and she made a mental note to keep an eye on both of them.

Kalindi turned her lovely dark eyes on Devora. "Cream and sugar, *memsahib*?"

"Both, please." Devora sank down into a cushioned chair, then started at the sight of a small lizard scurrying along the wall. "Gerald, there's a lizard inside!"

He glanced up. "Yes, I know. They often find their way inside. You'll have to get used to them. The good thing about them is that they eat mosquitoes."

He waved his hand toward Rohan, who stood near the door. Devora was convinced that the servant was laughing at her as he picked up a whisk broom and shooed the lizard outside.

Kalindi handed Gerald and Devora cups of tea and plates with butter biscuits. Devora took a sip of the sweet tea.

"Quite good," she remarked.

"Yes, the Indians do make good tea," Gerald said. "When the hot season arrives, you'll be able to visit some of the tea plantations in the hill stations. They're rather interesting."

"Don't you go to the hill stations as well?" Devora asked.

"Not usually. I might be able to come and visit you, but like I said, I do have to work, darling."

"Yes, I know." Devora glanced toward the door, where Rohan had resumed his post after driving away the lizard. He reminded Devora of a statue, all stone and implacability.

"Does he go to the hill stations?" she asked, addressing the question to Gerald, but making it loud enough for Rohan to hear. She wondered what it would take to spark a reaction from him.

"Who, Rohan? No, he'll stay with me. One mustn't let the servants have too much freedom, you know." Gerald chewed on a biscuit thoughtfully. "Remind me to pick up some paints and paper for you the next time I'm in town," he said. "I imagine you'll want to do your little paintings here."

"Of course I will. I brought several sketch pads and pencils with me, but no paints." Devora had had a love of painting and drawing since childhood, although it remained a hobby rather than a serious craft. She was, however, looking forward to painting the hills and trees of India, not to mention the exotic people.

Her eyes went to Rohan again. She would dearly love to capture his strong, refined features on paper. And then he turned ever so slightly, catching her gaze with his, and the look in his eyes sent a shiver of fear right down her spine.

"What is she like?"

Kalindi turned from the window to look at the woman who lay sprawled, naked, on the cot in the small one-room apartment. Lota's body glistened with a light sheen of sweat as she languidly ran a comb through her long, dark hair. The hot, heavy air was redolent of sweat and coconut oil.

Kalindi lifted her shoulders in a shrug as she thought of the fair new mistress of the Hawthorne household. Devora Hawthorne had light brown hair and brown eyes fringed with thick lashes. She also had lovely skin, pure and succulent. "She's young and quite pretty," she replied in Hindi. "Very fair."

She stretched out on the cot next to Lota, looking down at her own brown arms. Her skin tone had always been the bane of her existence. She couldn't even call herself "wheat-colored" since her skin was darker than wheat. Her entire family worried about being able to find her a suitable husband, since men greatly preferred fair women.

Lota was fair, with tan skin the color of milky tea. She had voluptuous, rounded hips and large breasts that recalled ancient Indian sculptures of goddesses and nymphs. Kalindi loved touching her, loved cupping those full breasts in her hands and teasing the nipples to tight points. She reached out now and rubbed her finger around one of Lota's aerolae, watching the dark skin crinkle and compress. Lota murmured a low sound of pleasure, lifting her arms above her head so that her body curved in a graceful line.

"Is she nice?" Lota asked.

Kalindi shrugged again. "I suppose so. She's snooty like all the rest of them, but at least she doesn't seem nasty."

"What's she like with the *sahib?*"

"I don't think they've been married long," Kalindi replied. "I did see him go into the bathroom while she was bathing, so I assume that they're glad to be with each other physically again."

A little rush of jealousy went through her at the thought. The new *memsahib* was much prettier than Kalindi herself— there was no question about that. But that didn't mean that Kalindi had to like her.

"Hmm, I wonder what they do together in bed," Lota mused.

"The usual, I imagine," Kalindi said dryly.

"No, I mean I wonder if they do things that are strange and different."

"I doubt it," Kalindi said. "The *sahib* never did anything strange or different with me, although he did once want me to take him in the bum."

Lota gasped. "And did you?"

"No, it hurt too much. But he didn't try and force me."

"I wonder if he does that with *her*."

"I don't know." Nor did Kalindi really care, at least not when the air was thick with the scent of womanly lust.

She bent her head and pressed a kiss against Lota's shoulder, licking up a few salty droplets of perspiration. When she was with Lota, Kalindi didn't have to worry about men, what they wanted from her, or what they expected from her. All she had to do was sink into the fragrant, lush pleasure of the other woman. Their clandestine assignations in the late afternoons were like bright little jewels in the tedious mediocrity of their daily chores.

Kalindi slid her palm down the swell of Lota's belly, rubbing the soft skin until her fingers encountered the crisp hairs of Lota's mons. Dipping her fingers into the hot fissure between the other woman's legs, Kalindi thought of how erotic it was to make love to another woman. Pleasuring seemed only a matter of doing, as if they already knew everything there was to know about each other physically. Her heart began to pulse with the advent of need, warmth gathering in her sex. She adjusted her position so that she could ease herself between Lota's thighs. She gazed in rapture at the sight of the moist spread flower of Lota's vulva, loving the musky scent that rose from her arousal. Drops of moisture clung to the labia lips, begging to be swept up with the touch of a tongue.

Lota propped herself up on the pillows, her expression languid as she gazed at Kalindi. Kalindi knew how much Lota loved to watch herself being pleasured. She stroked her tongue over the crevices of Lota's sex and up to her swollen clitoris, her head filled with the scent and taste of the other woman.

"Oh!" Lota's hips bucked upward at the first touch of Kalindi's tongue. She cupped her full breasts in her hands, plucking at her nipples with long, tapered fingers. "Yesssss, like that . . . lick me just like that . . ."

Kalindi opened her mouth and drank fully of Lota's taste. The flavor of Lota's juices on the surface of her tongue was an aphrodisiac like no other. Squirming, Kalindi rubbed her own sex against the rough sheets of the cot, her bottom thrusting as she tried to ease the increasing pressure in her clit. She hooked her hands underneath Lota's rounded thighs, pushing her legs farther apart to open up the creamy slit of her vagina. With a moan, Kalindi thrust her tongue deep into the other woman's body and sucked up the overflowing honey. Thrusting a hand between her thighs, she began to frantically manipulate her own clitoris, giving a muffled cry when a web of vibrations shuddered through her body. Seconds later, Lota pushed her sex fully against Kalindi's face, screaming out her own pleasure. Kalindi's tongue worked industriously to lick up the copious fluids of Lota's sex.

She pulled herself up the length of Lota's body, allowing their sweat-slickened breasts to press together as she bestowed a long, wet kiss on the other woman. Lota drew on Kalindi's tongue to taste the flavor of her own nectar. With a sigh of pleasure, Kalindi sank down next to Lota, letting the heat of the afternoon cover them like a canopy.

"Are we still going to be able to do this with the new *memsahib* there?" Lota asked.

Kalindi nuzzled her face against Lota's damp shoulder. "I don't see why not. Particularly if she goes off for tea in the afternoons like they all do."

"Well, they never seem to care what we do in our personal lives as long as we carry out our duties," Lota pointed out.

"No. They never ask."

"They haven't asked you to be the *memsahib*'s maid, have they?" Lota asked.

"No, no one has said anything. I don't know if she wants one, but I'm sure that Rohan would have said something if that were the case."

"Did you ever tell the *sahib* that you and I were lovers?" Lota murmured.

Surprised, Kalindi shook her head. "No, of course not. I would never tell him that."

"Why? Do you think he would fire us?"

Kalindi chuckled. "No, I think he would ask to join in."

chapter two

"It's a pleasure to meet you." Devora shook hands with the major, a short, rather dumpy older man with a shock of gray hair and a bushy beard. Gerald had told her that Major Cuthbert had a penchant for collecting insects, and he peered at Devora now as if she were some sort of rare specimen.

"Gerald tells me you've just arrived in India," Major Cuthbert said. "You've still got that fair English complexion, haven't you?"

"I suppose I do." Devora crushed a yawn between her teeth and tried to focus on the major. She felt as if she were back attending one of her aunt's tea parties, a scenario in which she had to act as polite and demure as possible.

She glanced around the vast green lawn of the Thompsons' garden, which included both a Victorian gazebo and a porch swing. Men and women dressed in casual-but-elegant suits and dresses stood around with glasses of wine and martinis, acting as if they weren't in the middle of one of the most complex and exotic countries. Only the presence of Indians, both as servants and guests, served as a reminder of their colonial situation.

"Excuse me, Major, but I want to introduce Devora to some of the other women." Mrs. Thompson, a busty older woman with an air of total confidence about her, glided down from the steps of the bungalow to Devora's side. She bestowed a sweet smile upon the major general before grasping Devora's arm and hauling her away.

"So, how do you like our little district?" Mrs. Thompson asked.

"I think it's wonderful," Devora replied. "India, I mean."

"Yes, well, you'll get over that," Mrs. Thompson said with a chuckle. "Thank heavens we've been able to recreate a bit of England here. Have you been to our club yet? We have a number of cricket games there."

"No, not yet. I'm just starting to meet people."

"Well, I must warn you that you need to be careful of some of these women," Mrs. Thompson said in a conspiratorial tone. "For instance, Marcia Smithton is notorious for attempting to steal other women's husbands."

She nodded meaningfully toward an attractive, dark-haired woman sitting on the porch swing. "Be careful of her."

"I will." Devora's gaze traveled to several of the Indian men, many of whom were dressed in military uniforms made all the more intriguing by their turbans. "Who are the Indians you've invited here?"

"Oh, they often work with my husband or hold some office here in the state," Mrs. Thompson explained, waving her be-jeweled hand in the air. "We don't really associate with Indi-ans, but we occasionally like to stay on good terms with those of the upper-class. Politics, you know. Some of them report to the Maharaja, so we try and treat them well."

"The Maharaja?"

"Yes, he's the ruling prince of Varitsar, which is a small free state right next to this one. He lives in a palace there. Quite a luxurious place, if I do say so myself. He often hosts very lavish dinner parties. Bit of a show-off, I think. Trying to prove that he's as good, if not better, than the British."

"Is that the only socializing he does?" Devora asked.

"Yes, as far as I know. He's an odd figure." Mrs. Thomp-son's voice dropped to a whisper. "Rumor has it that his wife committed suicide last year because she couldn't stand to be subject to his strange desires."

A jolt of shock shuddered through Devora's body. She stared at Mrs. Thompson. "You're joking."

Mrs. Thompson pressed her lips together and shook her head. "I most certainly am not. I'm not surprised, though. Indian men have very hot blood. You must be careful of them, particularly the servants. There have been . . . shall we say, *incidents* with them."

Devora frowned. "What kind of incidents?"

"Sexual incidents," Mrs. Thompson hissed. "They get terribly excited around Englishwomen, and sometimes they simply can't restrain themselves. I think it must have something to do with all the spicy food they eat, not to mention all those erotic sculptures constantly influencing them. They're a very lascivious people."

Devora thought of the restrained, regal Rohan and had to bite her lip to keep from smiling. As far as she could tell, the man didn't have a lascivious bone in his body. In fact, she wasn't even certain he had any emotions whatsoever.

"I'll be careful," she assured Mrs. Thompson.

Nodding her head with satisfaction over having carried out her cautionary duties, Mrs. Thompson led Devora around and introduced her to several of the other women. The women looked the newest member of the community up and down, scrutinizing everything from her clothing to her fingernails before deciding that, as Gerald's wife, she would have to do.

"I'll leave you all to get acquainted," Mrs. Thompson trilled, wafting off in the direction of her bungalow.

Devora smiled at Adele and Louise, both of whom were wearing the latest fashionable clothing and fanning themselves. "So, how long have you been in India?"

Adele, a tall, elegant blonde, rolled her eyes dramatically. "Too long. Hideous place. Hot, with too many bugs."

"Don't listen to her," Louise told Devora. "India is a fascinating country, heat and bugs notwithstanding."

Devora decided that she liked Louise better than Adele. Louise had a mop of reddish curls and blue eyes that seemed touched with the slightest sense of anxiety. However, she also appeared to be much friendlier.

"So, what do you do for entertainment around here?" Devora asked.

"We have bridge parties every Thursday and sometimes we go on picnics on the weekend," Adele said. "Other than that, it's parties and keeping an eye on the servants."

"Are there any local sites?" Devora asked. "I do quite a bit of drawing and painting, so I would love to see some temples and sculptures."

Both Adele and Louise laughed suddenly. Devora looked from one to the other.

"What's the matter?"

"The most well-known local temples are in Khajuraho," Louise explained. Two spots of color bloomed on her cheeks. "They're extremely . . . um, sexual temples and sculptures."

"Oh." Devora was intrigued in spite of herself. "Have you been there?"

"Heavens no!" Adele said, her eyes widening in shock. "I hear the sculptures are just disgusting, what with women spread out all over the place and engaged in really filthy activities."

"Well, there must be a reason for that," Devora said. "The Indians can't have built such temples just for the fun of it."

"Of course not," Adele said. She took a dainty sip of white wine. "I'm sure it's for religious reasons or whatever, but you do have to wonder about a country that would put *that* kind of image on their religious structures. I mean, can you imagine a Christian church with sculptures of people fucking?"

"Oh, Adele, don't say such things," Louise muttered.

"I'm just pointing out how hideous it all is," Adele replied. "This country is so bloody uncivilized."

Devora didn't bother telling the two women that she herself would be very interested in seeing the Khajuraho temples. Instead, she murmured some polite words about seeing the women at one of their Bridge Thursdays. She went in search of Gerald, hoping that she could convince him to return home. She was still worn out from her travels, and she certainly wasn't in the mood for arguing about the merits of India. Particularly since she still had to discover them for herself.

She went into the Thompsons' bungalow to freshen up a little. Their place was much larger than Devora and Gerald's, complete with a dining room with a table big enough for at least eight people. Devora walked down a small hallway, stopping in her tracks at the sound of panting and grunting. A moment passed before she registered what, exactly, the noises sounded like. She couldn't help grinning. She told herself to turn around and walk back outside, but her voyeuristic instincts got the better of her. Silently, she stepped forward, peering around the corner. Her eyes widened at the sight before her. Mrs. Thompson, for all her decorum, was pushed up with her back against the wall and her legs wrapped around the thrusting hips of none other than Major Cuthbert. Mrs. Thompson's skirt was hiked clear up to her waist, giving Devora a view of her fleshy cunt and the thick, pistoning stalk of the major's penis.

Devora clamped a hand over her mouth, trying to prevent herself from bursting out laughing. The major's face was red with exertion, grunts issuing from his mouth in a steady stream as he thrust away to his heart's content. And to Mrs. Thompson's content, too, from the looks of things. Her eyes were closed, her entire body jerking rhythmically against the wall as she moaned in rapture.

So much for lascivious Indians, Devora thought, chuckling silently to herself as she moved away and left Mrs. Thompson and the major to their lusty copulations. She walked back outside and found Gerald talking to an Indian man with a thick black beard and a white turban.

"Ah, there you are, love." Gerald held out his hand solicitously to greet Devora. "Are you having a good time?"

"Yes, I've been enjoying myself. It looks as if others are enjoying themselves as well."

"This is Ram Banerjee from Calcutta," Gerald said. "He's here on business."

Devora exchanged pleasantries with the friendly man before she and Gerald said their good-byes and began walking back home.

"Have you heard of this prince of Varitsar?" Devora asked as they walked down the street lined with trees and bungalows. "Mrs. Thompson was telling me about him."

"Oh, yes, the Maharaja," Gerald said. "I met him once at a dinner party. Rather stoic fellow. Friendly, but a bit reserved."

Devora eyed her husband assessingly for a moment. "What about the Khajuraho temples?" she asked. "I've heard they're very interesting."

To her amusement, Gerald glanced away uncomfortably. "Some people have gone there out of curiosity, but I hear it's quite filthy. Not the sort of thing a British lady should see. Mrs. Thompson will know of some other temples that are far more suitable."

Devora thought back to just how unladylike Mrs. Thompson had been acting when the major was screwing her against the wall. She stifled a giggle.

"I'm sure she will."

"Did you meet some nice people?" Gerald asked. "I'd hate for you to get bored here, but the ladies always have some sort of activity going on."

"Oh yes, it looks as if I'll have plenty to do."

Rohan was waiting at the top of the bungalow steps for them, giving Devora cause to wonder what the man did when she and Gerald weren't around. She knew that the female servants took care of the cleaning and cooking, so heaven only knew how Rohan occupied his time. As they passed him in the doorway, Devora made the mistake of glancing at him again. He returned her gaze unflinchingly and without expression, but

Devora still couldn't prevent the shiver that rippled over her skin.

"I don't like him," she told Gerald after they had ensconced themselves in the privacy of their bedroom.

"Who?" Gerald tugged absently at his tie and went to pour himself a small glass of water from the decanter on the dresser.

Devora stripped off her dress and hung it in the chiffarobe. "Your servant. Rohan."

Gerald lifted his eyebrows. "Rohan? He's very loyal. No reason to dislike him at all."

"I don't know. He gives me funny looks."

"He's just not used to you being here yet," Gerald said. "Give him a chance."

"I'm not so sure I'll be comfortable with him in the house when you're gone," Devora said, sitting down at the dressing table to unpin and brush her hair.

"Darling, please don't be difficult about this. Rohan is a very decent sort of chap. He's been with me since I first arrived here."

"If you say so," Devora muttered.

"Now don't sulk about it." Gerald paused behind Devora and gazed at her reflection in the mirror. "I know it's an adjustment having servants about, but you'll get used to it. You're just still weary from traveling and socializing."

"Perhaps."

Gerald put his hands on her shoulders and massaged her muscles gently. "Come to bed. We can talk about this in the morning."

His hands moved down to caress her breasts through the fine fabric of her slip. Devora's body reacted instantly, her nipples hardening into stiff peaks against her husband's hands. She looked at the movement of his hands in the mirror, finding it highly erotic to watch him touching her. He rolled her nipples between his thumbs and forefingers, then pressed his groin against her back so that she could feel the stiffening bulge in his trousers. Rotating his hips slightly, he rubbed his pelvis against her spine in a sensual movement that sent a wave of pure warmth to Devora's lower body.

"Come to bed," Gerald repeated in a husky voice.

He moved away from her and stripped off his clothes to reveal his slender, muscular body. Devora looked at him in the mirror, admiring the lean lines of his muscles and the shaft of his cock projecting forth from the nest of curls. Gerald pushed aside the gauzy mosquito net that hung over the bed like a canopy.

Devora stood, letting her slip fall from her shoulders and onto the floor in a silken puddle. The way that Gerald was looking at her with such hunger heightened her own arousal tenfold. She went and placed her palms flat against his hairy chest, toying with the flat coins of his nipples, kindling the spark between them that had lain dormant for so long. Her blood began to pulse with fervor as Gerald lowered his head and pressed his lips against hers.

With a moan, Devora parted her lips to let him inside, loving the way his tongue stroked over the glossy surface of her teeth and licked the corners of her mouth. She grasped his penis in her hand as they sank down onto the bed, bodies sliding together with a desire that seemed intensified by their months apart. She almost felt as if she were exploring his body for the first time, discovering the small mole on his hip, the configuration of his muscles, the fuzzy sacs of his testicles.

"Ah, how good you feel . . ." Gerald stroked his tongue over Devora's neck, licking a little path of fire over her skin and to her breasts. He sucked on her nipples, biting down on them gently and tracing her dark areolae as his hand slid down her moist abdomen.

Devora parted her legs and allowed him to dip his fingers into the hot fissure between her thighs. Gerald's breath rasped heatedly against her breasts as he began to stroke the folds of her labia, drawing forth an abundance of juices in readiness for his penetration. Devora had almost forgotten how wonderful it felt to touch and be touched by a man, and she sank willingly into the myriad sensations evoked by their carnality. Gerald thrust his finger back and forth in her humid passage, then moved down to the tight ring of her anus. After lubricating it with her fluids, he probed gently at the untried aperture. Devora gasped, tensing at first, but then Gerald pushed his finger into her, and a wealth of sensations fluttered through her body with such force that she cried out in pleasure.

"Oh, God, Gerald, do it," she whimpered. "Fuck me now."

Grasping his cock, she urged him toward her. Her body throbbed with heat, her nerves tightening like rubber bands as her tension began to mount. She rubbed the head of his penis over her oiled labia and the nub of her clit, a movement that caused Gerald to groan low in his throat. Slowly, he slid into her, filling her channel with slow, lush ease. Devora clutched his buttocks and pulled him against her. She arched her back as he began pumping inside her, creating a slick, easy rhythm that burned in her blood.

"Oh . . . harder . . ." Devora dug her fingernails into Gerald's buttocks as his hips worked frantically.

Gerald bent over her, rasping his tongue over her breasts, licking at the swollen pink crests. He thrust into her once so hard and fast that Devora's body jerked in surprise and her eyes flew open rapturously. Gerald braced his hands on either side of her head as he began a firm, steady plundering of Devora's cunt. Devora fairly squealed her pleasure, her hips pumping upward to match his every stroke.

"Oh . . . Gerald . . . yes, like that," she panted.

Her hand slipped down to the damp curls between her legs, and she rubbed frantically at the swollen nub of her clitoris as her throat arched and her expression grew strained. For a second, her entire body hovered enticingly on the precipice of rapture, and a final thrust from Gerald sent her over the edge. A scream broke from Devora with unrestrained abandon when violent trembles wracked her body. As Devora was still convulsing, Gerald pulled out of her and grasped his penis again,

stroking the shaft rhythmically in his clenched fist before he
groaned hoarsely and spurted milky streams of seed onto Devora's pale mons.

"Oh, Christ." With a grunt, Gerald flopped down next to
Devora, his chest heaving. "God, Devora, you're incredible."

Devora smiled languidly, stroking a hand down her damp
body. Such uninhibitedness from a man who had fairly blushed
at the idea of erotic sculpture. Devora was beginning to have
a very clear idea of what kind of hypocrisy seethed underneath
the proper British veneer.

Gerald reached out and took Devora's robe from a chair on
which it was folded. "Put this on in case one of the servants
should happen to come in at night. We don't want to give them
any ideas."

Devora slipped into the robe. "I thought they already had
plenty of ideas of their own," she said. "According to some of
the women at the party, the Indians have very lascivious na-
tures."

"Well, I don't know about that, but this isn't the most civilized of countries," Gerald replied. "It's best to be on guard."

Devora rolled onto her side to look at her husband. She
stroked her palm down his chest and touched the decreasing
tumescence of his penis. "So, what have you done with yourself
these last six months?" she inquired.

"Worked, of course."

"I mean sexually."

"Devora, really."

Devora lifted herself onto one elbow and gazed down at him.
"I'm serious. Have you had a mistress?"

"I'm not going to discuss this with you."

"Was it that servant?" Devora persisted. "Kalindi?"

"Devora, for heaven's sake." Gerald glared at her and swung
his legs over the side of the bed as he reached for his dressing
gown. "I'm getting a drink."

He stalked out of the bedroom, closing the door behind him.
Devora rolled onto her back and stared up at the mosquito-net

canopy. She was surprised to realize that she didn't particularly care if Gerald had been unfaithful to her. Instead, she was somewhat intrigued by the idea of him and the Indian woman. She wondered what they must look like naked together, how Gerald's pale skin would contrast with Kalindi's darker tones. And she wondered what they would do together, if Kalindi really did have some sort of innate eroticism that spilled forth in hot displays of carnality. And where had they done it, right here on the bed? Devora ran her hand over the wrinkled sheets, still warm from her and Gerald's passion.

As she closed her eyes and began to drift into sleep, an image of her husband and the Indian woman appeared behind her eyelids. Limbs tangled together, moans emerging from their throats, sweat bathing their skin. A tendril of arousal uncurled in Devora's belly, spreading fingers through her loins. Furtively, she slipped her fingers through the damp curls of her mons and into the furrow of her sex. The vision of her husband and the servant unfolded rapidly, images of Gerald's thrusting hips, his cock sliding in and out of the woman's tawny vulva.

Devora gasped, pressing her fingertips hard against her clit as her arousal intensified. She worked the slippery button faster and harder as her mind swam with images of Gerald and Kalindi. With a cry, she thrust a finger into her slit as an orgasm rocked her body, shuddering through her like hundreds of little firecrackers. She sank back against the pillows and absorbed every last sensation.

Heavens, she thought, two intense orgasms within the span of an hour. Maybe there was truth in the statement that India brought out the carnal nature of a person. How utterly delicious.

chapter three

Gerald stepped out onto the veranda, filling his lungs with the humid, spicy air of India. He'd been thrilled to receive a posting here, knowing that it would not only further his career, but that the experience would simply appeal to his sense of adventure. And, of course, it didn't hurt having Devora with him now. Over the past six months, his physical needs had been well met by Kalindi, but he'd missed Devora's rather lusty nature. He just hoped she wouldn't make a habit of complaining about the servants. Or of pressing him about his extramarital affairs.

He turned at the sound of Rohan's soft footsteps and eyed the tall Indian. Whatever Devora's problem was with the man, Gerald was certain that it must be her imagination. Why, Rohan had barely spoken to Devora, let alone exhibited any cause for concern.

"*Sahib,* a messenger from the Maharaja's palace in Varitsar is here. He wants to know if you plan to attend the Maharaja's dinner party on Saturday evening."

"Oh yes, I'd forgotten about that. Yes, you might as well tell him that we'll be there. Devora will enjoy visiting a prince's palace."

Rohan hesitated.

"What?" Gerald asked.

"I don't believe the lady was invited."

Gerald frowned. "What are you talking about? Of course she was invited. She's my wife."

"Yes, but the invitation arrived a month ago, before she was even here," Rohan replied.

"Well, then, send a message that I'll be attending the dinner party with my wife," Gerald snapped. "Good God, the Maharaja wouldn't uninvite me because of that."

"Yes, *sahib*." With a slight, respectful bow, Rohan went back into the house to convey the message.

Gerald turned back toward the yard and caught sight of Kalindi coming up the narrow pathway that led to some of the servants' quarters. She had a water pot tucked underneath her arm, and even from a distance, Gerald could hear the soft tune she was humming.

She glanced up and saw him standing on the veranda, then smiled and approached him. "Good afternoon, *sahib*."

"Hello, Kalindi."

"Your wife is enjoying herself?"

"Yes, thank you. She admires India very much."

Kalindi paused at the bottom of the steps and looked up at him. She was quite an attractive young woman, the curves of her breasts and hips clearly evident beneath the folds of her sari. Gerald had vivid memories of sliding his hands and lips over those very curves.

"I am not seeing you in a few days," she said.

"I've been busy."

"I know. Perhaps you will come this evening?"

"No, I don't think so," Gerald replied, thinking that at least the girl had realized that any future liaisons wouldn't take place in Gerald's bedroom.

"Gerald?"

Gerald swore softly under his breath at the sound of Devora's voice. He turned and saw her step onto the veranda. She looked both cool and pretty in an off-white dress with a broad, floppy hat dangling from her fingers. In the week that she had been in India, a sprinkling of freckles had decorated her nose. They gave her a very charming look.

Devora's gaze went from Gerald to Kalindi. "Hello."

"Memsahib," Kalindi murmured deferentially.

"I was just instructing Kalindi on her duties for the afternoon," Gerald said.

"I see." Devora sank down into one of the wicker chairs and crossed her legs. "How thoughtful of you to inform her yourself rather than telling Rohan, as you do for all the other servants."

Gerald frowned. "Don't start, Devora."

Devora looked at Kalindi assessingly, as if she were trying to determine something that wasn't readily apparent. "Where are you from?" she asked.

"A town called Cawnpore."

"And what brings you here?"

"Work, *memsahib.*"

"Ah, I see. Lots of work available, I imagine."

"Devora!" Gerald snapped out her name.

Her eyes went innocently to his. "I'm just asking questions, darling."

"Kalindi, that will be all for now." Gerald waved his hand in a dismissing motion. "You may leave."

Kalindi nodded and walked off, the tune of her humming drifting on the slight breeze. Gerald gave Devora a hard look.

"Devora, I won't have you interrogating the servants, do you understand?" he said. "I told you that you shouldn't associate with them, and I mean it. Do you understand me?"

She looked as if she were about to respond with a retort, but then her mouth compressed into a thin line. She nodded.

"Yes, I understand."

"Good. Now, I don't want to have this conversation again." Gerald removed his cigarette case from his jacket pocket and took out a cigarette. He tapped it against the case and lit it, drawing in a deep rush of smoke. "Now, I have some good news."

"What good news?"

"The Maharaja has invited us to a dinner party this Saturday at his palace in Varitsar."

Devora's eyebrows lifted. "A dinner party at the palace?"

"Yes. Everyone from around the district will be there, I'm sure, including British dignitaries."

A spark of excitement lit Devora's expression. "Really? We're going to the palace?"

Gerald smiled. "Yes. I hope you brought some evening dresses to wear."

"Oh, I certainly did. My goodness, how exciting this is. Mrs. Thompson was just telling me about the Maharaja."

"Really? What did she say?"

"Well, she mentioned the rumor about his sexual perversities," Devora said.

"Devora! You shouldn't be talking about things like that."

She blinked, giving him an innocent look. "I didn't start the conversation, Gerald. Mrs. Thompson was all too eager to volunteer the information, including the part about his wife committing suicide because she couldn't stand his sexual inclinations."

"Oh, for heaven's sake, that is the most salacious thing I've ever heard," Gerald said disparagingly. "People just love to spread rumors about him. He's a perfect gentleman in my estimation."

"Your estimation appears to be based on only two or so meetings," Devora remarked.

"That's still more than Mrs. Thompson has had, I dare say," Gerald replied. "Now, don't go about spreading those kinds of rumors about the Maharaja. He's a politically astute figure, and we can't risk upsetting relations between him and the British. I would hate to have him discover that the assistant controller's wife is one of the gossipmongers. Am I making myself clear?"

Devora yawned, patting her hand daintily over her mouth. "Yes, darling. Forgive me, but I fear I'm still suffering a bit from the journey."

"No doubt. I thought you were going to the ladies' bridge party this afternoon."

"Yes, that's at three." She rose, brushing the wrinkles out of her skirt. "Perhaps I'll take a little nap before then."

"Good idea. And, Devora?"

She looked at him. "Yes?"

"Don't cause trouble."

Devora smiled and walked over to give him a kiss on the cheek. "Oh, darling, of course I won't. You simply worry too much."

"Heavens, I've got butterflies in my stomach." Devora secured her final hairpin and examined herself critically in the mirror. She wore her best dress, a deep blue silk gown with a beaded bodice. A strand of pearls decorated her neck. She turned to look at Gerald, who looked quite stunning in a tuxedo and bow tie.

"You look lovely, darling. I've never seen you look so beautiful." Gerald patted Devora on the buttocks, then gave them a quick squeeze.

"What does one call a Maharaja? Sir? Your Highness?"

"I've always called him 'sir,' so I believe that's appropriate unless you hear someone call him something else."

"Must we take a carriage there? The roads are so dusty."

"No, I've managed to procure a car for the evening." Gerald pulled out his watch and flicked it open. "Darling, we'd better leave or we'll be late."

"All right, I'm ready." Devora powdered her nose one last time, picked up her pocketbook, and followed Gerald outside. To her surprise, their previous driver wasn't waiting at the car for them. Instead, Rohan stood next to the open car door. He looked rather magnificent in a white jacket and black trousers, his expression as stoic as ever.

"What's he doing here?" Devora whispered to Gerald as he helped her up into the car.

"He drives when we're going somewhere particularly important," Gerald replied. "It has to do with prestige among the servants, I believe."

Devora settled into her seat, gazing out at the landscape, the ribbons of orange and gold that were just starting to paint the sky. The sun hovered like a huge, golden bubble above the distant hills. They drove through the town of Calipore, a bustling mecca of noise and activity. White, sacred Brahmin cows wandered the streets placidly amidst the frenzy of the marketplace. Stalls lined the main street, each one filled with flowers, vegetables, silver jewelry, and bowls of colorful spices and dyes. Devora couldn't stop staring at the people, the Muslim women dressed entirely in black, the middle-class Indians wearing suits, the toothless beggars and poverty-stricken children. The sights alone encompassed more uniqueness than she had ever imagined of India.

After they made their way through the town, Rohan drove for another hour before they finally arrived at the palace, which rose above the landscape like a sudden hallucination. Magnificent in simplicity and splendor, it was situated on the west bank of a large lake, alongside which numerous cars and carriages were parked. The palace was reddish in color, with three towers topped by domes, and dozens of bracketed windows, ornate balconies, and balustrades. Palm trees sprouted around the grounds like sentries guarding their station, and the gardens seemed to radiate for miles.

Devora glanced at Gerald. "When was this palace built?" she asked.

"Sixteenth century, I think," Gerald replied.

"Seventeenth, *sahib*," Rohan corrected from the driver's seat. "It was built of red sandstone by the Maharaja Ramit Singh. It is a perfect example of Rajput architecture and consists of five stories and more than two hundred rooms, with imported Italian marble and stained glass."

"How wonderful," Devora breathed, leaning forward in her seat to get a closer look at the sight before them.

"Apparently, Rohan is also a historian as well as a servant," Gerald muttered.

"My apologies, *sahib*."

Devora glanced at Rohan, meeting his gaze in the rearview mirror. To her surprise, she could have sworn that a twinkle of amusement appeared within the fathomless depths of his black eyes, but then it was gone so quickly that she was certain she had imagined it. She doubted that Rohan had a humorous bone in his body.

Rohan stopped the car at the entrance and got out to hold the door open for them.

"I will go and park the car, but I will be here when you are ready to return home," he said.

"Thank you, Rohan." Gerald took Devora's arm as they walked toward the palace entrance.

Devora felt as if she had been transported back to the Seventeenth century as they walked past guards dressed in white uniforms, sashes, and silk turbans. The sound of a multitude of voices emerged from the reception room to the left of the entrance. Devora gave her wrap to a servant, her heart pounding as they entered a vast room of glittering silk, spicy scents, and lilting music. About forty guests meandered about the hall like slow-moving ships, British gowns and tuxedos contrasting with Indian saris and turbans. At the far end of the room, several people flanked a man dressed in a beautifully embroidered *kurta* and black trousers. He appeared to be in his mid-fifties, and he carried himself with such a regal bearing that Devora knew instantly that this was the Maharaja.

"Oh, good, you're here!" Mrs. Thompson, dressed in a long, sequined gown, floated over to them. "Have you met the Maharaja yet?"

An image of Mrs. Thompson spread out indecently against the wall appeared in Devora's mind like a moving picture. She smiled, hoping that her amusement would be mistaken for friendliness. "Not yet. We've just arrived. I expected there would be many more people."

"The Maharaja always plans sit-down dinners, so there is a limited seating arrangement," Mrs. Thompson explained. "It makes it rather nice, I think."

"We'll go and introduce ourselves to him," Gerald said. "Nice seeing you, Mrs. Thompson."

Taking Devora's arm again, Gerald led her over to the Maharaja and his court officials. Devora gazed at the man curiously, intrigued by his bearing and history. He wasn't an extraordinarily handsome man. Nor was he particularly slim, no doubt due to a constant array of wonderful foods. He did, however, have an air of command and control about him that made him rather fascinating.

"Sir, I don't know if you remember me, but my name is Gerald Hawthorne," Gerald said. "Assistant Controller. This is my wife, Devora. She arrived from England the week before last."

"Of course, Mr. Hawthorne, I do remember you." The Maharaja shook Gerald's hand heartily before turning to Devora. "And your charming wife, how lovely to meet you. Welcome to my home."

"Thank you for inviting us. It's beautiful."

"You may look around, if you like. Dinner will be served shortly." With that, the Maharaja moved on to greet another guest.

"I'm going to speak to John Fielding," Gerald said. "You'll be all right on your own?"

"Of course."

Gerald headed off in the direction of a man dressed in a British military uniform. Devora glanced up and saw Louise heading in her direction, her eyes bright with excitement.

"Oh, Devora, isn't this fun?" she asked. "Imagine, us at the palace of a Maharaja."

"What's his name, do you know?" Devora asked.

"I've no idea. Can you imagine what this place must be worth?"

"He gave me permission to look around," Devora said. "Will you come with me?"

"Will I! Let me tell my husband that I'll meet him before we go in to dinner." Louise scurried off, reminding Devora of a jittery rabbit.

Devora wandered around the reception room, which was lined with paintings of Indian Maharajas in history. She wondered what, exactly, the current Maharaja's role was, given the fact that most of the country was under British control. It seemed to her that he would be rather ineffectual, even if he was the ruler of a free state.

"Okay, I'm ready." Louise returned, clutching her pocketbook.

The two women headed off along a mezzanine that overlooked an inner courtyard. The courtyard was lovely, filled with flowering plants and decorated with a trickling stone fountain.

"Is he married, do you know?" Louise asked.

"Not that I'm aware of." Devora thought briefly of repeating the gossip she had heard about the Maharaja's wife, but decided against it. "I'm surprised he's not, though. I imagine that all these rulers want sons and heirs."

"Look at the workmanship of this!" Louise paused to touch an intricately carved marble screen that separated a room from the mezzanine. "This is all they used to separate the room."

"Probably because it's always so hot here," Devora said. "I wouldn't think they would need to block out the cold like we do in England. What kind of room is it?"

She peered around the corner of the screen at a room filled with embroidered silk pillows and *morahs*. The faint scent of incense clung to the air. "It looks like a lounging . . . oh my."

She caught sight of a stone sculpture against the wall. A full-breasted woman straddled a standing man, her legs spread wide as he supported her and thrust his penis into her. Devora's eyes widened. "Some kind of lounging room, indeed."

Stepping into the room, she started toward the sculpture to get a closer look.

"Devora, should you be going in there?" A thread of worry ran through Louise's voice. "I mean, we're in his private residence."

"He said I could look around." Devora peered at the sculpture, fascinated by the voluptuous curves of the woman and the outright lasciviousness of the couple.

Her gaze went to some framed paintings on the walls, each of which contained another explicit, erotic scene of couples in a multitude of positions. She stared at one of a richly outfitted man and five women, one of whom was straddling him, his penis inside her. Two other women sat near each of his feet, their legs spread as the man penetrated their vulvas with his toes, while he used his hands to finger two other women. One of the women by his feet even held up a mirror so that the man could watch himself. "Goodness. I knew the Indians had a tradition of erotic art, but I didn't know that it was *this* erotic."

"Isn't eroticism one of the greatest pleasures of life, though?"

The sudden male voice caused Devora to look up with a start. Louise gave a gasp of dismay as they both turned and saw the Maharaja standing in the doorway.

"Oh, we didn't mean to be snooping," Louise said quickly. "We're terribly sorry."

"No need for apologies," the Maharaja replied. "I appreciate your interest."

"Do all palaces have a room dedicated to erotic art?" Devora asked.

Louise gasped. "Devora!"

The Maharaja chuckled. "No, no, that's quite all right. The answer, Mrs. Hawthorne, is probably not. I, however, rather enjoy it and so"—he spread a hand out to encompass the room—"I decided to put some of my collection in this room."

Devora's eyebrows lifted. "You mean you have more?"

"But of course. I have an extensive collection of art, both erotic and non-erotic. Perhaps you would like to see the rest of my collection one day."

"I would," Devora agreed. She and the Maharaja gazed at each other for a moment before Devora turned away. She noticed a simple stone pillar with a circular base standing in one corner of the room. "That's erotic, too?"

"Of course. That is the *lingam,* the phallus. It's used for religious purposes."

Devora gave him a skeptical look. "Religious?"

"Yes. The *lingam* symbolizes the god Shiva and the potency of the divine. In some areas, the sacred *lingam* is still used to deflower a bride before her wedding night. She belongs first to the deity."

"You must be joking," Louise gasped. "That's disgusting."

"Not really," the Maharaja replied. "Do not your Christian nuns take a vow to belong to their God? The principle is much the same."

"Yes, but they don't deflower themselves with a phallus!" Two bright spots of color appeared on Louise's cheeks as her agitation increased.

"Oh, Louise, don't be so puritanical," Devora admonished.

"I deeply regret having offended you, Mrs. Moore," the Maharaja said, bowing slightly in Louise's direction. "Please forgive me. Won't you both come in to dinner?"

He stepped aside, allowing the two women to precede him along the mezzanine and back to the reception room. The guests were all making their way into the dining room, which was dominated by a vast carved table topped with flower arrangements and settings of fine china.

Devora found Gerald and sat down next to him.

"Where have you been?" he asked.

"I was just looking around," Devora explained, spreading her napkin out on her lap. "This palace is just beautiful."

"Well, please tell me if you're planning to go off again," Gerald said. "I dislike not knowing where you are."

"Yes, darling," Devora murmured.

The Maharaja stood from his place at the head of the table

and lifted his wineglass. "Ladies and gentlemen, I welcome you to my home. And I toast to the continuing good relations between the British and the Indians."

Everyone stood and lifted their own glasses, the men murmuring, "Hear, hear." Devora sipped the rich red wine and glanced at the Maharaja. To her surprise, he was looking directly at her. He lifted his glass again in a silent toast, drank, and resumed his seat.

Somewhat unnerved, Devora sat down. She tried not to look in the Maharaja's direction again as the servers brought out plate after plate of *pakora,* curries, *dahl,* and chutney, with mint-flavored yogurt to cool the heat of the spices.

"Darling, it's not too spicy for you, is it?" Gerald asked.

"No, I'm fine." Devora thoroughly enjoyed the food, the flavor of which burst onto her tongue with a multitude of tastes. The meal finished with sweet, milky desserts of *gulab jamun* and *sandesh* that counteracted the spicy meal. Devora thought it was quite ingenious of the Indians to create foods that both complemented and contrasted one another so very deliciously.

After dinner, the warmth of the evening air drew everyone outside onto the terrace overlooking the lake. A group of five men from the Maharaja's court were seated on a small platform at the end of the terrace, playing *sitar* and zither music that floated like raindrops on the night air.

Devora leaned against the marble railing and gazed out at the black velvet circle of the lake. She could see the cars parked alongside the lake, and the shadowy figures of the drivers as they lounged around the banks and ate food brought to them by the Maharaja's servants. For a brief instant, Devora imagined that she could make out the figure of Rohan, but of course that was ridiculous given that they were at such a distance.

"You are welcome back here at any time, Mrs. Hawthorne."

Devora looked up to find the Maharaja standing next to her at the railing.

"I appreciate your interest in Indian culture," he said.

"Thank you."

"Devora, I think we should be going now." Gerald approached them, carrying Devora's wrap. "Sir, thank you for your hospitality."

"Yes, thank you," Devora repeated. "We had a lovely time."

"Then I am very happy."

To Devora's surprise, the Maharaja bent to kiss her hand in farewell. She murmured her good-byes and took Gerald's arm as they walked back out to their car.

"He's an interesting man," she remarked.

"Yes, well, it's best to be a bit cautious of the Indians, as I've said to you. Whether they are servants or Maharajas."

"Gerald, I think the British are much too cautious," Devora said. They approached their car, where Rohan was waiting for them.

"You had a good evening?" he asked.

"Very nice," Gerald replied.

"I mean, it's not as if they're animals," Devora continued as she and Gerald got into the car. "They just have different philosophies and a different culture. For example, this whole idea of erotic art."

"Devora, I told you to leave that alone," Gerald said.

"It's a religious philosophy, Gerald, not a perversion!" Devora was getting exasperated. She'd been in India for only two weeks and already she was tired of British puritanism. "I'm sure there's a very deep history involved."

"No doubt," Gerald replied. "However, I don't want you to be running about researching this history. It's not becoming of a lady."

With a sigh, Devora crossed her arms and stared out the window.

"Now, Devora, don't sulk."

"Gerald, stop talking to me as if I were a child," Devora snapped.

"Look, next week I have to leave on a trip to Delhi," Gerald said. "Before I go, maybe we can take a trip to Agra and see the Taj Mahal. Also, we'll buy more sketch pads and water-colors for you so that you'll have something to keep yourself occupied."

Devora didn't respond. How was she going to last in India for years if she couldn't even attempt to understand the country? She continued staring out the window until the faint sound of Gerald snoring told her that he had fallen asleep. She looked at the back of Rohan's head for a moment, wondering suddenly what his thick, black hair would feel like under her fingertips. The thought startled her.

She leaned forward, bracing her arms against the front seat. "Rohan, how long have you been working for Gerald?"

"Eight months."

"And has he been having an affair with that woman Kalindi?"

A moment of silence filled the air between them. "I cannot answer that, *memsahib.*"

Devora snorted. "You mean you won't."

Rohan didn't reply. Devora sat back in her seat, feeling both irritated and restless. She glanced at Rohan in the rearview mirror and wondered what it would take to provoke some sort of reaction from him.

"Well, maybe I should have an affair of my own, then," she mused. "To find out if there really is something to this worship of the phallus."

He didn't reply.

"It doesn't surprise me, really," Devora went on. "The worship of the male member, that is. I wonder if anyone would think to worship the female part instead. After all, that's where life begins."

"Very true. The female counterpart is called the *yoni.*"

Startled, Devora met his gaze in the mirror. "The *yoni*? Do Indians worship the *yoni*?"

"I certainly do."

chapter four

You're leaving for two entire weeks?" Devora disliked the
petulant tone in her voice, but she couldn't even fathom
how bored she would be without Gerald. At least when he was
home, they could talk, go out sightseeing and to parties. Without him, she would be stuck playing bridge and gossiping with
a bunch of uptight British women.

"Darling, I'm sorry, but it's unavoidable," Gerald said. He
tossed his shaving kit into his suitcase and zipped it up. "We
have to go on tour to obtain a census of the Indians in this
district. I can't simply let the other men handle it alone."

Devora flopped back onto the bed and looked out the window at the threads of dawn just beginning to weave through
the sky. "Well, why can't I go with you?"

"Devora, I'm working. And census-taking is no place for a
woman."

"No, the place for a woman is at a bridge table," Devora
muttered.

Gerald sighed and ran a hand down his face. "Are you going
to be this difficult every time I leave?"

"I'm not being difficult, I'm just getting terribly bored," Devora replied. "Every time I want to do something or explore
something, you tell me it's not appropriate. I can't even be
friends with any Indians."

"You've got your sketch pads and pens," Gerald said. "You'll have plenty of time to do as many drawings as you like. And there's needlepoint and bridge games, not to mention visiting the club. They have a library with a number of English books. You'll enjoy that."

"I suppose."

"Oh, darling, you know I hate it when you're unhappy." Gerald sat on the side of the bed and reached out to run his fingers through Devora's hair. A hint of dismay lit in his blue eyes, making Devora feel even guiltier for her behavior. "I was worried that you'd be bored in India, but I did so want you with me."

Devora took her husband's hand, trailing her fingertips over the lines in his palm. "I know. And I wanted to be with you, too."

"Listen, I know I promised you a trip to the Taj Mahal, but I won't be able to take you at least until next month," Gerald said. "I heard that the Thompsons might be organizing a trip there for some of the others. Perhaps you could join them. Rohan and several of the servants will accompany you for protection and to take care of the details, but I'm sure you'll have a wonderful time."

Devora turned that idea over in her mind and found it highly appealing. Traveling with Mrs. Thompson might prove to be exasperating, but at least she would have an opportunity to see other parts of the state. Not to mention the Taj Mahal, which had always fascinated her.

Gerald rubbed his knuckles over Devora's cheek. "Does that sound like something you might enjoy?"

Devora nodded. This really wasn't Gerald's fault. Heaven knew that he was just abiding by convention like all of the other British colonizers. "It does, Gerald. It sounds lovely."

"Good." Gerald gave a definitive nod and stood. "I'll send a message to Mr. Thompson before I leave to let him know that you'd like to do that. He can help you take care of everything, and I'm sure he'll be thrilled to have you along."

"All right. Thank you." Devora continued watching him pack. Rohan wasn't going with him. The thought of being alone with the Indian man made her more than a little nervous, particularly after their brief conversation on the return from the Maharaja's palace. Rohan hadn't treated her any differently in the few days since their brush with royalty, but that didn't make Devora any less uncomfortable around him.

"Do you want some breakfast before you leave?" she asked Gerald. "I'm sure you'll be on the road for a long time."

"Kalindi fixed me some tea and toast about an hour ago," Gerald replied. He looked in the mirror and ran a comb through his hair.

"Kalindi, hmm?"

"Devora, she's a servant. That's what she does."

"Serve you, you mean?"

"Devora!"

"Sorry." Devora couldn't figure out what was the matter with her. In addition to being bored, she was feeling incredibly snippy lately. Maybe a short separation between her and Gerald would actually be a blessing in disguise.

Gerald turned to look at her, his gaze raking over her figure sprawled indecently on the bed. "You're becoming a bit obsessed with that woman, aren't you?" he mused.

Devora's heart quickened a few beats at the husky, sexual undertone to his words. "Am I?"

"You're always asking me about her."

Devora lifted her shoulders in a shrug. "I'm just curious, that's all."

"About Kalindi or women in general?"

Now it was Devora's turn to be shocked. She stared at Gerald for a moment, uncertain if she had even heard her straitlaced husband correctly. "Excuse me?"

"You heard me."

Devora's lips parted as she drew in a breath. Her skin prickled with excitement at the mere thought of what he was implying. "God, Gerald."

He approached her, his eyes gleaming with a sexual wickedness that she had never before witnessed in him. "Well, Devora? Does it excite you, the idea of another woman?"

"I don't know," Devora whispered.

"I think it does. Or else you wouldn't be commenting on other women so much."

Devora couldn't move. Her gaze locked to Gerald's lewd expression as he lifted his hand and traced the scooped neckline of her nightgown. His fingertips barely brushed against her skin, but Devora's nipples hardened as if he had just enclosed them with his lips. Her heart began to thud hard against her rib cage. She glanced down at Gerald's trousers. Heat quivered through her at the sight of his hard penis pressing against the material. The knowledge that he was excited by the thought of her and another woman made Devora both aroused and slightly unnerved.

"Would you like that?" Gerald murmured, his eyes fixed on her neckline as he began to draw the sheer material down to expose her breasts. "Being with another woman? Kissing her, touching her?"

He took one of her nipples between his fingers, then tweaked it so hard that Devora winced. She couldn't believe how aroused she was in such a short time. Her sex was already damp, her clit pulsing gently and craving pressure. She watched the movement of Gerald's hands as he pushed her onto her back and began pulling her gown up over her thighs. His palms stroked over her thighs, moving toward the heated fissure of her sex.

"Maybe you'd like a woman's hand between your legs for a change, is that it?" Gerald's chest heaved with his own excitement as he leaned over her with that feral expression.

His groin pressed against her vulva, his penis pushing insistently against her as if Gerald were forcing her to remember that he was a man. Devora shifted her hips and rubbed her exposed sex against the tight bulge, delighting in the way the rough material of his trousers chafed against her sensitive folds. With a groan, she writhed lewdly against him, stimulating the growing pressure in her loins. Gerald bent his hand and sucked hard on one of her tight nipples as she continued to pleasure herself against him.

Devora let her eyes drift closed, her mind swimming with images of herself naked with another woman. Cupping another woman's breasts in her hands, delving her fingers into the soft sex, tasting the musky flavor of womanly secretions. Ah, Devora couldn't help but think how delicious such a union would be. Blood pounded through her veins with a force made all the more potent by her sapphic thoughts.

"Do you want me to fuck you instead?" Gerald's voice grated roughly in her ear as he lifted himself away from her.

His obscene words only served to excite Devora all the more, quickening pulses of heat through her entire body. Opening her eyes, she gazed at her husband, thinking that she had never seen him quite this forceful. His eyes blazed blue fire as he stared down at her, a pulse throbbing violently at his temple.

"Come on, Devora, admit it," he hissed. "Is that what you've been wanting? Is that it?"

"Oh, Christ . . ." Devora closed her eyes again when Gerald thrust a finger roughly into her, his passage eased by the fluids of her arousal. She grasped the front of his shirt for stability as his thumb began to circle her clitoris. Sensations wrapped her in a hazy mist, one that included nothing else save for the touch of Gerald's hand and the image of herself entwined with another woman. Gerald pushed his finger back and forth a few times before Devora felt the head of his cock pressing against her sex. A momentary fear fluttered through her, startling her. She had never had reason to fear Gerald.

Devora looked up at Gerald, wondering suddenly if she even knew the man who was her husband, and then he started to pump inside her with a rhythm she had come to know instinctively. His expression softened to one of lust. Devora's fear dissipated quickly and was replaced by growing ripples of excitement that tugged at her pelvis and demanded release. She stretched her arms above her head to let herself be thoroughly ravished, her body jerking rhythmically with every thrust.

Gerald lifted Devora's legs over his arms, pushing her thighs back as far as they could go so that he could penetrate her to the hilt. Luscious it felt, this slick thrusting edged with the mere notion of forbidden lesbian pleasures. As the pressure built, waiting to burst forth in a glorious explosion of rapture, Devora turned her head toward the door. Her heart leaped into her throat at the sight of a dark-haired man visible between the crack of the slightly open door. And then he turned and disappeared.

Devora stilled so suddenly that Gerald paused in his movements. He drew in a ragged breath and looked at her. "Devora?"

She shook her head, putting her hands on his chest to push him away. "Rohan."

"What about him? What's the matter with you?"

Devora gestured toward the door, almost unable to get the words out. "He was there. Just outside the door."

"So what?"

"Gerald, the door was open."

"Oh, Christ." Gerald pulled away from her, breaking any remnants of lust. He stalked across the room and slammed the door closed, then grabbed his trousers off the floor. "I have to leave, or I'll be late."

Devora stared at him. She wrapped her dressing gown around her unfulfilled body and tied the belt tightly. "Gerald, you can't leave now."

"Devora, I have work to do."

"Gerald, I'm telling you he saw us!"

"Look, I don't like that idea any better than you do, but it's our own damn fault for not being careful." Gerald buttoned his trousers and shrugged into his jacket. "I told you that you have to watch your step around them."

"So now we can't even fuck each other in the privacy of our own bedroom?" Devora snapped. She paced back and forth furiously, pushing her hair away from her face.

"Don't talk like that." Gerald laced his shoes and picked up his hat. "Listen, Devora, this isn't London. We need to conduct ourselves accordingly given that we're in a different country."

"Fine, and now you're going to leave me alone in a house with a man who just saw me in the most indecent of positions." Devora was so angry that every muscle in her body felt tight. She whirled around to glare at her husband. "You tell me I can't even walk around in my dressing gown because it's indecent, and here your servant just saw you fucking me!"

"Devora, that's enough." Gerald closed his eyes for a moment and took a deep breath. "Listen, I'm sorry that happened, but you have nothing to worry about where Rohan is concerned. In fact, you should be grateful for his protection since you'll be alone here."

"I don't feel very grateful."

Gerald approached Devora and put his hands on her shoulders. "Darling, please don't make a big deal out of this, all right? I love you. You're the sexiest, most passionate woman in the world. If I could, I'd stay here and make love to you twenty-four hours a day. However, I suspect the British government would balk at paying me for such an activity, no matter how delightful."

A reluctant smile tugged at the corners of Devora's lips. "One can always hope, anyway."

"I'll call Mr. Thompson straight away to arrange your trip to Agra." Gerald bent to press a kiss against Devora's lips. "And, if it will make you feel better, I'll ask him if someone can come here and stay with you."

"Thank you, but I'm sure I'll be fine."

"Behave yourself while I'm gone," Gerald said. "I love you."

"I love you, too," Devora murmured. She watched Gerald leave the bedroom, closing the door behind him.

She stood in the middle of the room for a moment and tried to collect her thoughts after such a shocking end to an intense sexual experience. She wondered how long Rohan had been standing outside the room. The idea alone made her face flame with humiliation. How must she have looked, spread out and exposed so wantonly?

Devora groaned and wrapped her dressing gown around her body as she went into the bathroom. She took a quick bath, masturbating almost furtively to rid her body of the lingering tension, then dressed in a conservative light blue dress and matching shoes. After fixing her hair, she went into the sitting room. A three-month-old English newspaper and a pot of tea rested on the sideboard. Devora poured herself a cup and sat down at the table to read the news.

"You wish something to eat, *memsahib*?"

Devora looked up at the sound of Kalindi's lilting voice. The servant stood before her, dressed in one of those saris that Indian women wore with such grace. She was such a pretty little thing, with delicate features and richly brown skin. A sudden image of herself and Kalindi appeared in Devora's mind, another erotic picture of them naked and writhing together.

"*Memsahib?*" Kalindi prompted.

"Oh." Devora flushed. "Yes, I think a boiled egg and some toast, please."

"Very well." Kalindi padded off toward the kitchen.

Devora pressed a hand against her chest, surprised to discover that her heart was beating rapidly. Good Lord, what was the matter with her all of a sudden? One day she was discussing sacred phalluses with a Maharaja and just a few days later she was imagining herself naked with a female servant. She would have thought she was going crazy were it not for the fact that everything felt oddly logical and very, very real. She felt as if the hot sun of India, the dry plains and wheat fields, the crumbling, ancient temples and multiarmed gods had all given her permission to feel and experience every licentious thought.

After eating breakfast, Devora picked up her teacup and wandered over to the bookshelf that rested against the side of the wall. She hadn't taken the opportunity to examine the shelf's contents, but it occurred to her that there might be some texts dealing with Indian religion and philosophies. Perhaps even this notion of the worship of the phallus. After perusing several English novels and books about Indian history, Devora found a small volume on the bottom shelf entitled *The Kamasutra of the Vatsyayana*.

Taking the book, she sat down on the sofa and leafed through it. She had heard of the Kamasutra before, of course, but she'd never known exactly what it contained. All she knew was that it was a fourth century text about the sacred act of love and union. And she certainly hadn't known that the book was filled with such sexual detail, focusing on the range of positions available, the erogenous zones, even such matters as how to hold the phallus in one's mouth. Devora was certain that some of the sexual postures illustrated in the book were completely impossible between normal people, but, oh, what imagination! She never would have imagined such positions. Her couplings with Gerald, no matter how raw, had always been with her lying on her back and him over her. What would it be like to actually sit astride a man, or to bend over, or to turn away from him . . .

"*Memsahib,* you have a visitor."

Startled, Devora looked up at Rohan. "Excuse me?"

"Mrs. Thompson is here to visit you."

"Oh. Please send her in."

Rohan nodded, but not before glancing down at the book in her lap. A hot flush colored Devora's face as she realized that the book was open to a number of illustrations about sexual postures. She slammed the book closed and thrust it back onto the shelf, giving Rohan a haughty glare.

"I said send Mrs. Thompson in," she ordered.

Rohan turned and went back outside. Devora fought the urge to make a face at his retreating back. She hated what he must think of her, and she was equally annoyed with herself for even caring what he thought. He was just a servant, hardly a person of importance. What did it matter if he thought she was a libido-driven tart? Heavens, maybe she was even turning into one.

Devora couldn't help smiling at the thought.

"Oh, my goodness, would you feel how hot it is already?" Mrs. Thompson strutted into the room, sporting a flowing chiffon dress and a flowered hat. "I must say, I do long for the rain."

"Hello, Mrs. Thompson, what a pleasant surprise." Devora stood to kiss the other woman, catching a whiff of talcum powder. "What brings you here?"

"My husband told me that you might want to join us on our Agra trip while Gerald is gone," Mrs. Thompson replied. She sat down heavily in a chair and began fanning herself with her hat. "Dear, have you got any tea brewed?"

"I'll have Kalindi brew a fresh pot." Devora rang the servant's bell and instructed Kalindi to bring out tea and cookies. She settled down across from Mrs. Thompson. "Yes, I thought that going to Agra was a wonderful idea. I've been wanting to visit the Taj Mahal, and with Gerald gone for two weeks, I thought I would be quite bored. He suggested that a trip might be great fun."

"Yes, I suppose it will be."

"Have you been?"

"Oh, of course. Several times. We usually take the train into Delhi, but it's a rather horrible city. Very crowded and with beggars everywhere. Then we take a car to Agra, which is, of course, infinitely more pleasant. At least there are a number of British people around."

"When are you planning to go?" Devora asked.

"We were hoping to go this coming weekend, since that's when Reginald can take some time off. I'm not comfortable going without a man, you understand."

"Quite."

Kalindi returned with a tea tray and poured two cups, glancing at Mrs. Thompson. "One lump or two, *memsahib*?"

"Two." Mrs. Thompson accepted the tea and watched Kalindi leave the room. "She's a young one, isn't she?" she said to Devora.

"I imagine she's at least twenty. That's not so young."

Mrs. Thompson chuckled. "And how old are you, my dear?"

"Twenty-eight."

A thinly penciled eyebrow rose on Mrs. Thompson's fore-head. "Oh."

"What?"

"I thought you were younger than that. Having been married only a year and all."

"Yes, I know, I was in danger of being a spinster before Gerald came along and rescued me," Devora said dryly.

"Now, now, there's no need to be sarcastic," Mrs. Thompson replied. "Just remember that when there's a younger woman in the house, regardless of the fact that she is Indian, the men are in danger of temptation." Her voice rose and fell on the word *temptation*, resulting in a little singsong tone that Devora found particularly irritating.

"I'll remember that," she muttered.

"So, my dear, you enjoyed our little visit with the Maharaja the other day?"

"Yes, I found him to be very engaging." Devora debated whether or not to tell Mrs. Thompson about the erotic art room, but decided that such a revelation would only give the other woman more fodder for gossip. "His palace is beautiful."

"And he's quite a dashing man himself, in a regal sort of way. Not handsome really, but poised and . . . oh, I don't know. Refined."

"That's an interesting observation considering the rumors about his sexual behaviors that seem so prevalent," Devora said.

Mrs. Thompson's eyebrow shot up again, no doubt due to Devora's sardonic tone. "Well, the persona that one presents to the public is quite different from the one that exists behind closed doors, is that not the case?"

Devora had to smile and concede the point. "Yes, that is indeed the case."

Mrs. Thompson suddenly glanced at the doorway, where Rohan stood in all his stoicism. "Does he always just stand there?"

"Well, no. Sometimes he drives the car." Devora couldn't hold back a grin. She looked at Rohan, hoping that her condescending words would take him down a peg or two.

Mrs. Thompson lowered her voice to a whisper. "Be careful around him. Don't let him wash your undies or anything. Some of these Indians get so excited about white women's undies."

Now it was Devora's turn to lift an eyebrow. "He's not a *dhobi*," she said. "He's the head servant."

"Good. Still, it might behoove you to count your underclothes and keep track of them. There have been cases of stealing, you know."

"By women or men?" Devora asked dryly.

"Both, of course. The women want to keep them, and I'm sure the men want to do disgusting things with them."

"Really? What kinds of things?" Devora watched with amusement as Mrs. Thompson's skin grew a rosy shade of pink.

"For heaven's sake, Devora, I'm not going to *explain* them to you. Just don't let the men steal your undies."

"I'll do my very best to prevent such a mishap."

Mrs. Thompson glanced at Rohan again. "I hope you don't let him run the place when Gerald is gone. We'll have to find someone to stay with you."

"Actually, that's really not necessary. I'll be fine alone." Devora wasn't entirely convinced of her own words, but she also didn't want a nanny. She changed the subject so that Mrs. Thompson wouldn't press the issue. "Isn't there a picnic tomorrow or something?"

Mrs. Thompson's expression brightened. "Oh yes! We'll come pick you up around noon. We're going to a nearby temple site, so you should bring your sketch pads or paints or whatever it is you use."

"Oh, good. I've so been wanting to visit a temple."

"Now, you know, dear, that you can call on myself or Reginald for anything you need. I just hate to think of you all alone here."

"I'll be fine. Thank you for stopping by." Devora walked Mrs. Thompson back outside and stood on the porch watching as the horse and carriage chugged away in a cloud of dust.

She turned to go back inside. Rohan was standing right behind her near the doorway. Devora gazed at him for a moment, never failing to be intrigued by the sculpted planes of his features and the depth of his eyes.

"Where are you from?" she finally asked.

"Punjab, *memsahib*. In the north."

Devora knew that was why he was taller than most other Indians and had fairer skin. "Is your family still there?"

"My parents are both dead. My sister is married and living in the city of Jaipur."

"I see. I'm sorry. About your parents, I mean."

"What for? Death is simply a move into a different existence."

"That doesn't mean you can't be sad about it."

"That would be pointless."

Devora shrugged and moved past him. "To you, all emotion seems pointless."

She wasn't surprised when he didn't reply.

"He's practically left her all alone." Kalindi poured a small pool of coconut oil into her palms and began to massage it through Lota's long black hair. "Can you imagine?"

"Rohan stays in the servants' quarters at the back of the house though, doesn't he?" Lota asked. She was sitting on the floor at Kalindi's feet, glancing through the pages of a magazine that the *memsahib* had given them. Neither Kalindi or Lota could even read Hindi, let alone English, but the pictures were quite lovely.

"Yes, but I'm surprised that the *sahib* entrusted his wife

solely to Rohan's care," Kalindi explained. She picked up a comb from the bedside table and tugged it carefully through the tangle of Lota's hair. "Although I did hear that fat cow Mrs. Thompson telling the *memsahib* that they should get someone to stay with her."

"Really? Do you think they will?"

"Probably. You know Mrs. Thompson. She's such a busy-body."

"What does Rohan think of this whole situation?"

"I don't know," Kalindi replied. "He only talks to me to give me orders."

"Has the *sahib* visited you at all since his wife arrived?" Lota asked.

Kalindi gave an unladylike snort. "No. I think he's afraid of what she would do if she found out about us. They've been spending a lot of time in the bedroom, though."

Lota chuckled. "I can't imagine why. Maybe she's satisfying him enough so that he doesn't need you."

Kalindi yanked hard on a particularly tight tangle in Lota's hair, causing the other woman to give a yelp of pain.

"Ow!" Lota grabbed her head protectively. "That hurt."

"Sorry."

Lota glowered at her. "Kalindi, you can't have thought that he would still be with you when she arrived."

Kalindi shrugged. Truth be known, she had hoped exactly that. Of course, she didn't harbor dreams of romance with a British man, but she had enjoyed her occasional visits to his bed. "No, I guess I didn't."

"Didn't they go to dinner at the Maharaja's palace recently?" Lota asked, returning her attention to the magazine.

"Yes, just a few days ago. I heard the *memsahib* telling Mrs. Thompson that she found the Maharaja to be very interesting."

"Really? I wonder what she means by that."

"Every woman finds the Maharaja interesting," Kalindi said. "With all that money, how could he *not* be interesting?"

"I wonder if she knows about his harem and all his sexual preferences," Lota mused.

"I'm sure she's heard rumors."

"I know. I wonder if she believes them."

chapter five

Devora squinted as she gazed at the sun-burnished stone temple. The surface of the large temple was covered with richly detailed sculptures, although none with the kind of explicit eroticism that apparently characterized the Khajuraho temples. The sculptures were chipped and broken, some even appearing to have been vandalized by warring religious factions. They consisted of a multitude of gods and animals, with several large-breasted female *yakshi* figures. The entire temple had fallen into disrepair, overgrown with weeds and vegetation. Still, it made for a very picturesque vista.

This country is like an ancient history book. Devora wrote the words on a fresh page in her journal. *It's very mysterious and everything seems alive, as if gods and spirits are embedded so deeply within the fabric of the country that they are a part of daily life. There is holiness, to be sure, but a comforting kind of holiness, one that seems to inspire love rather than fear or simple awe.*

"Devora, would you like another sandwich?" Louise held out a plate of cucumber sandwiches.

Devora looked up from her journal. "Oh, thank you."

She took a sandwich and closed her journal. They had spread a picnic blanket out underneath a tree near the temple, and several of the women had brought more food than they could possibly eat. Their party consisted of about eight people, all of whom were draped lazily over several embroidered Indian pillows.

"What is it you're writing, Devora?" Reginald Thompson was leaning against the tree trunk, puffing on a pipe. He was a plump, jolly man with a thicket of gray hair and a handlebar mustache that curled at the ends.

"Only my journal, that's all."

"You know, you shouldn't be alone in your bungalow without Gerald around."

"I'm all right," Devora replied. "He's only been gone for a day."

"Perhaps Billy should come and stay with you. He's our son, you know. Back from a journey to Banares for the week."

"No, that's really not necessary." The last thing Devora wanted was another man staying with her. She reached for her bag and took out a pencil. "Besides, it's giving me time to work."

"On what?"

"Some drawings and watercolors." Devora opened her journal again and sketched the outline of the temple. She would have to return here alone to capture more detail, but she was grateful for the opportunity to at least do some sketches.

"You're coming to the cricket match at the club tomorrow, aren't you?" Mr. Thompson asked.

Devora barely suppressed a sigh. "I'll have to think about it."

"Oh, you must come," Louise said. Her reddish curls, tossed by the wind, made her look like a blue-eyed doll. "Cricket matches are always so much fun. And there will be a lovely luncheon, too, of course."

"Of course."

"Devora, I meant to tell you that I'll be happy to accompany you ladies to Agra this coming weekend," Mr. Thompson said. "You'll love the architecture of the Taj Mahal. One of the few things the Indians have done right."

"I think all of their architecture is beautiful," Devora said. "And very unique."

"Of course, dear. Just a bit primitive is all. I mean, these people still worship gods in the form of animals, if you can believe that."

Devora leveled a long look at Mr. Thompson. "What's wrong with that? Many cultures worship animals."

"It's uncivilized, that's what's wrong with it," Mr. Thompson replied. "Not to mention all of their monstrous gods. Very violent religion, Hinduism. Contains a great deal of blood shedding."

Devora's mouth twisted derisively. "Well, Christianity does, too. For example, look at the Crusades, and the mere idea of nailing a man to a cross."

Louise's eyes widened in shock. "Devora, there's no need to be blasphemous."

"I'm not being blasphemous," Devora protested. "Simply pointing out that Hinduism isn't the only religion that involves bloodshed. Just because it's an Indian religion doesn't make it uncivilized."

"Good God, Devora, you're turning into an Indian sympathizer, aren't you?" Mr. Thompson said. His mustache quivered slightly. "If they're so civilized, then why do they need the British presence to keep things in order? If it weren't for us, they would be in total chaos."

"They managed fine without us for hundreds of years," Devora murmured.

"You're an impertinent young woman, did you know that?" Mr. Thompson sniffed. "I really can't believe that Gerald has left you alone."

"I'll be fine, thank you. And Gerald appreciates the fact that I have opinions about things." Devora didn't exactly believe her own words, but she also didn't want Mr. Thompson to think that her marriage was a conflicting one.

"That doesn't mean you should be criticizing the British presence here," Mr. Thompson retorted. "Dissent in our own ranks, even from a woman, is the last thing we need."

"That's quite true, Devora," Louise agreed. "We must be loyal empire-builders."

Devora turned her attention back to the crumbling stone temple. A bird alighted on one of the outstretched arms of a sculpture.

"I do understand that, but don't you think it would behoove us to learn something about Indian culture?" she asked.

"Frankly, some of these curries are about all the Indian culture I can handle," Mr. Thompson replied.

"How long have you been here, Mr. Thompson?"

Mr. Thompson blew out a puff of smoke. "Nearly ten years now. I've put in for a transfer back to England, but it's been refused. Looks like they need as many of us on the civil lines as they can get."

"Why?" Devora asked. "Have there been threats of revolt?"

"There are always threats of revolt," Mr. Thompson said. "Ever since the Sepoy Mutiny, we have to keep an eye out for violence. There are also a number of gangs who run about looking for trouble. This is what I'm talking about when I tell you the Indians are uncivilized."

Devora didn't even bother to argue the point, knowing that Mr. Thompson's opinions were unchangeable, no matter how irrational they were. "What does the Maharaja have to say about that?"

Mr. Thompson snorted. "Say about that? I suspect he's funding them."

Devora's eyebrows lifted. "Funding the gangs? Whatever for?"

"To cause trouble, of course. The Maharaja would love to see the British ousted from India."

"I thought he wanted to keep relations positive."

"That's what he says," Mr. Thompson replied. "What he does is, I believe, an entirely different matter."

"Then why does he even bother inviting us to dinner and the like?"

"To put up a cooperative front," Mr. Thompson said. "But he doesn't trust us, and we don't trust him."

Devora didn't find his words terribly difficult to believe. She was, however, surprised that she found the idea of a rebelling Maharaja more intriguing than worrisome.

"Kalindi, would you keep this place dusted, please?" Devora drew her finger over the sideboard and held it up coated with dust. "This is unacceptable."

"Sorry, *memsahib*. I'll tell Lota to dust while I start preparing dinner."

"Please do." Devora stalked out of the bungalow onto the back veranda, where Rohan sat writing up a shopping list. He stood immediately when Devora stepped onto the veranda.

"*Memsahib*."

"Kalindi is failing to carry out her duties," Devora said icily, crossing her arms over her chest. "Simply because the *sahib* isn't here is no reason to stop working. I intend to keep this place in order."

"Of course, I'll speak to Kalindi straight away."

"Please do. And I want you to trim these hedges." Devora waved her hand toward the abundant junipers growing by the veranda railing. "Do that by the end of the day, please."

"Yes, *memsahib*." Rohan turned, glancing toward the road that led to the front of the house. "I believe you have a visitor."

Devora followed his line of vision to the sleek black car speeding up the road. She frowned. "Whose car is that? I don't think I recognize it."

Rohan stepped off the veranda and starting walking around to the front of the house. Curious, Devora went after him. They both paused to watch the car pull up near the steps and come to a halt. A driver dressed in a pristine, white turban and a silk jacket got out of the car to open the back door.

To Devora's shock, the Maharaja himself emerged from the vehicle. Dressed in a dark blue embroidered *kurta* and *jamas,* he fairly exuded regality. Devora stared at him, wondering what on earth he was doing here.

"Ah, my dear Mrs. Hawthorne." The Maharaja approached Devora with his arms outstretched and a smile on his face. "How delightful to see you."

"Thank you, sir," Devora replied. She nodded in greeting, painfully conscious of Rohan's presence beside her. "To what do I owe the honor of your presence?"

"I've heard that your husband is away, and I simply cannot stand for the idea of you being alone here," the Maharaja replied. "I came to see if you needed anything or if I could be of any service whatsoever."

"Thank you, but I'm fine," Devora said. "May I offer you a cup of tea?"

"I would be delighted."

Devora looked at Rohan, who was already heading back inside to start the tea. She led the Maharaja inside, silently cursing Kalindi for not having cleaned the place thoroughly this morning. Still, she was pleased when the Maharaja commented on the tastefulness of the decor.

"Please, my dear, you must not hesitate to call upon me if you require anything while your husband is away," the Maharaja said as he settled onto the sofa. "I am at your service."

"Thank you very much, but Gerald will only be away for a short time. I'm quite fine, really." Devora perched on the edge of a chair, somewhat nervous at suddenly having this man in her house. "You didn't have to come all this way just to check on me."

"I also came to see if you will do me the extreme pleasure of having lunch at my place tomorrow afternoon."

"Oh." Devora was taken aback. "Lunch?"

The Maharaja chuckled. "Yes. I would be greatly honored. I can send a car to pick you up around noon, if that would be suitable."

Devora had a feeling that the answer no would simply not be acceptable. One didn't say no to a Maharaja. Not that she had any intention of doing so.

"I'm flattered, sir. I would love to have lunch with you tomorrow."

"Good."

Rohan appeared with a tea tray, glancing once at Devora before pouring tea for them.

"Rohan, I'll be lunching with the Maharaja tomorrow," Devora said. "Please cancel my plans for the day."

She knew perfectly well that she had nothing scheduled for tomorrow, but it wouldn't hurt if the Maharaja thought she would cancel plans to have lunch with him.

Rohan nodded. "Yes, *memsahib.*"

Devora settled back in her chair and sipped her tea. "I greatly enjoyed your dinner party the other night."

"Thank you. I enjoyed your company. And how do you find India?"

"As you know, I'm very intrigued by it. I think it's fascinating."

"And have you been sight-seeing yet?"

Devora shook her head. "Not really. Gerald hasn't been able to take me because he's working constantly, and most of the British people prefer to have cricket games. We were thinking of taking a trip to Agra, but I'm afraid I'm at the mercy of other people."

"No, you couldn't go alone," the Maharaja agreed. He set his teacup down and stood. "I'm afraid I shall have to take leave of you now. I have other people to call upon, but I will see you tomorrow afternoon. I do look forward to a nice, long visit with you."

"Thank you for the invitation. I look forward to it as well."

Devora walked him out to his car, then returned to finish her tea. She glanced up when Rohan entered the sitting room.

"*Memsahib,* I must tell you that it might not be wise for you to lunch with the Maharaja without your husband present."

Devora rolled her eyes. "Oh, Rohan. Don't tell me you believe all those rumors about him."

"It is not a good idea."

"Other people will be there," Devora said. "He's just gone to invite others, so I won't be alone. For heaven's sake, Rohan, you're not my keeper. Please don't tell me what to do."

"I apologize." Rohan bowed slightly. "I am only telling you my opinion, as your husband entrusted you to my care."

"I'm not a child!" Devora said in exasperation, suddenly sick to death of everyone thinking they knew what was best for her. "I don't care what my husband told you. You're a servant, not my nanny. Is that clear?"

"Yes, *memsahib*." Rohan turned and left.

Devora glowered at his retreating back. Regardless of their nationality or class, men always seemed to think they had to protect women. Between that and the prejudices of the British community, Devora decided that she'd had more than enough of convention.

She went into her bedroom and began examining her dresses, finally deciding on an elegant beige dress. After ringing for Kalindi, Devora thought briefly about calling Mrs. Thompson for her opinion, but decided not to in case Mrs. Thompson wasn't invited.

"Kalindi, would you iron this, please?" Devora asked. "I'll be wearing it for lunch tomorrow."

"Oh, yes, Rohan told me that you are going to lunch with the Maharaja!" Kalindi's eyes were bright with excitement as she took the dress. "How exciting."

"Yes, it is rather," Devora agreed.

"I am hearing that he has a harem of fifty women," Kalindi said eagerly.

Devora looked at her. "Where on earth did you hear such a thing?"

"Oh, everyone around here has heard that. He has his pick of the most beautiful women in the land, and he keeps them in one of the palace rooms so that he can choose whichever woman pleases him."

"That's ridiculous," Devora said, even though her mind swam with images of Eastern harems saturated with beautiful women and the scent of perfume. "Those are old stories and rumors. This is the twentieth century, Kalindi. People don't do that sort of thing anymore."

"Yes, but money can buy a man anything," Kalindi said. "Including a harem of fifty women."

"Kalindi, go and do your work," Devora ordered, shooing the younger woman away. "I have a great deal to do before tomorrow. Now hurry along and don't go spreading gossip."

Kalindi dashed off with the dress. Devora spent the evening washing her hair and filing her fingernails, her thoughts constantly drifting back to the Maharaja and his vast palace. She wondered what he did during the day, not to mention how he entertained himself at night. What if he really did have a harem of women to choose from?

Her nervousness grew the following morning as she waited for the Maharaja's car to pick her up. She checked and rechecked her hair, then paced the sitting room until she heard the sound of the car engine.

"*Memsahib,* I do wish you would let me accompany you," Rohan said.

"There is no need, Rohan. I'll return before dark." Devora hurried out to the car, where the driver was already holding the door open for her.

Settling against the plush seats, Devora had to smile. Finally, something exciting was happening! She was lunching with a Maharaja, and without Gerald around to prevent her from asking about Indian erotic art and philosophy. Now maybe she could get some questions answered.

The sandstone palace gleamed red in the hot sun, with the lake appearing like a sparkling mirror before it. Unlike the other night, there were no other cars or carriages parked beside the lake. Realizing that she was the first one there, Devora approached the entrance with a small amount of trepidation.

"Mrs. Hawthorne, I'm so glad you've arrived." Smiling, the Maharaja bent to kiss her hand gallantly. He wore no turban today, and his dark hair was shot through with threads of gray. "What a pleasure to welcome you to my home once again."

"I'm the first one to arrive, am I?" Devora asked.

The Maharaja's dark eyebrows lifted. "Oh, I'm sorry. I thought I made it clear that you were to be my only guest."

"No, I hadn't realized that."

"I do hope that doesn't cause you discomfort."

"No, not particularly." In truth, Devora was rather flattered that the Maharaja had invited only her to lunch with him. "Is there a reason you've only invited me?"

The Maharaja spread his hands out in a gesture of supplication. "You are alone, are you not? I thought surely an intelligent woman such as yourself must be bored with nothing to do and no husband to take you anywhere. Am I correct?"

Devora gave him a rueful smile. "Yes, you are correct."

"Come and sit." The Maharaja led her inside the palace, which was no less splendid during the day. "I sometimes dine out on the terrace, but I'm afraid that the sun hits it directly during this time of day. I thought you would be much more comfortable in the courtyard."

They walked into the plant-filled inner courtyard. The air brushed against Devora's skin, feeling deliciously cool due to the shade and the light mist from the fountain. A musician sat on a carpet in a corner of the courtyard, his delicate sitar music accompanied by the trickling of the water.

"Please, sit down." The Maharaja pulled a chair away from the round table that had been set up near the fountain. "I've had the cooks prepare a delicious lamb curry and *dahl*. I hope you enjoy Indian food."

"I do. I love it."

The Maharaja took his seat and waved for the servants to

bring out the food and wine. "So, my dear Mrs. Hawthorne, do tell me about yourself."

Devora looked at him in surprise. "About myself?"

"Yes. What you like to do, that kind of thing."

"I enjoy painting and drawing," Devora said. She delved into her food, delighted by the spicy flavors. "I was hoping to be able to sketch some of the temples around here, but so far I've only been able to see one of them."

"You have not been to Khajuraho?"

Devora shook her head, aware of a slight flush coloring her cheeks. "My husband says that it wouldn't befit a lady to go there."

"Nonsense!" the Maharaja said emphatically. "Complete nonsense. The temples there are beautiful, and they are part of India's complex history. You cannot leave India without seeing the Khajuraho temples."

"Yes, but I've heard they're quite sexually explicit."

"But of course!" the Maharaja replied. "Such is the Kamasutra, is it not?"

"So I've heard." Devora suspected that it wouldn't be wise to confess her own interest in the Kamasutra. "Still, I have little hope that I'll see the Khajuraho temples."

"Well, you must allow me to escort you there," the Maharaja insisted. He waved a hand at a servant, who immediately came to refill Devora's plate with curry and rice. "It will be our little secret, yes?"

"Oh, I don't know if that's a very good idea."

The Maharaja shrugged, as if to say, what does it matter?

"Your husband is not here, and you've told me yourself that you want to visit the temples. Why not take advantage of my hospitality?"

"I really don't want to inconvenience you." In truth, Devora dearly wanted to see the temples. The Maharaja's offer was difficult to reject. She spooned some mango chutney into her mouth, nearly groaning aloud at the splendor of its taste.

Everything about India seemed to seethe with sensual pleasure. "And I know that my husband would not approve."

"Ah, but your husband would disapprove of you dining alone with me, would he not?"

"Probably," Devora admitted.

"And yet, here you are," the Maharaja said, as if that settled everything.

Devora couldn't argue with that point. "Well, maybe just a quick trip wouldn't hurt," she said. "Are the temples far from here?"

"Approximately two hours by car. If we left in the early morning, we could return by nightfall."

"I appreciate the offer," Devora said. "I'll have to think about it, of course."

"Of course," the Maharaja replied smoothly. "Think about a day next week that suits you. Before your husband returns, of course. Now, tell me about your life in England. I was educated at Oxford, you know, and I do miss the country."

Devora was only too happy to return the conversation to familiar ground. She told him about the apartment she and Gerald had rented before moving to India, her family, and her previous job as a bookkeeper. The Maharaja seemed to be very interested in everything she had to tell him, as he listened intently and asked questions. Devora ate until she couldn't eat any more, a situation that seemed to please the Maharaja greatly.

"I find you very appealing," he said, as the servants cleared their plates and brought out cups of tea.

"Me?" Devora said in surprise. "Appealing?"

"Yes. You have a great deal of life in you. Energy."

Devora had never thought of herself in that way before. "I'm quite ordinary, actually."

"No, you're not. No one with such interests as you have could possibly be ordinary." The Maharaja sipped some tea and pushed back his chair. "Come. We will have dessert later. I want to show you the rest of my art collection."

Devora followed him into an open room separated from the courtyard only by a lattice screen. She stopped in the doorway at the sight of the numerous sculptures and paintings. Stone and bronze sculptures of all sizes sat upon specially designed pedestals, while framed paintings lined the walls.

"It's like a museum," Devora breathed.

"It is indeed my own private museum," the Maharaja said with evident pride. "My father was not an art collector, but I started this collection when I was in my early twenties. Over the years, I have acquired some wonderful pieces."

Devora reached out and rubbed the corpulent belly of Ganesha, the elephant god. She gave the Maharaja a smile. "I've heard it's good luck to rub his belly."

"It is indeed," he agreed.

"How old are the sculptures?"

"Oh, they date from almost every period of India's history. This one is from the fifth century." The Maharaja led her around the room, explaining the styles and the content of the sculptures, which consisted of every subject from the god Shiva poised in a posture of dance, to the goddess Durga slaying the buffalo demon. There were three large sculptures of Shiva and his consort Parvati, who seemed to always be depicted as an incredibly voluptuous woman with large breasts and rounded hips. Devora paused in front of one sculpture in which Parvati was seated on Shiva's knee.

"All of the women in Indian art appear to be very seductive," she remarked.

"You mean their naked bodies?" the Maharaja asked. "These are signs of fertility, you know. Large breasts and hips mean that a woman is very fertile, which connects her with the earth and the mother goddess."

Devora gave him a skeptical look. "That's it? You mean they're not considered sexual?"

The Maharaja laughed, a deep, rich laugh that resounded off the walls. "Oh, my dear Mrs. Hawthorne, they are considered sexual indeed. Sexual union is necessary not only for procreation, but for pleasure as well. The Hindu Tantric philosophy relies heavily on the notion of divine union."

"As does the Kamasutra."

"Ah, a scholar of ancient erotic texts, are you?" The Maharaja's eyes twinkled as they stopped in front of a series of erotic paintings. "Many of these paintings are illustrations of the Kamasutra."

Devora's heart leaped as she gazed at the small, finely detailed paintings. Men and women, often still partially clothed in exotic saris and *kurtas,* lay sprawled in a multitude of positions. Their legs were often spread wide, giving the spectator a clear image of the man's penis penetrating the woman. The women all had large, beautiful breasts and curved hips, their bodies ornately decorated with gold jewelry. Devora gazed at the paintings with fascination, aware of the growing warmth collecting in her lower body.

She glanced at the Maharaja, unnerved to find him looking at her rather than the paintings.

"Um, perhaps I should leave now," she suggested.

He looked dismayed. "Mrs. Hawthorne, please tell me I haven't offended you. Come, we will sit and have some tea and sweets. You know, it is considered rude in Indian custom to visit a person's home and not partake of sweets."

Devora didn't know whether or not to believe him, but she went with him up the stairs to the balcony. They entered the same sitting room Devora had discovered with Louise, the one with large, cushy throw pillows scattered around the room and more erotic sculptures and paintings. The cloying scent of incense still clung to the air.

"Please, sit down," the Maharaja invited. "You will not be uncomfortable on the floor, I hope?"

"No, not at all." Devora sank down into a nest of pillows, unable to keep herself from relaxing against their softness. She felt utterly replete from their delicious lunch, not to mention somewhat stimulated from viewing the Maharaja's art collection.

She turned her head to look at him as he settled beside her.

"What's your name?" she asked.

He looked at her in surprise. "My name?"

"Yes, your real name. Everybody only calls you the Maharaja."

He smiled, reaching out to trail his fingers down her bare arm. Startled, Devora jerked away from the sudden touch.

"My apologies," the Maharaja said. "I do not mean to make you uncomfortable."

"No, that was just unexpected."

"You dislike me touching you?" He stroked his fingers over her arm again. This time, Devora didn't pull away.

"My name is Hastin Singh," the Maharaja said.

"Hastin Singh," Devora repeated. She leaned her head against the pillows, her head filling with the rich scent of sandalwood incense. The touch of his fingers was light and teasing. "That's a nice name."

"Thank you."

Devora gazed from afar at the erotic painting she had seen the other night, the one consisting of one man and five women.

"Are there other erotic temples in India besides Khajuraho?" she inquired.

"Yes, there are, often based on the Kamasutra as well. The Kamasutra penetrates many areas of Indian life."

"I have a copy of it at home," Devora confessed. "I'll have to read it more thoroughly."

"You know, there is a section on how a virtuous wife should behave with her husband," the Maharaja said.

Devora lifted an eyebrow. "Is that right? What does it say?"

The Maharaja lifted his hand and rapped out a few words in Hindi to a nearby servant. Within a few seconds, a servant standing near the door brought him a bound copy of the sacred text. The Maharaja opened the book to the fourth chapter.

"It says that you must act in accordance with your husband's wishes as if he were a divine being," he said. "And in his absence, you must wear auspicious jewelry and observe fasts."

Devora thought of the abundant meal she had just eaten and couldn't help giggling. "Well, I don't think my jewelry is auspicious, and I love Indian food too much to want to fast."

"You also should not leave your house unless you are accompanied by your husband's servants."

Devora rolled her eyes. "Don't show that to Rohan. He'll hold it up as the divine law."

"And you are required to do everything for your husband's welfare," the Maharaja said.

"Well, heavens, I don't think I've followed those rules at all."

The Maharaja put the book aside and leaned back against the pillows. "I suppose that means you're not a virtuous wife then, doesn't it?"

Devora didn't know whether he was being serious or joking, but she chuckled anyway. "I suppose it does. Oh, well. Virtue can be boring."

She closed her eyes, suddenly feeling very relaxed and even sleepy. "I know that book doesn't completely make women the attendants of men," she said with a yawn. "In fact, I distinctly remember that several of those details involve pleasuring a woman."

"Oh, indeed," the Maharaja said. "A man would be remiss if the woman did not obtain pleasure from their union."

Devora turned to look at him, realizing that he was much closer to her than he had been before. Oddly enough, she didn't find his proximity alarming. Instead, she merely gazed at him for a moment.

"I don't know how people do it, to be honest with you," she said.

"Do what?"

"All those positions, even just for hugging and kissing. I can't remember how many different types of kisses there are."

"There is the straight kiss." The Maharaja moved closer to her, and then his lips barely touched hers. He lifted his hands to the back of Devora's neck, his fingers sliding into her hair as he tilted her head slightly. "Then the bent kiss."

Devora's heart pulsed in her throat, but she didn't pull away from him. He tasted like spices and curry, the touch of his mouth totally different from Gerald's familiar kisses.

"And this," the Maharaja murmured, as he captured her lips between his. "Is called the clasping kiss."

Devora gasped inwardly, her fingers clenching around the edge of a pillow as the Maharaja began to slowly plunder her mouth with his. A hundred thoughts splashed around in her mind, the most prominent one being that she should pull away from him. And yet, something inside her refused to obey. Instead, she fairly sank against him, parting her lips to allow him to enter her more thoroughly. So different from Gerald. This man exuded sensuality and lust as he stroked his tongue slowly over her teeth and licked the inside of her lips. Desire sparked in Devora's blood, a desire kindled by painted visions of men and women engaging in acts of pure carnality.

She felt the Maharaja draw slightly away from her. She opened her eyes, her breathing hard as she turned to look at a woman who stood before them. An incredibly beautiful woman, dressed in a dark green silk sari and draped with gold jewelry. Her eyes were lined with kohl, and a small diamond pierced her nose. She wore dozens of gold bracelets and rings, including several on her toes. Devora stared at her as if she were a vision out of nowhere. Good God, what if this was the Maharaja's wife?

"Who . . ." Devora swallowed hard and tried again. "Who are you?"

The woman looked at the Maharaja, who nodded slightly.

"My name is Channa," she replied, her words hesitating and tinged with a heavy Indian accent. "I come to please you, yes?"

Devora looked from Channa to the Maharaja and back again, suddenly getting a sick feeling in the pit of her stomach as she realized what Channa was implying. "No!"

"Wait." The Maharaja put his hand over Devora's, shaking his head as he started to laugh. "She means that she will bring us tea and sweets," he said.

Devora's heart was pounding so hard that she could hear it inside her head. "That didn't sound like what she meant."

The Maharaja said a few words in Hindi to the woman, who padded off in a rustle of silk and gold. "I'm sorry, Mrs. Hawthorne. Her English is not very good."

A thought suddenly occurred to Devora as she recalled Kalindi's words. "Is she part of your harem?"

The Maharaja laughed again, that deep, throaty chuckle. "You've heard of my harem, have you?"

"Yes. Do you have one?"

"I do enjoy women, if that's what you mean," the Maharaja replied.

"Does that mean yes?"

The Maharaja shrugged slightly and waved his hand toward one of the servants. "I fear I have frightened you."

Devora didn't reply, although she acknowledged that he had. She suspected that this situation might present her with more than she had bargained for. Excitement was one thing, but to be confronted by a harem woman was quite another. Devora remembered her and Gerald's last coupling when he had questioned her about her interest in other women. The mere memory caused a rush of heat to flood her body.

A servant brought them cups of tea and a silver platter filled with milky sweets. Devora popped one of the sweets in her mouth and sipped her tea, trying to collect her thoughts. She licked sugar off her finger and eyed the Maharaja.

"What exactly do you want from me?" she asked.

"Why, nothing at all, Mrs. Hawthorne."

Devora smiled at the innocent tone to his voice. "Now why don't I believe that?"

The Maharaja pressed a hand against his chest as if she had mortally wounded him. "I want to be your friend," he said. "Can you accept my friendship?"

"That kiss felt a little more than friendly."

"You didn't like it? Then I will never attempt such a brash act again."

Devora smiled again. Such melodrama. She surprised herself with her next words. "Well, I didn't say that," she said.

The Maharaja glanced at her. "You would like it again?"

"Possibly." Devora didn't know what she was thinking, but she did know that the Maharaja's kiss had been a heady one. She didn't even really consider the notion that she was being unfaithful to Gerald, for it felt as if she were in a completely different world, one removed from the conventions of Western propriety.

When the Maharaja leaned toward her again, she didn't pull away. She let him touch her lips with his again in a kiss that again deepened slowly. Devora sank back against the pillows, her bones going weak as she let him move over her. Men had touched and kissed her before Gerald, but none possessed the same kind of seductive heat as the Maharaja did.

His hands skimmed lightly over her body, lingering at the hard points of her nipples and the curve of her waist. His touch was feather light, almost purposely gentle, as if he were afraid of scaring her away. His body pressed against hers. He was a large man, hardly slender, and the weight of his physique pushed Devora against her bed of pillows until she felt wholly surrounded by him.

She had never been so close to a man like him before, and her senses spun with a myriad of sensations. Her legs parted almost unconsciously to accommodate him, her blood surging as she felt his erection pressing against her thigh. She closed her eyes. The Maharaja slid his lips to her neck, flicking his tongue into the hot hollow of her throat. Sweat broke out on Devora's forehead as she became immersed by heat, scents, and spice. The Maharaja's hands slipped underneath the wide straps of her dress, pulling them over her arms as he slowly bared her body to his gaze.

Devora's breath caught in her throat as she realized the sheer magnitude of what was about to take place. She couldn't have stopped him even if she wanted to, for she felt as if the tides of the ocean itself were rising inside her. Some dim, rational part of her mind made her turn toward the door to see if the servant was still standing there, but the room was empty. Sunlight filtered through the marble lattice. Devora pushed aside any lingering inhibitions and gave herself up to the pure sensuality of her surroundings and her lover. As the Maharaja cupped her breasts in his hands, he began murmuring words in Hindi that sounded exotic and musical.

Devora experienced a momentary fear that her slender, small-breasted body, so wholly different than the voluptuous Indian fertility goddesses, would be displeasing to him. The Maharaja soon alleviated her fears by fairly worshipping her body, stroking his hands and lips over her skin with a kind of reverence. He pushed her dress off her body, then threaded his fingers through the dark curls between her legs. Devora lay back and let him touch her, awash in the feeling of another man's hands on her. Warm and slow, the Maharaja's hands caressed her as if he had never touched a woman before. Devora wanted to tell him to take off his clothes, but then she recalled the paintings that contained images of half-dressed people. Maybe it was an Indian custom that men remained clothed during lovemaking.

The Maharaja soon disproved Devora's theory when he moved away from her and unfastened his *kurta*. His dark eyes burned with an edge of lust as he then pushed off his trousers to reveal the short, thick stalk of his penis. Devora's gaze raked over him, his barrel-like chest and heavy belly, the darkness of his skin, the lush mat of black hair. His stocky physique was not one that she would have normally considered beautiful, but then there was nothing normal about this situation. Need boiled inside her like an overflowing teapot. She wanted to be crushed and taken by him, to feel the weight of his body on hers and his penis inside her.

A moan of pleasure escaped her when the Maharaja leaned over her, his cock seeking out the humid fissure between her legs. Devora wrapped her arms around him, touching the abundance of his flesh and the strength of his body. His chest hairs rubbed deliciously against her nipples, creating a most delightful friction. With a grunt, the Maharaja slipped his hands underneath her thighs to push her legs farther apart. His hot breath rasped against Devora's lips as he began edging forward, the knob of his penis rubbing against her labia.

Devora gasped, pushing her hips upward with the need to feel him inside her. She clutched his shoulders as he positioned himself and thrust into her. The sensation of his penis immersed in her snug channel was enough to make Devora cry out. He wasn't as large as Gerald and thus didn't fill her as thoroughly, but oh, what pleasure it was be so totally possessed by him. Her broken moans filled the air as the Maharaja began thrusting into her, each thrust accompanied by a heavy grunt. He was heavy and hot above her, and Devora reveled in the sheer weight of him. She wrapped her legs around his thighs and gave herself up to their raw carnality, only to be startled when the Maharaja pulled out of her.

Devora looked at him in surprise. "What happened?"

"We will try another position, of course." The Maharaja settled back against the pillows and wrapped his hand around his cock.

Mesmerized, Devora stared with unabashed curiosity as the Maharaja began to stroke his own flesh. She was fascinated by the rhythmic movement of his hand.

"Another position?" she repeated.

"Yes. Like the Kamasutra says. Lovemaking consists of many different postures and pleasures, not merely one."

"What do you want to do now?" Devora asked. Her sex fairly quivered with anticipation.

"Come here," the Maharaja said. "Straddle me."

Devora's heart slammed against her rib cage. She had been thinking of this position just yesterday. Had it only been yesterday? It felt like such a terribly long time ago. She moved toward him, her gaze fixed on his jutting penis. She straddled his pelvis, bracing herself on the wide expanse of his chest as she leaned back into him. He put one hand on her hip, while guiding his cock toward her with the other hand. Devora groaned with pleasure as she sank down onto him. In this position, he seemed to fill her more completely, sending heat throbbing through her inner walls. Moreover, her clit rubbed against him, stimulating her own arousal to unfathomable depths.

"Oh, God." Devora didn't quite know what to do, but she went with her instincts and began to move up and down. She looked down at the Maharaja's languid expression, his harsh breaths telling her that she was doing this right.

This was an oddly liberating position, allowing her to create a rhythm of her own liking rather than always leaving it up to the man. Devora toyed with the Maharaja's nipples as she lifted her body and brought it down again, spurring herself toward her release. She began to ride him more and more frantically as the pressure built. She cried out loudly as an explosion of rapture rained through her body, writhing her hips to derive every ounce of pleasure. Letting the Maharaja's penis slip out of her, Devora moved back on his thighs and grasped his shaft. She stroked his oiled cock from base to tip in a quick, fast rhythm. Within seconds, the Maharaja grunted, his seed spurting from him in milky jets. Devora continued stroking him until he became flaccid again.

"I've never done that before," she admitted, rolling back onto the pillows. Her breath came in heavy gasps as she tried to catch her breath. "That position, I mean."

"Straddle a man?" The Maharaja turned to look at her.

"No, never." Devora couldn't believe that she had just done that with the Maharaja, of all people in the world.

"Pity," the Maharaja said. "That position is exquisite for both the man and the woman."

"Yes, it is." Devora looked at the sweaty roundness of the Maharaja's face. "You're not going to tell anyone about this, are you?"

He pressed a hand against his chest. "My dear Mrs. Hawthorne, of course not. This is our secret. I am honored that you trust me enough to attempt a new position with me."

"Yes, well, there are a number of postures I haven't tried, at least if the Kamasutra is anything to judge me by."

"Then you're missing many of the greatest sensual pleasures," the Maharaja said. "Attempting different postures is most fulfilling."

"My husband is passionate, but not very experimental."

"Then perhaps you require a different teacher."

chapter six

Devora crept up the steps to the front door, feeling like a teenager who was trying to sneak into the house past curfew. She'd stayed with the Maharaja until well past nightfall, and now it was close to ten. Stepping inside, she was relieved to find the bungalow dark and silent. She wouldn't have put it past Rohan to be sitting up waiting for her.

Devora went into her bedroom and kicked off her shoes. Her body still quivered with the remnants of passion, and her sex felt deliciously sore. In spite of the Maharaja's somewhat small size, the difference of positions seemed to have touched previously unreached places in her, leaving her feeling thoroughly taken. A shiver of delight raced through her at the crudity of the thought. How terribly clandestine and rebellious it was to have done what she did.

"*Memsahib,* you're back."

Devora whirled around at the sound of Rohan's voice. He stood in the doorway, wrapped in shadows like some sort of demon.

"Yes, I am, thank you. You may leave now."

"I might suggest that returning after dark is dangerous," Rohan said. Disapproval threaded his voice. "There have been incidents of gangs attacking people on the road."

"Well, as you can see, I have arrived safe and sound," Devora replied coldly. "Thank you, however, for your concern."

"Also, it is not a good idea to stay at the palace alone at night," Rohan continued.

"Don't tell me," Devora said, wondering just how much Rohan suspected about her activities with the Maharaja. "There have been rumors of the Maharaja's crazed orgies or something."

"I am required to look after your safety."

"Has it ever occurred to you that I can look after my own safety?" Devora said in exasperation. "I told you that I'm not interested in being treated like a child."

"Then perhaps you should act like an adult."

Devora gasped with outrage. "How dare you speak to me like that? I'll have my husband dismiss you when he returns!"

"I am only concerned with the matter of your reputation, which of course reflects on that of your husband."

Devora clenched her hands into fists, fairly trembling with fury. "Excuse me? My reputation is none of your business. You're nothing more than a servant, and I will not have you talking to me like that!"

"I will have to insist that I accompany you on your next outing."

"You will do no such thing! Don't you countermand my orders!"

"My orders come from your husband."

"Not when he's away, they don't!" Devora was even angrier that Rohan didn't appear irritated in the slightest. His expression was as unreadable as ever, his words spoken without infliction. She was ready to slap him to see if that at least would provoke a reaction.

"I said you may leave now," she snapped.

Rohan looked at her for a long moment. Then, without another word, he turned and left.

Furious, Devora slammed the door behind him and stripped off her clothes. Who did he think he was? Just because Gerald was gone, that gave him no right to question her like that.

So why did his obvious disapproval bother her so much? Devora scowled at her reflection in the mirror as she brushed her hair. She wished she had an answer to that question. She didn't even like the man, so why did it matter what he thought of her?

Devora climbed into bed, suddenly exhausted from the events of the day and her confrontation with Rohan. She fell into a deep sleep, saturated with lovely dreams of herself being kissed and touched with extraordinary reverence.

"Devora?"

Devora opened her eyes to the gauzy fabric of the mosquito netting. She yawned and blinked as she focused on Louise's slender figure behind the net.

"Louise, what are you doing here?" Devora buried her face in the pillow and closed her eyes again, wanting to sink back into the lushness of her dreams.

"I wanted to see if you're still coming to Agra with us." Louise pulled aside the netting and sat down on the edge of the bed. "Kalindi told me you were still sleeping."

"Mmm, I've been awfully tired." Devora yawned again. She squinted as sunlight brushed against her eyes. The morning sun spilled through the lace curtains, creating an intricate pattern on the hardwood floor. "What time is it?"

"Past nine. You're not feeling sick, are you?"

Devora latched on to the explanation. "Well, I do have a rather bad headache. When are you leaving for Agra?"

"Tomorrow morning. Have you forgotten already?"

"No, but I'm afraid I won't be able to go," Devora said. The last thing she wanted to do now was spend several days in the company of the Thompsons and other British people. "I'm not feeling up to it."

"I hope you're not coming down with malaria or anything." Louise reached out and put her hand on Devora's forehead.

"You do feel a little warm. Maybe I should stay here with you."

"No, I'd really rather be alone, thanks," Devora said, thinking that it would be a perfect opportunity to see the Maharaja again if the Thompsons and Louise weren't around to keep an eye on her or to question her whereabouts. "You go and have a good time. I'll see the Taj Mahal some other time."

A crease of worry appeared between Louise's eyebrows. "You're sure? I hate to think of you here all alone."

"Really, Louise, I'll be fine. I'll just sleep a lot over the next few days. You'd be terribly bored hanging around here."

"Well, all right. I do wish you could come with us, though."

"I'll come on the next trip."

"I hope so. I'll leave you to get some sleep, then."

"Thank you for stopping by. Please give my regrets to the Thompsons."

"I will. Take care of yourself." Louise let the mosquito net fall back into place as she left the room.

Devora rolled onto her back, feeling guilty over having lied to her friend. Still, having Louise and the Thompsons out of town for a few days was exactly what she needed. The British community could be decidedly suffocating.

She got out of bed and went to take a bath, aware of a lingering soreness between her legs. As she sank into the hot water, she let her thoughts drift back to her day with the Maharaja, a day of pure carnality. Just before she had left to return home, the Maharaja had said that he hoped to see her again and to take her to the Khajuraho temples.

As she slid the soap over her body, the scent reminding her of the sandalwood incense in the palace, Devora acknowledged that she hoped he would, too. Of course, she felt guilty over being unfaithful to her husband, but then, he had also been unfaithful to her. And it wasn't as if she had any intentions of ruining her relationship with Gerald. All she wanted to do was explore avenues that she would probably never have a chance to explore again.

"So, *memsahib,* you enjoyed lunching with the Maharaja?" Kalindi asked when Devora sat down at the dining table. "What was it like?"

"It was very nice, Kalindi. Please bring me some toast."

"Did you find out about the harem?"

Devora shot the young woman a disapproving look. "Kalindi, I don't care to discuss this. Please go about your work."

Kalindi looked disappointed, but she nodded and returned to the kitchen. With a sigh, Devora sipped her tea and read a newspaper from the British government. She was surprised to see an article about an Indian gang who had just broken into the British governor's home near Delhi. Apparently, the crime was thought to be committed by a gang known for roaming the countryside committing acts of violence against the British. Devora recalled that Mr. Thompson had said they even suspected the Maharaja of funding such gangs.

A shiver rained down Devora's spine, and she pushed the newsletter aside. Whatever politics were involved, it was probably better that she didn't know too much about them. At least, not if she was planning to see the Maharaja again.

After getting dressed, she went out onto the back veranda. Rohan, clad in his usual uniform of a white jacket and black trousers, was in the garden trimming dried flowers off the rosebushes. Devora watched him for a moment, then descended the steps to approach him.

"I thought there was a gardener on staff who did that," she remarked.

Rohan glanced up at the sound of her voice. "There is," he said. "I merely enjoy gardening, so I sometimes do it myself."

Devora remembered what he had said to her just last night, and she fought a sudden rush of anger. She wouldn't find him so irritating if he would at least display some sort of emotion, but his complete impassivity annoyed her to no end. It made him seem somehow inhuman.

"Heavens," she murmured. "I didn't realize that you actually could enjoy something."

He clipped another flower and didn't reply.

"Maybe you should enjoy yourself a little more," Devora suggested. Her gaze roved over the hard lines of his profile. The sunlight glinted off his black hair, shredding it into luminous strands. "Not be so rigorous."

Rohan dropped the faded flowers into a bucket at his feet. "Thank you for your advice."

"Are you married?" Devora asked.

"No, *memsahib*."

"Why doesn't that surprise me?" Devora murmured.

Rohan straightened and leveled his dark gaze on her. "Was there something you wanted?"

Devora gave him a beatific smile. "No, I'm just curious. I suspect that women are rather frightened of you."

"Is that right? Are you?"

The question startled Devora. "No, of course not. I think you can be a bastard, but I'm not afraid of you."

"I'm only carrying out orders."

"Of course you are." Devora recalled the other morning when she had caught Rohan standing outside her and Gerald's bedroom door. Her heart pulsed as she thought again of what he had witnessed and how she must have looked. She wondered what kind of images were burned into his mind.

"You're good at that, aren't you?" she asked. "Carrying out orders."

"So I have been told."

"Good, then why don't you bring me a glass of lemonade? It's getting rather hot out here."

"Yes, *memsahib*." Rohan dropped the clippers into the bucket and headed toward the house with his long-legged stride.

Devora smiled and returned to sit on the veranda. Maybe it was about time she showed him who was boss, regardless of whatever Gerald had told him. She lowered herself into a wicker chair and stretched her legs out in front of her. A trickle of sweat ran down between her breasts. She picked up a bamboo fan and began fanning herself. Her limbs felt loose and relaxed after last night with the Maharaja. Moreover, she felt deliciously wicked. She unbuttoned the top two buttons of her dress to let the air circulate.

She watched Rohan approach her with a glass of lemonade on a tray. He set the tray on a table next to her and handed her a napkin.

"You require something else?" he asked. His gaze darted to the valley created by her unbuttoned dress and the gentle swell of her moist breasts.

A surge of pure triumph rose in Devora as Rohan looked quickly away from her. Hah. So he wasn't as stoic as he appeared to be. He was a man just like any other man. All he needed to express that was a push in the right direction. After all of Devora's wondering about what it would take to provoke a reaction in him, it turned out to be the exact same thing that would provoke a reaction in any other man. She might even have been disappointed by that realization if she weren't so thrilled by it.

"So, why don't you sit down and rest for a moment?" she said, waving her hand toward another chair. She sipped the sweet lemonade gratefully.

Rohan sat down, averting his gaze from her to look out at the garden.

Devora crossed her legs, surreptitiously hiking her skirt up a few inches. She'd show him who was in control here.

"So, how long have you been a servant?" she asked in a conversational tone.

"Since I was fifteen."

"And how old are you now?"

"Thirty-five."

"You've always worked for the British, have you? That must be why your English is so good."

Rohan nodded and glanced at her. His eyes wandered over the curve of her calf before he cleared his throat and stood. "I'm sorry, *memsahib,* but I must return to my duties."

"Of course," Devora murmured. She sucked on a piece of ice and watched him return to the rosebushes.

With an instinct as old as time, she knew their relationship had just taken on a whole different dimension.

"Devora, I don't want you visiting him alone again." Gerald poured himself another brandy and gave Devora a severe look. He'd been home for less than twenty-four hours, only to discover that Devora had not just gone cavorting off to the Maharaja's palace alone, but also that she hadn't been attending any of the British functions. "I don't like it."

Devora sighed. "Really, Gerald, it's all perfectly civilized. I've simply had lunch with him several times."

"Several times? I thought you'd only gone once!"

Devora spread her hands out. "Once, twice, what's the difference?"

Gerald swallowed some brandy and eyed his wife suspiciously. The difference was that she *seemed* different. He didn't know why, but there was something rather too relaxed and secretive about her. She was such a lovely woman with those large brown eyes that could appear so innocent. Only Gerald had firsthand knowledge of the wickedness that lay within his wife.

"The Thompsons told me that you didn't even go with them to Agra," Gerald said. "That you were sick or something."

"Yes, I'm afraid I had a mild cold. I didn't feel up to traveling."

"Well, we won't have that happen again," Gerald said. "You probably caught something at the palace. I want you to promise me that you won't go there alone again."

"Oh, Gerald, I was just doing something unique." Devora stood and approached him. She slipped her arms around his waist and leaned her head against his chest. "I was so terribly bored without you, and the Maharaja came here specifically to invite me. I couldn't say no."

"Devora, I might be away rather frequently," Gerald said,

unable to keep himself from drawing in the scent of her hair. "I want to know that you'll be safe."

"I will be." Devora reached up to kiss his neck. "I promise. Besides, Rohan looks after me quite thoroughly."

Gerald didn't miss the somewhat bitter note in Devora's voice. He pulled back slightly to look at her. "What does that mean?"

She shrugged and toyed with the collar of his shirt. "He acts like my nanny rather than a servant," she replied. "Questioning my whereabouts and all that."

Gerald sighed. "Devora, I asked you not to make this difficult. Rohan is acting on my orders."

"Well, you don't have to order him to virtually keep me under lock and key," Devora muttered.

"Now that I know you've been visiting the Maharaja alone, I might do just that," Gerald snapped.

Devora pulled away from him, her eyes flashing. "Honestly, Gerald, who is the servant around here, me or him?"

"Devora, this isn't England! You can't run about alone here!"

"I didn't realize that you also could order me about like a dog!" Devora snapped.

Gerald ran a hand tiredly through his hair and tried to reign in his temper. It was true that Devora had to get used to more restrictions than she was comfortable with, but that didn't mean she could try and break them at every opportunity. "Darling, let's not fight. I can't ask Rohan not to keep an eye on you, and you must not make it difficult for him."

"That seems to be my main occupation here," Devora replied. "Not making things difficult."

"There are plenty of activities for you, if you'd only avail yourself of them," Gerald said.

"Yes, watching cricket matches and attending garden parties. I could do all of that back in London, but I certainly couldn't visit a Maharaja's palace there." She shook her head and sighed, turning away from him. "I'm sorry, Gerald. I don't mean to be upsetting you, but this is such a wonderful country that I can't abide being restricted from it."

"And I can't abide being constantly worried about your safety."

Devora nodded, a hint of guilt flashing in her expression. "I know. I'm sorry. I'll cooperate."

"Good." Gerald nodded and swallowed the last of his brandy, feeling somewhat vindicated.

"I'm going to bed." Devora tugged her robe around herself and stood on tiptoe to kiss him good night. "I'm awfully tired."

"Sleep well, darling."

"You, too." Devora went into the bedroom, closing the door behind her.

Gerald poured himself a bit more brandy and went to the doorway that led to the veranda. He stared out at the night sky, thinking that as long as he lived in India, he would never fully understand the country or its people.

"*Sahib,* if you wish nothing else, I'll retire for the night."

Gerald turned at the sound of Rohan's voice. "No, nothing, thanks."

Rohan nodded. "Good night then."

"Wait a moment." Gerald swirled his brandy in the glass and hesitated. "Besides her visits to the Maharaja's palace, have you noticed anything different about my wife?"

"Different? No. However, she appears to be very headstrong."

A smile tugged at Gerald's mouth. "Yes. She is that." He took another sip of brandy and returned to stare out at the night. "Rohan, I'm afraid I'm going to have to ask you to keep a closer eye on her when I'm away. I realize that you are the servant, but I'm a bit worried about her."

"I'm afraid she refuses to listen to me."

"Yes, well, perhaps you'll have to follow her a bit and listen in on conversations," Gerald said. "Just so that you have a better idea of what's going on, you understand."

"Yes, *sahib.*"

"Fine, thanks. That'll be all. Good night."

Rohan murmured another good night and left to return to the servants' quarters. Gerald finished his brandy and put the glass on the sideboard. Despite the alcohol burning through his veins, he still felt tense. He knew his tension wasn't only a result of his words with Devora, but also simply from having been without a woman for two weeks. He was in no mood to attempt amorous activities with his wife, so he went out onto the veranda and started in the direction of Kalindi's apartment on the outskirts of the village. A single oil lantern burned in the window of her room.

Gerald didn't bother knocking. He opened the door and let himself in, his passion surging at the sight of Kalindi's half-naked form lying underneath the sheets. Her dark skin fairly glowed in the dim light as she lay with her head propped on her hand, skimming through a magazine spread out on the bed. She wore a sleeveless cotton shift, and the bedsheet slid off her figure to expose her bare thighs.

Gerald closed the door hard, causing Kalindi to look up, startled.

"Sahib!"

"Hello, Kalindi." Gerald reached up to unbutton his shirt. His cock was half-hard already. "I've missed you."

Kalindi stared at him, her dark eyes sparkling with a hint of mutiny. Then, she pressed her lips together and nodded. "I am missing you, too."

Gerald cast his shirt aside and unbuttoned his trousers, reaching out to run his fingers through Kalindi's coconut-scented hair. "Come on, then, darling. Make me feel good."

Kalindi's throat muscles worked as she swallowed, lifting herself up to enclose the head of his penis between her lips. Gerald let out a groan as Kalindi began to take his stiff flesh into the hot, wet cavern of her mouth. Her lips slid slowly over him, her tongue teasing as she traced the veins of his shaft. She was a wicked one, Kalindi was. She knew how to please a man. She reached down to caress his testicles, rubbing the secret area between his genitals and his anus with a light touch that scorched his desire.

Gerald wrapped the length of Kalindi's hair around his hand, pumping his hips so that his prick slid in and out of her mouth. He loved watching Kalindi when she was doing this, the way her lips puckered up and her tongue flickered out of her mouth. He reached down to massage her breasts through her shift, rolling her large nipples between his fingers. He liked Kalindi's body, which was full, womanly, and very different from Devora's more slender figure. Ah, how delicious to have the best of two worlds.

Gerald moved away from Kalindi, his cock as hard as stone as he pulled the woman's shift over her head. He gazed for a moment at the lush curves of Kalindi's body, then straddled her abdomen and pressed his cock between her tits.

"Squeeze them," he said hoarsely, feeling as if he would explode then and there.

Kalindi pressed her breasts together, her abundant flesh surrounding and immersing his penis like warm pillows. Gerald's entire body stiffened with tension as he pumped his cock back and forth, his balls slamming against the undersides of Kalindi's breasts. A powerful pressure began to build at the base of his penis, and he pulled away from her before he lost control completely. He slid down the length of Kalindi's body, reaching to push her thighs apart and delve his fingers into the plentiful curls between her legs. Kalindi gave a little moan of pleasure, spreading her legs even wider to allow him access. Gerald pushed his erection into her slowly, savoring the sensation of her tight heat enclosing him. His blood was hot with the need for release, but he so enjoyed the act of fucking that he sought to prolong it for as long as possible.

Pushing Kalindi's legs almost up to her chest, he penetrated her as far as he could go, pushing in and out so hard that her body shook with each thrust. Whimpers spilled from Kalindi's throat in a steady stream. Gerald bent to capture one of her nipples between his teeth, licking thirstily at the salty taste of her skin. Ah, woman. He could drown in a woman's taste and scent and, oh yes, her cunt. Kalindi's inner muscles tightened around him in the way she knew he liked, stimulating his fire all the more potently. With a groan, Gerald pulled out of her, grasping his cock in his hand as he stroked it up and down. Within seconds, a shudder of pure rapture exploded through his body, and his seed spurted out onto Kalindi's dark mons.

"Oh, Christ." Gerald flopped down next to Kalindi, gasping as he tried to catch his breath. "That was wonderful."

Kalindi propped her elbow on her chest as she gazed down at him with a smile. "You are missing me, yes?"

"Sometimes, yes." Gerald put his hands on her shoulders and dropped a kiss on her forehead before pushing her gently away. He wasn't certain he liked Kalindi's growing possessiveness. "I must go now."

"You will return when, *sahib?*" Kalindi asked.

"I don't know." Gerald dressed quickly. Kalindi was wonderful when it came to satisfying his physical needs, but he had little use for her otherwise. Housekeepers and cooks were readily available in this godforsaken country.

Kalindi watched him dress, skimming a hand down her naked body.

"Good night, Kalindi." Gerald dug into his pocket and tossed a few rupees on the bedside table before he turned and left.

chapter seven

H onestly, I simply can't understand it." Mrs. Thompson
shook her head and took another dainty sip of tea. "Your
husband is away at work every day, and yet you still won't
join us for our bridge parties. What is it you do all day long?"

"I've been working on my paintings," Devora said. She
waved a hand toward the dining table, which she had converted
into a veritable worktable. Her sketch pads, paints, and pencils
lay scattered over the entire table, and a half-finished painting
rested on an easel by the window. "I've done so many sketches
that I thought it was about time I turn them into paintings."

"Well, you can only do so much doodling," Adele said. She
was sitting on the piano bench, looking very refined and British
in a white dress and pearls. "Isn't Gerald leaving this weekend
again?"

"Yes, he has to take a trip to Delhi," Devora replied. "He
promises that the next time he goes, he'll take me with him."

Mrs. Thompson chuckled. "Oh, my dear, they always say
that. But, don't worry. You'll get used to living with an absent
husband. We all do eventually."

Devora glanced at Adele, who nodded in agreement. "Yes,
we do."

"Well, Gerald is different," Devora said. "He has no intentions of simply leaving me here to rot."

"Oh, no, they never have the intention of doing that," Adele replied. She turned to the piano and began to play a light, delicate tune. "Somehow, though, that's what always seems to happen. That's why we have to occupy ourselves with bridge parties and luncheons."

"Speaking of luncheons . . ." Mrs. Thompson leaned forward as if she were about to hear news of great import. "We heard that you dined with the Maharaja himself recently."

Devora's eyebrows lifted. "Really? Where did you hear that?"

Mrs. Thompson waved her hand in the air. "Oh, you know, dear. Servants gossip, don't they?"

"So I've been told," Devora replied dryly.

"Well?" Mrs. Thompson's double chin fairly quivered with excitement over the possibility of hearing the news from the main source. "Is it true? You dined with the Maharaja?"

Devora nodded. "Yes, it's true. He invited me to have lunch with him a few weeks ago. It was all very proper, I assure you."

"I don't doubt it," Mrs. Thompson said. "But, my goodness, Devora, you must have more caution. This is how rumors get started, and with the Maharaja's reputation, you can't be too careful."

"It was a very simple lunch," Devora said, knowing perfectly well that she was about to be the subject of rumors herself, probably ones started by Mrs. Thompson.

"The mere idea is highly irregular, you know."

"We also heard that you returned after dark," Adele said, pinning her gaze on Devora as if daring her to dispute the fact.

"Yes. We had car trouble on the way back, I'm afraid. These things do happen."

"Yes, but not often when one is returning from a Maharaja's palace," Adele said.

Devora made a big show of looking at the clock. "My goodness, would you look at how late it is? I'm so sorry we didn't have a longer opportunity to visit. I do hope we can get together next week sometime."

"Yes, and I might suggest that you do join us for bridge." Mrs. Thompson collected her gloves and hat, giving Devora a pointed look. "You wouldn't want people to think you are unsociable, now would you?"

"That's the last thing I want," Devora agreed. "Thank you both for stopping by."

She saw them out, then rang the servant's bell for Kalindi to clear away the tea things. She considered the idea of giving Kalindi a lecture on gossiping, but she knew it would be a futile effort. Instead, she went to her easel and resumed work on her painting. She had drawn a sketch of a full-breasted female statue, and she was in the process of making a small painting from it.

"*Memsahib,* you require something?" Rohan stopped beside the table.

Devora glanced up. "Oh, no, I just wanted Kalindi to clear the tea things," she replied. "Thank you."

Rohan nodded and turned to leave. A sudden thought occurred to Devora as she looked at the broad expanse of his back.

"Rohan?"

He turned toward her again. "Yes."

"Can I draw you?"

"I beg your pardon?"

"Draw." Devora gestured toward her sketch pads and pencils. "I would like to draw a portrait of you."

"I don't think that would be a good idea."

Devora sighed. "Do you think *anything* is a good idea?"

"Begging your pardon again, please?"

Devora put down her paintbrush and approached him. She placed her hand on his arm, realizing that this was the first time she was actually touching him. His arm felt warm and strong underneath his jacket. Devora guided him to a chair and told him to sit.

"*Memsahib,* I must return to my duties."

"Oh, sod your duties for a change."

"Excuse me?"

Devora couldn't help smiling. He looked as if she had just asked him to strip naked and dance the waltz. "All you have to do is sit there, Rohan. I'll do all the rest."

She turned one of her sketch pads to a fresh sheet of paper and picked up a sharpened pencil. After gazing at the lines of Rohan's face, she turned her attention to the paper and began sketching what she saw. His face was made for representation on paper. A strong jawline; high, broad cheekbones; a sensual mouth; eyes as dark as midnight and filled with mystery. Devora drew his black hair with long, sweeping strokes, pleased that a few locks of his hair fell over his forehead. Somehow, the wayward strands humanized him.

"Wait. Move your head to the right a little."

Devora stood and put her hands on either side of his head, turning his head slightly. His hair felt delicious against her hands, and she fought the urge to stroke her fingers through the thick strands. Her heart leaped as she glanced at him and saw that his eyes were on a direct line of vision to her breasts. And that he was looking at them. Devora's nipples hardened against her dress so suddenly that she was shocked. She quickly moved to sit back down, unnerved by how she had reacted to a simple leer that any man would have made in the same circumstance. Clearing her throat, she resumed the sketch.

Although she usually tried to capture an expression on her subjects' faces, she knew that such a feat would be impossible with Rohan. His implacability would transfer even to paper. Devora spent an hour rendering his likeness on her sketch pad before she put her pencil down.

"All right, that's all I need," she said. "Thank you."

Rohan nodded shortly and stood. "May I see it?"

Devora hesitated, but opened the pad and showed him her work. Rohan looked at his image. In that moment, Devora realized she was holding her breath as she waited for his verdict.

"Very good," he finally said.

"Thank you." Devora snapped the sketch pad closed and leveled a look at him. She was almost annoyed by how much his words pleased her, for it reinforced the notion that she cared what he thought of her. Which, of course, she didn't. At all.

Devora moved to stand in front of her easel again. "You may leave now."

After he had gone, Devora looked at the sketch again. He had the most intriguing face, full of character and strong planes. If he would exhibit his emotions more readily, his face would be alive with life. As it was, his expression remained as unmovable as a statue. Devora didn't think she could capture his humanity even if she tried.

She put down the sketch pad and went after him. "Rohan, wait."

He turned from the doorway leading to the kitchen. *"Memsahib?"*

"Do you ever smile?"

"Excuse me?"

"Smile. Do you ever smile?"

"I have no reason to."

Frustration rose in Devora like a wave. "Everyone has a reason to smile. Smiling is part of . . . of everyday life, for heaven's sake."

"I will remember that."

"God, you are such a . . . a machine," Devora said, her hands clenching into fists at her sides. "Nothing moves you, does it?"

"I'm afraid I don't know what you mean."

"No, I didn't think you would." Devora looked at him and shook her head. "Never mind. Go about your duties. Tell Kalindi to draw me a bath, please. I need to dress for dinner."

"Yes, *memsahib.*" With a shrug, Rohan disappeared into the kitchen.

Devora stood there for a moment, biting down on her thumbnail. She had never been one to back away from a challenge, particularly one as intriguing as Rohan.

She turned and went into the bedroom and sat at her dressing table. Her skin had already turned a shade darker from the sun, despite her use of hats and parasols. She unclipped her hair and brushed it out, then went to take a bath. After scrubbing away the never-ending dust of India, she slipped into a silk dressing gown and went back to the bedroom. Gerald would be returning home shortly, an event that Devora had begun to anticipate. At least when Gerald was home, she had someone to talk to besides the tiresome British women.

Settling on the bed, she opened the English copy of the Kamasutra and began to read. The Maharaja had been correct when he said there was a section on the behavior of virtuous wives, although Devora wasn't surprised that the book lacked a similar section for virtuous husbands. Instead, there were sections on using the fingernails during sex, and the various ways to bite one's partner. And, oh, the postures of sexual intercourse, including the "support" congress up against a wall and the "yawning" position in which a woman put her legs on the man's shoulders.

Devora chuckled. If a woman actually yawned in the yawning position, then she was with the wrong man. She leafed through the pages, not surprised that many of the commandments didn't put women in a very favorable light. Nor was she terribly thrilled with some of the names of the types of union, including the "congress of the cow" if a woman was on her hands and knees.

Although, Devora thought, as she pushed the book aside, *she would like to try that, regardless of the name.* A quiver rippled through her body at the thought of being so wholly exposed while Gerald pounded into her from behind. Ah, how she hoped that she could convince Gerald of the pleasures of experimentation. The mere idea made her sex pulse. She lifted her arms above her head in a long stretch, allowing her muscles to lengthen gloriously. Her limbs felt loose and weak after her soak in a warm bath, and she closed her eyes to enjoy the sensations.

With images of sexual congress swimming behind her eyelids, Devora slipped a finger between her thighs and gently teased the outer lips of her labia. Her skin was still damp from the bath, but the heat of her skin began to evaporate lingering water droplets. Devora sighed with pleasure as she teased her sex with a finger, stroking the plump lips and toying with the dark curls. As much as she loved being with a man, there was something so personally intimate about touching oneself. She relaxed against the pillows and probed a little deeper with her finger just as a noise sounded at the door.

Devora lifted her eyelids halfway and fixed her gaze on the shadowy figure behind the bedroom door. She froze as her heart leaped into her throat. It had to be Rohan watching her again. A rush of anger broke through her shock. She might have believed that the last time was an accident, but what if he were actually seeking her out and waiting to witness her most private moments? What if all those rumors about Indian men were correct? Watching her sexually must be the only thing that made Rohan respond.

And wasn't that what she had been wanting? His response?

Devora hesitated for a minute, but then her fingers began working almost of their own volition at her sex again. She couldn't believe she was actually doing this with the knowledge that Rohan was standing just behind the door. The knowledge of his presence, however, inflamed a rush of desire over her veins. She spread her thighs wider, drawing in a breath as she slipped her finger into the moist folds of her vulva. Closing her eyes again, she let her head fall back against the pillows as tension began to tighten in her lower body. Her thumb brushed against her swollen clit and sent a twinge of delight through her body.

Slowly, she pressed her finger into her humid passage, her arousal intensified with the knowledge that Rohan was watching her. She lifted her other hand to her breasts and plucked at her nipples through the silk fabric of her dressing gown. Then, she tugged at the belt and let the gown fall open, exposing her naked body to a dark, heated gaze. Devora's heart pounded hot blood through her veins as she thrust her finger back and forth, thrilled at the sensation of her inner walls clenching around her finger. A moan escaped her throat as she pressed harder on her clit, her hand moving with increasing frenzy as she spurred herself toward the ultimate release. She imagined that she could even feel Rohan's gaze pinning her to the bed, painting trails of fire over her skin as the pressure built to unfathomable depths. With a cry, Devora broke through the invisible wall into a world of pure sensation. An orgasm rocked her body, her sex swelling with a rush of moisture.

Gasping, Devora sank against the pillows and drew in a deep breath, urging the final sensations out of her body. She opened her eyes slowly to look at the doorway. As she expected, Rohan had gone.

Devora lay on the bed for a long moment, wondering about that strange, inscrutable man who trimmed rosebushes and spoke such perfect English, yet revealed nothing about himself.

"Devora?" Gerald's voice rang through the house.

Devora grabbed her belt and tied her dressing gown around herself just as Gerald entered the bedroom. He paused in the doorway, his expression concerned.

"Darling? Are you feeling all right?"

Devora nodded, pushing her hair away from her face. "Yes. Yes, I'm fine. I just had a bath, and I must have fallen asleep."

"Oh, I see. Bloody hot day out there." Gerald entered the room, tugging at his tie. "And the damn Indians can't seem to keep their paperwork straight."

"I'm sorry, love."

"Yes, well, one gets used to it." Gerald dropped a kiss on Devora's forehead. "Are you looking forward to going to the club this evening? I hear they're putting on a musical show."

"Yes. That should be quite entertaining." Devora tried to instill a note of enthusiasm in her voice as she took a pale green silk dress from her chiffarobe.

"I want to have a bath myself before dinner."

"Wait, and I'll tell Kalindi to draw one. I'll fix you a drink while you're waiting." Devora dressed quickly and went to find Kalindi again. She poured Gerald a gin and tonic and brought it to him.

"What have you been doing today?" Gerald asked.

"Mrs. Thompson and Adele came over for tea this afternoon," Devora said. "And I've been painting."

Gerald nodded his approval. "Good. Those are exactly the kinds of activities you should be involved in."

"So you've said." Devora smoothed down her skirt. "I'll just go check on dinner."

She gave Kalindi further instructions, then stepped out onto the veranda to find Rohan. He was watering the potted geranium plants, pausing to clip the dried flowers.

Devora cleared her throat.

Rohan glanced up. "Yes, *memsahib*?"

"Is the carriage ready for our trip to the club this evening?"

"Yes, of course."

"Good." Devora let her gaze travel over him, thinking that he always looked so crisp and correct, his white jacket bearing no smudge of dirt and his hair perfectly in place.

"There is something else you require?" Rohan asked.

Even after witnessing her most private moments, there was not a single crack in his implacable veneer. Devora might have found it amusing had she not been mildly insulted. One would think that such an experience would cause a man to at least look at a woman differently. Particularly if the man were Indian and the woman British.

"No," she replied curtly. "Go about your work."

She went back inside, wondering if the balance of power in her relationship with Rohan was starting to shift. And not in a direction that would be favorable to her.

"What are we eating for dinner tonight?" Gerald came out of the bedroom, buttoning up his waistcoat.

"Mutton pies," Devora said. "I'm sorry, it's not very interesting, but I thought we should eat quickly if we're going to the club."

"Quite right, my dear."

They sat down to eat, their conversation focused around the activities of the British community and Gerald's work. Afterward, Rohan drove them to the club, a lavish, Victorian building built in the nineteenth century for the purpose of allowing the British a place to congregate apart from the Indians. The only Indians allowed were the servants and guards, who stood at strategic locations like statues.

"Devora, darling, how nice to see you here!" Mrs. Thompson approached Devora in the lobby, her eyes bright. "Do come in and have a sherry."

Gerald went off to have brandy and cigars with the men, while Mrs. Thompson led Devora toward the enclave of women. Several of the women gave Devora haughty looks and turned away without greeting her.

"Don't worry, dear, it's just that they've heard about your visit to the Maharaja," Mrs. Thompson said. "I did warn you that that was highly irregular. Word has gotten around, you know."

"I'm not surprised." Devora sat down next to Louise in one of the rattan chairs, accepting a small glass of sherry from a servant.

"Well, I think it's rather exciting," Louise said. "I mean, when has the Maharaja ever invited a British woman to his house for lunch?"

Mrs. Thompson pursed her lips. "That is precisely my point."

"Well, I don't really care what anyone thinks," Devora said. "It was a very proper luncheon."

"What did Gerald have to say?"

"He's forbidden me from going again, of course. Frankly, I think he was just a bit jealous that he wasn't invited."

"My dear, I suspect you and Gerald are going to be living

in India for some time to come," Mrs. Thompson said. "I suggest that you don't make things difficult between you from the
outset."

"That isn't my intention, Mrs. Thompson."

Devora stifled a sigh as she gazed across the lobby at the
group of men seated near the bar. While it was true that she
didn't want to create difficulties between herself and Gerald,
she couldn't help thinking that he would always be the same
kind of man. Caring and, on occasion, passionate, but basically
uninteresting. Not even living in India could entice Gerald
away from his set ideas and opinions. He simply lacked a desire
for adventure. And lately, it seemed as if Devora had a desire
for nothing *but* adventure, in all its myriad forms.

chapter eight

Devora clipped the stems of the roses and arranged them in a glass vase on a side table. The flowers weren't as full or dewy as English roses, but they still carried a nice scent. She opened two of the windows to allow a cross breeze to enter the room. The sky was heavy with thick, dripping clouds that looked as if they would break open any minute with a torrent of rain. At least that might cool the air a little, Devora thought as she went to dispose of the stem cuttings in the kitchen. She paused at the sight of Kalindi rolling out bread dough on the counter.

Kalindi looked up a the sound of Devora's entrance. "*Memsahib*, you require something?"

"No." Devora tossed the stems into the rubbish bin and leaned against the counter. She watched Kalindi pounding and kneading the dough with practiced movements, sending puffs of flour flying in every direction. "What kind of bread are you making?"

"It's called *poori,* you will like it very much."

"I'm sure I will." Devora's gaze tracked over the younger woman's delicate features and creamy skin. "Are you engaged to be married, Kalindi?"

"Oh, no, *memsahib.*" Kalindi wagged her head from left to right in that peculiar movement that all Indians seemed to possess. "You know that we have arranged marriages in India. I fear my parents are having difficulty finding me a husband."

"Really?" Devora took a few walnuts from a jar on the countertop and began chewing on them. "Why is that?"

"Too dark skin." Kalindi held up her arm to demonstrate. "Men are preferring women with fair skin."

"I've heard that about Indians."

"Englishwomen, too, is it not?" Kalindi asked. "That is why you all wear hats and carry . . . what is the word?"

"Parasols," Devora replied. "Yes, that's true, I guess. We want to protect our skin from the sun."

"When one is born with dark skin, *memsahib,* even a parasol cannot help." Kalindi ripped a piece of dough off and began rolling it into a small ball.

"Well, surely there must be someone who wishes to marry you," Devora said. "You're very pretty."

Kalindi flashed her a smile. "Really? You are kind to say so."

"What will you do if your parents can't find you a husband?"

Kalindi looked startled, as if she hadn't even considered that possibility. "Oh, I think I will be working," she said, waving her hand in the air, sending a cloud of flour onto the floor. "But every woman marries. That is our duty."

"Yes, I see." Devora popped another walnut into her mouth. "Do you live with your parents?"

"No, *memsahib.* I did, but I have four younger brothers and sisters. There is no room."

"So where do you live now?"

"I have a small room in the village. It is quite sufficient."

"You live there alone?"

Kalindi became very busy rolling the dough into balls. "Yes. Alone."

"How can you afford it?"

"I am managing."

Devora suspected that Gerald had something to do with paying for Kalindi's room, but she didn't press the issue. She dusted off her hands and headed for the door. "Make sure you sweep the floors thoroughly today, do you hear? Yesterday they were still rather dirty."

"Yes, *memsahib.*" Kalindi dropped the dough balls into a metal bowl. "I also must go into the village to pick up vegetables."

"All right. You can sweep when you get back."

Devora went out onto the back veranda and sank down into a chair, picking up an English novel she had been reading. Yet, as much as she loved reading, she couldn't concentrate on the book. She hadn't heard from the Maharaja since their last lunch together, although she decided that it was better that way. He probably knew that Gerald was back in town and was playing it safe. As she should be.

Devora leaned her head against the back of the chair and closed her eyes. Ah, well, it wasn't as if she had any feelings for the prince. She simply liked what he could do to her, not to mention the fact that he was an exotic adventure. She harbored no romantic notions that he would carry her off to live in his palace with him. Besides, she'd never seen the allure of such fairy-tale dreams. Palace life seemed to be a rather boring existence overall. She would merely become very fat and spend most of her time dressing up lavishly in silk and jewels. No, that wasn't the route she wanted her life to take.

Not that she knew what that route was. Devora let out her breath in a long sigh. She would figure that out soon enough. If there were any place in the world where she could come face-to-face with herself, it was India.

Delicate piano music began to invade her dreamy state of mind. Mozart. She recognized the lively passage almost immediately. Mozart's "Concerto in A Major, Number 23." The way the third movement began, with such a simple declaration and then an excited response, never failed to elict a warm smile from her. Her eyes opened slowly and focused on the garden. Where was the music coming from? She turned her head toward the sitting room, frowning at the sight of a male figure at the piano bench. His body swayed as the music spilled effortlessly from his fingertips. Devora stood and moved to the doorway.

Her heart leaped as she realized that Rohan sat at the piano bench, playing Mozart as if it were second nature. Devora stifled a gasp and pressed a hand against her chest. What on earth was he doing? And where did he ever learn how to play the piano at all, let alone with such fluent beauty? She could have watched him play for hours, but then Rohan looked up and saw her there.

He froze, standing so quickly that the piano bench almost tipped over. For the first time, surprise flared in his expression. *"Memsahib*, I apologize. I didn't realize you were home. I thought you went to the village with Kalindi."

"No, I've just . . . I was sitting on the veranda." Suddenly flustered, Devora gestured outside as if Rohan didn't know where the veranda was. "I . . . I'm sorry for interrupting you."

He shook his head. "No, it is I who is at fault. I should be working."

He turned to leave the room, but Devora stopped him.

"Wait." She approached him with rapid steps, irrationally feeling like he would disappear forever if she didn't stop him now. "Where did you learn to play the piano so beautifully?"

Rohan glanced at her, seeming uncomfortable. "I took lessons when I was a boy."

"Lessons? Where?" Devora had been under the impression that the servants came from villages and poverty-stricken homes in which mere literacy was considered unusual. Certainly piano lessons must be unthinkable.

Rohan didn't speak for a moment, but then his shoulders lifted in a slight shrug.

"My father was a city magistrate in Delhi, where I grew up," he said. "I took piano lessons when I returned home from school in the afternoons."

Devora stared at him, trying to reconcile his position now

with the boy he had once been. "Your father was a magistrate? What . . . how did . . ." Her voice trailed off.

A slight smile curved Rohan's lips. "How did I become a servant, you mean?"

Devora nodded.

"My father died when I was thirteen. I had no mother, as she died when I was less than one year old. My sister and I were sent to separate orphanages after the death of my father. There, they found me work as a *dhobi*. I have been working for the British ever since."

Devora couldn't believe what she was hearing. "But . . . but, surely you continued your education?"

"In a sense. For five years, I worked at the household of a family that allowed me to use their library. On occasion, the *memsahib* also allowed me to use their piano. She sometimes found it amusing to ask me to play for her friends."

"You never went to school again?"

Rohan shook his head. "No."

Not an ounce of self-pity threaded his words. He simply appeared to be very complacent about the route his life had taken.

"What about your sister?" Devora asked.

"As I said, she is married and living in Jaipur. Her husband is a shopkeeper. I believe the orphanage arranged the marriage."

"Have you seen her at all?"

"Two, perhaps three times over the years."

Devora shook her head and tried to absorb the entirety of what he had just revealed to her. She had barely even considered the idea that the impassive Rohan had a past at all, let alone one filled with tragedy and incongruities.

"I apologize again for using the piano."

"No, no. Don't apologize. Have you used it often?"

He hesitated, but then nodded. "Over the months when the master has been away, I have used it frequently."

"You may continue to do so."

Rohan looked at her for a very long moment, his dark eyes

seeming to see right through her and into her very soul. Then, he nodded again and bowed slightly in her direction.

"My thanks, *memsahib.*" He turned and headed for the servants' quarters.

Devora watched him leave, remembering the sound of the concerto that still seemed to reverberate in the air like an echo.

"No," she murmured to the empty room. "My thanks."

"Yes, he came to me the other night." Kalindi ran her hand down Lota's body, pausing to dip her finger playfully into the other woman's navel. "I told you that he would."

Lota gave a mild snort. "How long did he stay?"

Kalindi didn't reply, not wanting to admit that the *sahib* had stayed with her for less than twenty minutes, if even that. Instead, she pressed her lips against Lota's shoulder.

"I don't expect him to marry me or anything," she said. "I know why he wants me."

Lota shifted onto her side and gazed at Kalindi. "And you like it that way?"

Kalindi shrugged. "It's not the same as us, of course, but it's something."

"Does the *memsahib* know about you?"

"I think she suspects, but she hasn't ever come right out and asked me."

"How does she treat you?"

"Fine. Better than most *memsahibs*, anyway." Kalindi recalled her earlier conversation with the *memsahib*. "She told me that I'm very pretty."

Lota ran her fingers through Kalindi's dark hair. "You are. Although I'm surprised that she would have told you that. The British women never think that Indian women are attractive. Maybe she's interested in you the way that the *sahib* is."

"Oh, Lota, don't be silly." Even as she denied it, Kalindi couldn't help being more than a little intrigued by the thought. She wondered what Devora Hawthorne would look like naked, if her slender body would be as pleasing to the touch as Lota's fuller figure was. Kalindi cupped one of Lota's breasts in her hand, rubbing her thumb over the thick nipple. "Besides, even if she did like women, I suspect she would be attracted to British women."

"Well, I'm not," Lota declared. "I think they're all too skinny, and they have practically no breast. That is probably why the *sahib* prefers you."

Kalindi smiled. "Well, I do enjoy his visits, although if I had to choose between him and you, I would choose you."

"You would?"

"Of course." Kalindi bent to kiss the other woman, stroking her tongue gently over Lota's lower lip. Lota tasted delicious, like honey and spices. And she was so warm and accommodating.

"I like men," Kalindi murmured. "But they can also be rather brutish, don't you think? Women like you are always so soft."

"Women also know each other's bodies much better than men do," Lota agreed. She encircled Kalindi's waist with her hands, her fingertips stroking lightly. "Men so often want their own pleasure, while women enjoy the act of giving pleasure."

"I like to give you pleasure," Kalindi agreed.

She urged Lota's lips apart with her own and slid her tongue into the warm, wet cavern of Lota's mouth. Kalindi felt her blood begin to flow hotly through her veins as the embers of passion sparked with such readiness. She sank against Lota with an ease borne of familiarity, their breasts pressing together as they surrendered to their mutual lust. Kalindi loved the sensation of Lota's hard nipples rubbing against hers. She slid her hand down Lota's belly and into the damp fissure between her legs. Lota gave a little groan of pleasure, spreading her legs wider to allow Kalindi easy access. Kalindi rubbed her finger over Lota's sex and pushed her finger gently into the tight passage, delighting in the way that Lota's inner flesh closed around the slender digit.

"Wait," Lota gasped. "I want to touch you, too."

She eased her body out from underneath Kalindi's, pressing

Kalindi gently onto her back. Kalindi closed her eyes and let herself succumb entirely to the pleasure of Lota's touch. With gentle, exploring fingers, Lota caressed her breasts and abdomen, stroking her palms over the curves of Kalindi's hips. Kalindi let out her breath in a contented sigh. No man ever touched her the way that Lota did. In fact, no man was ever as concerned with her pleasure. Lota spread a series of light kisses over Kalindi's body, circling the buds of her nipples with her tongue and lips. A rainfall of sensations spilled through Kalindi, centering in the aching crevice of her sex. She twined her fingers through Lota's thick hair as the room became heavy with the scent of lust. The sheets slipped off their bodies, exposing their naked skin to the humid air.

Kalindi parted her legs to allow Lota to relax between them. Their cunts pressed together with an exquisite degree of pressure. Lota gave a little moan, rubbing her clitoris against the coarse curls of Kalindi's mons. Kalindi watched her lover with a heavy-lidded gaze and reached out to clutch Lota's hips as Lota began to quicken her movements. Lota put her hands on either side of Kalindi's head to brace herself, grasping the sheet in her fists as she strained toward release. Her breath emerged from her throat in harsh little pants. Kalindi adored the mere sight of Lota, her head thrown back, her skin slick with perspiration, her breasts swaying with the force of her movements. Lota let out a sudden cry. Kalindi dug her fingers into the other woman's hips, pressing her body downward when Lota trembled with rapturous vibrations.

"Oh yes . . ." Lota collapsed and buried her face in Kalindi's neck as she tried to catch her breath. "Oh, that felt good."

Kalindi smiled and stroked her hands down Lota's damp back, loving the scent of the other woman's sweat and lust. She squirmed when Lota dipped her tongue into the warm hollow of Kalindi's throat, painting a delicious pattern of heat over her skin. Lota lifted herself up and reached toward the night table. She grasped a long, thick candle that Kalindi often had to use when the power went out.

Kalindi's breath caught in her throat. "Just what are you going to do with that?"

Lota gave her a wicked look. "Don't you want to find out?"

"I most certainly do." Kalindi stretched her body out and lifted her arms above her head, letting Lota take control.

"I love your body," Lota murmured, rubbing her hands over the soft skin of Kalindi's inner thighs. "I love the way you look, the way you smell, and especially the way you feel."

She bent her head and licked lightly at the dewy folds of Kalindi's sex. A river of sensations twisted through Kalindi's body, making her limbs go weak with sheer pleasure. Her sex swelled with the onslaught of passion, and she couldn't resist bucking her hips upward to meet the touch of Lota's tongue. Lota teased her gently, entwining Kalindi in the delicious ropes of tension that began to wind around her body.

Then, Lota pressed Kalindi's legs farther apart and stroked the end of the candle over the crevices of her labia. The contrast between the hard wax and the soft touch of Lota's tongue was unlike anything Kalindi had felt before. Her heart slammed against her chest as Lota began to insert the candle into her, filling her with the thick, hard length. Kalindi clenched her inner flesh around the candle, drawing in a sharp breath at the luscious feeling. Lota moved up to kiss her, still holding the candle end as she began to draw it back and forth from Kalindi's body.

Lota smiled against Kalindi's mouth and thrust her tongue inside. "Does that feel good?"

"Oh yes," Kalindi gasped, clutching Lota to her as the candle began to tickle her sensitive nerve endings. "Harder."

Lota pumped the candle harder and brushed her fingers against Kalindi's swollen clit. Kalindi's body burned with such heat that she was certain she would melt the wax, but oh, how good it felt. She pushed her hips upward again to meet Lota's strokes, and then an orgasm rocked her. Her body convulsed violently around the makeshift phallus. Lota pulled the candle out and let it fall to the floor before sinking into Kalindi's arms.

Kalindi closed her eyes, absorbing the arousal still pulsing gently through her. She stroked her hands over Lota's rounded buttocks and let the heaviness of sleep overtake her.

A sudden knocking at the door startled Kalindi out of her slumber. She sat up, waking Lota in the process, and tried to collect her thoughts.

"Kalindi? It's Devora Hawthorne. Open the door."

Kalindi's heart leaped into her throat as she recognized the *memsahib*'s voice. She gasped and turned to stare at Lota in shock.

"What's she doing here?" Lota hissed.

"I have no idea! Get up!" Kalindi pushed Lota out of the bed and grabbed a white cotton shift. She pulled the shift over her head, realizing that there was nowhere Lota could go. Kalindi scrambled off the bed and went to the window in a panic, as if she could climb out and run.

"Kalindi!" Another knock rapped sharply at the unlocked door, and then the *memsahib* pushed it open with an impatient movement.

Kalindi's head plummeted as she turned to face the *memsahib*. Devora Hawthorne stepped into the room, looking quite English in a beige cotton dress and a silk shawl with a flowered hat perched on her head. Her gaze swept over the entire room in one glance, her eyes widening as she took in the rumpled bed and Lota sitting there clutching a sheet to her naked body.

Kalindi grasped onto the windowsill for support, feeling as if she might faint. How could the Englishwoman miss what was going on here, with two half-naked women and the air thick with lust?

"*Memsahib,* what are you doing here?" Kalindi choked.

"I came to speak with you." Devora looked from Kalindi to Lota and back again. Realization dawned slowly in her brown eyes.

"I am begging your pardon, please." Kalindi was terrified that the *memsahib* would dismiss her on the spot.

Devora was quiet for a moment before a light sheen of perspiration broke out on her upper lip. She shook her head. "No, Kalindi, that's all right. I shouldn't have rushed in without contacting you ahead of time."

"I . . . I am not knowing what to say." Kalindi glanced at Lota, who looked about as nervous as Kalindi felt.

"Never mind." Devora turned toward the door. "I'll leave you alone."

"Wait!" Kalindi had a sick feeling that if the *memsahib* left now, she would have far too much time to think about what she had just witnessed. Additionally, Kalindi had to find out why the British woman had come here in the first place, if only to be able to give her what she wanted. Then, perhaps the *memsahib* would think twice about dismissing her. "What was it you came for?"

"Oh, nothing. It's rather silly."

"I can make you tea," Kalindi said desperately, making a sharp gesture at Lota.

Lota scrambled to put on a shift, then went to light the stove. Devora looked at Kalindi and lifted her shoulders in a shrug.

"I was just speaking with Rohan," she explained. "I was wondering what you knew about him."

"Rohan?" Kalindi was startled. The last thing she had expected Devora Hawthorne to ask her about was the head servant. "I do not understand." She hurried to take some clothing off a chair. "Please, sit down."

Devora hesitated, but moved to sit down. "I really should leave. This isn't necessary."

"No, please stay. Please excuse the state of my home. I was not expecting you." Kalindi grabbed a hair clip and clasped her long hair at the nape of her neck, trying to pat the flyaway strands into order. "You asked about Rohan?"

"Yes, well, he was telling me about how he came to work for the British," Devora said. "Having lived in an orphanage."

"Yes, that is true. He told me that once."

Devora looked down at her hands, twisting her fingers together. With a start, Kalindi realized that the British woman was nervous.

"I suppose I was just wondering if you knew anything else about him," Devora said. "He's very . . . um, stoic."

"Stoic? What is that word?"

"I mean that he doesn't display his emotions," Devora said. "At all."

"No, he is a very cold man," Lota agreed. She brought Devora a cup of tea and sat down on the bed. "Very cold."

"Do you know why?" Devora asked.

"I know he was engaged to be married perhaps ten years ago," Kalindi said, wondering why the *memsahib* was so interested in Rohan. She hoped that Devora Hawthorne wasn't looking for a reason to dismiss him. "There was a rumor that the woman could not provide the dowry, but I do not think that is what happened. I am thinking her family did not want her to marry a servant."

Devora looked somewhat thoughtful. "I see. He was in love with her, then?"

Both Kalindi and Lota chuckled.

"Oh, *memsahib*, we do not marry for love," Lota explained. "Our marriages are arranged marriages. Our parents seek people from suitable families for us."

"But if Rohan came from an orphanage, his parents couldn't have found a possible bride for him," Devora pointed out.

Such a thought had never occurred to Kalindi. She looked at Lota, who appeared equally surprised.

"Perhaps it was the orphanage," Lota suggested.

Devora arched an eyebrow wryly. "When he was twenty-five years old, the orphanage sought to find a bride for him?"

"No, I am not convinced of that," Kalindi said. "An orphanage arranged a marriage for his sister, but she was fifteen years old. Maybe Rohan *was* in love with his fiancée. That would be unusual, though."

"Or maybe it was the British family he was working for," Lota said.

Kalindi laughed. "Lota, really. The British would never think to get involved with the Indians, and certainly not in their personal lives and marriages. They are too interested in themselves." She looked at Devora in horror, cursing her characteristic of speaking before she thought. "*Memsahib*, I am apologizing."

Devora smiled and shook her head. "Actually, you're correct, Kalindi. The British do not want to mix with the Indians. I seriously doubt that a British family would be concerned with the marital status of one of their servants."

"That is all I know of Rohan," Kalindi said. "He is a good man, but as Lota has said, a cold one. He does not like to talk, and he takes his duties with great seriousness."

"Yes, I've discovered that," Devora murmured. She stood, placing her teacup on the windowsill. "Thank you for the tea. I shall take leave of you now."

"I'm sorry again for . . . not being prepared for your visit," Kalindi said.

"Quite all right." Devora glanced from Lota to Kalindi. "What you do on your own time is your business. Good evening to you both."

She turned and left. Kalindi pushed aside the curtain to look out at the street, where Devora Hawthorne was climbing into a tonga pulled by a bicycle-riding driver.

"Goodness," Lota flopped back onto the bed with a sigh of relief. "That was unexpected. I wonder why she was asking about Rohan."

"I think she wants to get rid of him," Kalindi replied. "She doesn't like him, and I have heard them arguing."

"Why doesn't she just tell the *sahib*?"

"She has," Kalindi said. "I've heard *them* arguing as well. The *sahib* refuses to dismiss Rohan."

"Do you think the *memsahib* will succeed if she wants Rohan to leave?" Lota asked.

Kalindi watched the tonga *wallah* bicycle away. "I think she will. She is a woman who gets what she wants."

chapter nine

"You see, my dear, sexuality is innately divine in Indian philosophy," the Maharaja said. "In the Upanishads, the woman becomes transformed into a Vedic site of sacrifice so that the act of intercourse is also a great sacrificial performance."

"It's very complicated, isn't it?" Devora propped her head on her hand as she stretched out on the picnic blanket. The Maharaja spared no expense when it came to picnicking. The servants had arranged a number of silk pillows for their comfort and set out the food on fine crystal and china.

With Gerald gone on another short trip, the Maharaja had brought Devora to the Khajuraho temples accompanied by a veritable entourage of two cars and six servants. A number of British tourists, mostly men, wandered about the grounds of the six temples. Many of them were simply craning their necks to get a view of the sexually explicit sculptures.

"Very complicated," the Maharaja agreed.

"I find it fascinating that there is such an emphasis on the erect penis," Devora mused. She looked at the sketches she had drawn of the temple sculptures, several of which involved various gods displaying full erections.

"Yes, but the goddess is also highly revered," the Maharaja reminded her. "Many legends relate to the concept of divine

duality, as the gods all have a feminine side. There is even one
type of sculpture called the *Ardhanarishvara*, which consists of
a deity that is half-male, often with an erect penis, and half-
female."

Devora pushed herself to a sitting position and examined her
sketches. The temple sculptures were extraordinary, filled with
men and women in every conceivable posture of intercourse.
She had even drawn one of a standing man holding a woman's
legs over his shoulders, which wouldn't have been particularly
unusual were it not for the fact that the woman's back was
against his chest and her head twisted to suck his penis.

Devora couldn't help but find the sculptures stimulating. She
stood, brushing off her dress as she approached the temples
again. Such intricate detail and creativity! Some of the couples
were simply entwined and kissing, while others were contorted
into impossible positions. There were also scenes involving
three or more people, not to mention cunnilingus, masturba-
tion, and fellatio. Devora glanced at the Maharaja as he came
to stand beside her.

"Some of these postures aren't even possible," she remarked.

"Well, the contortion indicates the flexibility and suppleness
of the Devadasis, who are the female servants of the gods," the
Maharaja explained. "They were dancers and acrobats, and
certainly their extreme flexibility was greatly prized, as it en-
hanced pleasure during coitus."

"When were the temples built?"

"Most of the Khajuraho temples were built during the Chan-
dela dynasty," the Maharaja replied. "That was perhaps 1000
A.D., I think."

They walked around the temple grounds again, entering several of them to look at the sculpture of Shiva's mount, the bull
Nandi, as well as lingam and yoni sculptures. Devora still
wasn't certain she fully understood the concept of such explicitly erotic art, but she possessed a great admiration for a country that was not only so unashamed of sexuality, but also
highly valued it.

She paused before a sculpture of two women entwined in lust, and her thoughts went back to her encounter with Kalindi and Lota a couple of nights ago. Devora was certain that the two women were lovers, even if she only had their guilty expressions to judge them by. As it was, Devora had been more than a little stimulated by the notion of the two lovely women together. Her arousal had been intensified by the sight of their disheveled figures and the scent of passion. Even now, her sex surged as she stared at the stone image of two women and imagined them to be warm flesh and blood.

"Come, we will wait in the car while the servants pack up," the Maharaja said. "I fear the sun might be getting too hot for you."

Devora turned to him and nodded, patting her damp brow with a handkerchief.

"Thank you for bringing me here," she said as they returned to their car. "I never would have seen this if it hadn't been for you."

"My dear Mrs. Hawthorne, you honor me with your presence." The Maharaja bowed his head slightly in her direction. "It is purely my pleasure."

Devora had to smile at his continued use of the title "Mrs. Hawthorne" considering their own intimacy. She got into the car, leaning with a sigh against the plush seats. The Maharaja did know how to travel well.

"So, what are you going to do with your drawings?" the Maharaja asked.

Devora shrugged. "I don't know. I haven't really thought about it."

"Perhaps you could publish them."

"Believe me, no British publisher would be interested in publishing drawings of erotic Indian art," Devora said.

"Not even if they are drawn by a beautiful British woman?"

Devora smiled again. "Not even then."

"But you are not just any British woman, are you?" the Maharaja asked. "You have your own mind."

"So I've been told."

"Does your husband tell you that?"

"Everyone seems to tell me that," Devora replied wryly.

"Ah, then you must have your own opinions about the British presence in India, yes?"

"What about the British presence in India?"

"For example, how is it justified for the British to hold India?"

"I don't know that it is," Devora said. "It certainly seems to me that the Indians don't want the British here. Mr. Gandhi's movement is gaining force, from what I understand."

"Yes, yes, that is what I hear as well."

Devora shot him a glance. "Are you involved in it? The anti-British movement?"

The Maharaja shrugged philosophically. "Aren't all Indians involved in the movement in one manner or another?" He reached out and put his hand on her knee. "And you know well that the British always suppress the slightest hint of unrest."

"I believe the British try," Devora said. "I don't know that they always succeed."

The Maharaja smiled. "You use the word *they*," he said. "I find that most intriguing. All other British use the word *we*."

"I don't like to put myself in with that lot."

"But you *are* one of them," the Maharaja said. "It's painfully obvious, Mrs. Hawthorne."

Devora gave him an irritated look. "What is that supposed to mean?"

"No British woman in India is immune from the dreaded curse of the *memsahib*," the Maharaja said, his dark eyes glinting with amusement. "Rounds of gossiping, complaining, bigotry, and downright nastiness. Every British woman succumbs to it sooner or later."

"Well, I won't. I dislike the *memsahibs* entirely."

"Do you now? Surely you must enjoy the gossiping."

"No, I don't. I don't enjoy socializing with them, but it's my duty to do so. Also, it's important to keep abreast of British affairs."

"Ah, yes. Politics. No place for a lady, in my opinion, although I admire your interest in it. I expect that you've heard the British are planning a raid on a local village."

Devora looked at him in surprise. "No, I haven't heard that. Why?"

"A villager was accused of stealing from a British woman. Of course, that provoked a outcry among the British. This is their method of revenge."

"I've heard that the British are attempting to suppress Indian gangs," Devora said. "That might be the reason for a raid, not revenge."

A slight hint of triumph flashed in the Maharaja's expression, giving Devora an uneasy feeling in the pit of her stomach. She had never assumed that the Maharaja had romantic inclinations toward her, but she could easily believe that his motives were political ones. She made a mental note not to reveal anything else about what the British might or might not be planning.

"Well, I don't really know," she replied. "As I said, I don't enjoy gossiping."

"And that, my dear, is why I appreciate your company so much."

The Maharaja picked up her hand, pressing a series of light kisses across her fingertips. He really did have a sensual touch, Devora thought, as she watched him toying with her fingers. He lifted his hand to her face, caressing her cheek and sliding his thumb along her lower lip. Slowly, he pushed his thumb into her mouth in a suggestive movement that made Devora's blood start to race. Without thinking, she slid her tongue over his thumb and sucked on it lightly. Then, she grasped his wrist and pulled away from him.

"The servants . . ." she murmured.

"We have time," the Maharaja assured her, pulling her toward him for a heated kiss.

The interior of the car was hot and stuffy, but Devora didn't care. She felt wholly submerged in the eroticism and history that this country had to offer. She sank against the Maharaja, letting her fingers find the increasing bulge beneath his trousers. She massaged him gently as his penis hardened underneath her fingertips. He grunted and pushed his hips up toward her. Devora's mind still spun with the sheer carnality of the temple sculptures, and she suddenly wanted to attempt an act that the Devadasis performed with such finesse.

She glanced up at the Maharaja from beneath her eyelashes, noting the dull flush beneath his dark skin and the increasing force of his breath. Slowly, she unlaced the drawstring of his trousers and pulled them down to his knees to expose his jutting member. The sight of his cock never failed to fascinate her, projecting from the abundant nest of dark curls like a living creature. She wrapped her hand around the shaft and stroked it from base to tip as she knelt on the seat beside him.

"Ahhh, you do excel at that, my dear," the Maharaja murmured, leaning his head against the back of the seat.

Devora cupped the tight sacs of his testicles in her hand as she bent her head to take him in her mouth. She and Gerald had done this before, although for some reason he always stopped her before he had an orgasm. Devora slid her lips over the hard glans, flicking her tongue into the indentation at the tip as she licked up a drop of moisture. He tasted salty and spicy, the heat of his skin fairly throbbing against the surface of her tongue. With lush ease, Devora slackened her jaw muscles and began to take him in fully. His shaft slid easily into the warm wetness of her mouth.

The Maharaja groaned and pressed his hand against the back of her neck, twining his fingers through her hair. Devora almost choked when his penis hit the back of her throat. She started to pull back. The Maharaja's grip on her neck tightened suddenly.

"Take it in," he said, his voice hoarse.

A flutter of fear went through Devora as she tried to pull

away again and found herself unable to do so. She reached up to grab his hand and push him away from her, but he was stronger than she was. His grip became fairly inexorable, his fingers digging into her scalp until rays of tight tension began to spread across her head. Devora gave a muffled cry of distress, feeling as if he were suffocating her completely. Her nostrils filled with the scent of his semen, and panic rose like a tidal wave. Without thinking, she bit down hard on his penis. The Maharaja roared with outrage and yanked her away from his groin so hard that Devora banged her head against the car window.

"You bastard!" Gasping, Devora slammed her fist against the Maharaja's shoulder. An intense relief flooded through her, accompanied by a furious anger. "How dare you do that to me? How *dare* you treat me like that?"

The Maharaja glowered at her and clutched his groin with one hand and his shoulder with the other.

"Bitch!" he spat, "What did you think you were doing?"

"I couldn't breathe!" Devora snapped, swiping at lingering tears of panic. "Don't you ever do something like that again, do you hear me? Ever!"

She very nearly stormed out of the car, but then a servant knocked on the front window. Cursing, the Maharaja fixed his trousers and rolled down the side window.

"Drive!" he snapped. "We are ready to leave."

Devora sat as far away from him as she could, crossing her arms angrily over her chest. The silence stretched between them, taut with fury, for the entire car trip. Humiliation descended on Devora's shoulders like a heavy cloak.

When the driver pulled up to the steps of her bungalow, she gave the Maharaja a haughty look.

"Thank you for taking me to see the temples," she said icily. "I appreciated those, at least."

He didn't reply. Devora hurried out of the car and into her bungalow. She slammed the door closed, her chest heaving as she tried to collect her scattered thoughts.

"*Memsahib?*" Rohan appeared in the doorway leading to the kitchen. He frowned at the sight of her disheveled appearance. "You are all right?"

Devora drew herself up and tried to compose herself. She nodded, running a hand through her hair. "Yes, thank you. I'm fine."

"You were out with the Maharaja again," Rohan said, his disapproval still all too evident.

"Yes, I was," Devora snapped, suddenly sick to death of men. Either they were disapproving, apparently cruel, or just plain absent. "What do you have to say about that?"

"You know that I think it is not a good idea for you to be with him."

"Why do you even care?"

"Because you reflect on the status of this household," Rohan replied.

"Well, do you know what?" Devora said angrily. "I don't care what you think! You can disapprove of me all you want, but I really don't give a damn!"

"I only disapprove of women who do not keep their promises."

"Oh, stop sounding so bloody self-righteous! I never promised anything, least of all that I wouldn't see the Maharaja again."

"You have also disobeyed your husband's orders," Rohan continued, apparently not having heard a word she said. "He told you that you were not to see the Maharaja again."

"Damn his orders! I don't take orders from people, not even my husband. You know, I used to think that you people were a little more liberal when it came to human relations, but I can see now that I was sadly mistaken!"

Devora turned and stalked toward the bedroom, fighting an onslaught of tears. She hated having been frightened by the Maharaja, but she hated even more the fact that Rohan disapproved of her. With a sob, she threw herself onto the bed and buried her face in her arms. India had so much to offer, yet she still could not escape the confines of the British presence. And she realized now that she probably never would. A wave of self-pity washed over her, and she intended to wallow in it to the fullest extent.

After her tears dried, Devora rolled over and stared at the mosquito-net canopy overhead. She was becoming unbearably tired of being so out of place. She didn't fit into the British community, and she certainly didn't fit into the Indian community. In fact, she suspected that she would never understand the Indians, which is exactly what Gerald and the Thompsons had been trying to tell her all along. As much as she hated admitting it, Devora suspected that they were right.

"*Memsahib?*" Rohan's voice drifted through the closed door. Devora lifted her head. "Yes?"

"You wish some tea?"

"Yes, please. I'll come right out." Devora hadn't even realized it was teatime already. She climbed off the bed and went to the dressing table, grimacing at the sight of her tear-stained, smudged face. She splashed water on her face from the basin and powdered her nose, then brushed her hair and changed clothes. Finally feeling more presentable, Devora went into the sitting room, where Rohan was setting out a tea tray for her.

"You are expecting guests?" he asked.

"No, no one." Devora sat down and accepted a cup of tea from him. She suddenly wished that Mrs. Thompson or Louise would drop by to share tea with her. She would have appreciated someone to talk to.

"Rohan."

He turned from his way back to the kitchen. "Yes?"

Devora gestured toward the tea tray. "Would you like to join me?"

"That would not be proper, *memsahib*."

"It's just a cup of tea." Devora gave him a exasperated look, remembering that he recently had the gall to watch her as she was pleasuring herself. *That* was proper? Not that she had made an effort to prevent him from doing so.

"I have my duties to attend to."

"Don't tell me that you're disgusted by the thought of having tea with a woman who allegedly doesn't keep her promises," Devora said, her tone somewhat bitter.

"No. Servants do not socialize with the master or mistress of the household. It is custom."

"Oh, but servants do secretly watch the master and mistress when they're engaged in intimate acts," Devora snapped, finally so fed up that she was unable to prevent the words from escaping. She put her cup down so hard that the tea splashed over the edges. "Is that customary, Rohan?"

A flicker of surprise appeared in his eyes, but his expression did not change. "I'm afraid I do not understand."

Devora's hands clenched into fists at her sides.

"The hell you don't," she said angrily. "You're a hypocrite, Rohan. Did you know that? You're so damn self-righteous about my activities, and yet you're the worst kind of voyeur!"

Rohan was quiet for a moment, and then his broad shoulders lifted into a shrug. "If the person being watched is putting on a display, am I still considered to be a voyeur?"

Devora gasped in shocked outrage, her body trembling suddenly. She strode across the room and slapped Rohan hard across the face. "You bastard! How dare you say that to me?"

"It is simple fact, I believe."

"Don't you dare judge me!"

"I never said it was wrong. On the contrary, I enjoyed it very much."

Devora stared at him. And then, as his words penetrated her mind, she started to laugh. Never in a million years would she have thought that she would ever have such a conversation with the impassive Rohan. Yes, she had gotten herself into quite a muddle. The humor of it struck her all at once, and she sank down in her chair and laughed until her stomach hurt.

"*Memsahib?*" A thread of concern wove through Rohan's voice. "You are all right?"

"Yes, Rohan, I'm fine." Still chuckling, Devora reached for

a napkin and wiped away tears of laughter. "Actually, I might even be mildly flattered that you enjoyed yourself."

Rohan's mouth quirked upward at the corners in what would have been a smile in anyone else. "I suppose it would be little compensation if I told you that I happened upon you by accident. I was on my way to the back of the house."

"When I distracted you, is that it?" Devora shook her head and reached for her tea. She took a sip and closed her eyes. "Oh, never mind, Rohan. I expect that such activities aren't viewed with the same sort of puritanism as they are in England."

"*Memsahib,* your view of India is not entirely accurate," Rohan said. "Indians can be very backward in their way of thinking, particularly when it comes to matters of sexuality."

Devora opened her eyes and looked at him. "Is that right?"

"Indeed."

"What about the Kamasutra and fertility goddesses and all that?"

"Those are part of Indian culture, no doubt," Rohan explained. "However, Indians for the most part are much more . . . what was the word you used? Puritanism."

"Puritanical. Really?"

"Sexuality is acceptable in a historical sense, but it can cause people discomfort in daily life."

"I'm surprised to hear that."

Rohan shrugged. "Perhaps it is a result of so many years of British influence."

Devora couldn't help smiling. "Perhaps it is."

"You, however, are not puritanical," Rohan said. A hint of wickedness appeared in the fathomless depths of his eyes. "At least, not from what I have witnessed."

A flush rose to color Devora's face, but she couldn't bring herself to be offended by his words. Quite the opposite. "I suspect that my lack of puritanism is one of the reasons I don't fit in with the British."

Rohan lifted an eyebrow. "You don't?"

"You mean, you think I do?" Devora was surprised to discover that she was mildly dismayed by the thought. "You consider me to be just like them?"

"No, I don't consider that at all," Rohan replied. "You are different. There is little question of that."

"Well, being different is of no use, anyway." Devora put down her teacup and stood, brushing the wrinkles out of her skirt. "So far, all it has done is irritate me to no end. I think that conformity might be far easier."

"Easier, yes," Rohan said. "But it would not be nearly as interesting."

Devora looked at him, thinking that this was the first time she had ever spoken so easily and comfortably with him. And she did so enjoy hearing him speak with good-natured humor and honesty.

"Yes," she agreed, "conformity wouldn't be nearly as interesting." She paused to set the tea things back onto the tray. "I'd like to go into the village for a bit," she said. "Will you accompany me?"

"You are asking me to accompany you on an outing for a change?"

Devora gave him an amused look. "Yes, believe it or not. I'd like to purchase another shawl and perhaps some silk scarves. Try not to be so shocked."

Rohan bowed slightly. "I will be most happy to accompany you. Let me harness the horse to the carriage."

"No, wait. Let's walk. We can catch a tonga on the road."

"*Memsahib,* you will be more comfortable in the carriage."

"I'd prefer the tonga. The carriage is so British."

"I suspect that people will know you are British whether you are in a tonga or a carriage," Rohan said dryly.

"Pity, isn't it?" Devora glanced at Rohan with a grin.

To her utter surprise, he smiled at her. Her heart leaped with a wild rush as she stared at him, stunned by the way his entire face changed with the lovely display of even, white teeth. The air seemed to shift between them in that instant. And then Devora forced her gaze away from him, suddenly unsettled, and went to put on a hat and retrieve her parasol. "All right, let's go."

They went to the village market, which Devora always found overwhelming with scents of everything from cow dung to curry spices. She purchased a shawl, a small pair of earrings, and a bar of sandalwood soap. She was grateful for Rohan's presence as he obtained a fair price for her and told her which merchants sold the highest-quality goods.

Devora paused next to a man who was seated cross-legged on a mat, spreading a pastelike substance onto a large green leaf. He then placed a nut in the center and folded the leaf into a neat little package. After placing the folded leaf on a bamboo tray with several others, he started on a new concoction.

"What is that?" Devora asked Rohan.

"It is called *paan*," Rohan explained. "A betel nut wrapped in a leaf with a number of spices, such as cardamom, anise, and cloves. It is usually used to aid digestion after a meal."

"I'd like to try it."

"*Memsahib,* it is not appropriate for ladies," Rohan explained.

"Why not?"

"The taste is rather bitter and you must put in into your mouth all at once, or else the red juice stains your hands and clothes."

"I'd still like to try it," Devora said. She reached into her pocketbook and handed him a couple of rupees. "Get one for yourself as well, if you'd like."

Rohan shrugged and spoke in Hindi to the man, who gave Devora an odd look. He wrapped up two *paans* and handed them to Rohan in exchange for the rupees.

"Now, place it all at once in your mouth and bite down," Rohan said, handing Devora one of the wrapped leaves.

Devora did, her teeth crunching through the betel nut and filling her mouth with a tangy, bitter taste. She was startled by the flood of acridity, as well as the fact that it seemed to make her entire mouth go numb. She gave Rohan a surprised look as a trickle of liquid escaped her mouth.

He grinned and handed her a handkerchief. "Too bitter for you, I think."

Devora wiped her mouth, but gamely chewed down the rest of the *paan* and swallowed. "Yes, but certainly interesting. This is a common food among Indians?"

"Oh yes. It is very popular." Rohan ate his *paan* with practiced ease. "The British have not yet acquired a taste for it."

"I can see why." Strong bitterness lingered in Devora's mouth. She patted her lips again and tried to swallow the taste.

"Wait, I will get you something to drink." Rohan approached a stall and purchased a glass of mango juice, which he brought to Devora.

Gratefully, she drank the entire glass to wash away the taste and the numbness. "Thank you."

"Not many *memsahibs* would be willing to try a traditional Indian food such as *paan*," Rohan said.

"Well, I'm not 'many *memsahibs*,' " Devora replied.

He inclined his head in acknowledgment of her words. "I dare say you are not."

Pleased with his words, Devora continued walking alongside him as they made their way through the spice market.

"Do you come here often when you're not shopping?" Devora asked, glancing at Rohan as they walked through the bustling streets. Shouts and voices emerged from every direction. A cow plodded past them, followed by three women with bundles balanced on their heads.

"Memsahib, do be careful." Rohan touched Devora's elbow to steer her around a steaming pile of cow dung. "Yes, I come to a pub here in the evenings."

"Really?" Devora thought briefly about asking him about his alleged fiancée but decided that such a question would surely break the tenuous camaraderie that had developed between them. "You mean you have a social life?"

Rohan tossed her a wry look. "Don't you?"

Devora chuckled. "If you can call going to the club and cricket games a social life."

"That isn't all you do, though, is it?"

Devora looked at him, wondering if he was fishing for information about her and the Maharaja. The Maharaja whom she had no intention of ever seeing again unless it was at one of his crowded dinner parties. "You mean my lunches with the Maharaja? I assure you they were entirely uninteresting."

"I believe he took you to the Khajuraho temples, didn't he?" Rohan asked. "At least, that is what his driver told me."

Devora arched an eyebrow. "Then why ask me? And here I thought you didn't gossip."

"As I told you, I am required to make certain of your safety. The master told me as much."

"Well, I will assure the *master* that you've done your duty," Devora said. She climbed into the tonga ahead of him and settled into her seat. "Why don't we go to the club?"

"Yes, *memsahib*." Rohan rapped out a few words of Hindi to the tonga *wallah*, who began peddling in the direction of the British club. He drove past the Indian guards stationed at the gate entrance and stopped at the foot of the steps.

Devora climbed down and glanced back at Rohan, who remained seated in the tonga. "Well," she said. "What are you waiting for?"

"You know that Indians are not allowed into the club. I will wait outside the gates for you."

Horror filled Devora as his words struck her. "Oh, Rohan. I'm so sorry. I completely forgot. Do forgive me."

"As I said, I will wait outside the gates. When you are ready to return home, I will call for another tonga."

"No, don't be silly, I don't have to—"

"Devora, is that you?"

Groaning inwardly, Devora turned to find Adele standing at the top of the steps, peering down at her and Rohan. She was dressed in a silk evening gown with her hair arranged in the latest fashion, a glass of sherry in her hand.

"Devora, come inside!" Adele said. "They're starting a performance of *A Midsummer Night's Dream* in less than five minutes."

"No, I'm afraid I need to return home," Devora called. "I'm not feeling well."

"Oh. Didn't you just get here?"

"Yes, I feel sick rather suddenly. I'll call on you tomorrow, if you'll be home."

"Yes, of course." Her expression darkening slightly, Adele watched Devora climb back into the tonga next to Rohan. "Have a good evening."

"Oak Street, tonga *wallah*," Devora said.

The tonga jerked and moved back to the street. Devora crossed her arms and sat silently, aware of Rohan's stiff figure beside her.

"*Memsahib,* it is ridiculous for you to return home," he finally said.

"It's even more ridiculous that the club doesn't allow Indians," Devora replied.

"That is the way things work." Anger edged Rohan's voice.

"Yes, I know. But that doesn't mean I have to like it."

They were silent for the remainder of the trip home. Devora took her packages from Rohan as they walked back into the bungalow. She shot him a sideways glance.

"You seem angry suddenly," she said. When he didn't reply, she pressed the issue. "Why? Because the club doesn't allow Indians?"

Rohan glared at her. "No. Because you seem to think that somehow you are a martyr for the Indian cause."

"What on earth are you talking about?"

"Not even refusing to enter the British club tonight will prevent you from *being* British," Rohan said. "Making such a sacrifice is noble, I'm sure, but not one that Indians need."

Devora couldn't believe what she was hearing.

"You think that I made some sort of sacrifice by not going

into the club?" she snapped. "Believe me, Rohan, it's no sacrifice to avoid watching those people mutilate Shakespeare."

"All I am saying to you," Rohan said, "is that you needn't sacrifice yourself on my behalf."

With that, he turned and went toward the back door of the house. The door banged shut as he left to go to the servant's quarters. Devora stood in the middle of the room for a long minute after he had gone. She should have known that she would hurt his pride by not allowing him to simply do his duty. Rohan had a prideful streak as wide and deep as the Ganges river. He would take any concession on her part as an insult if it interfered with his role as the servant.

Devora almost went after him to try and explain, but decided that it was better not to. She felt as if she had already become more involved with him than was wise. Perhaps it would be better simply to let their relationship return to its normal dynamics. Not that Devora had any idea what those dynamics were.

chapter ten

Rain spilled incessantly from the sky, pattering on the bungalow roof and windows like a million tiny pebbles. Awash in heat and humidity, Devora gazed up at the gossamer mosquito net. Everything looked foggy and mysterious through the thin netting. Devora rolled onto her side and hugged a pillow to her chest, thinking that all English storms were so cold and frozen in comparison to this Indian torridity. She wished that Gerald was home. She liked rain in general, but this was the first real storm since she'd arrived in India and it made her somewhat edgy.

Devora pushed back the mosquito net and swung her legs to the floor. Moisture dampened her skin, causing her to feel both hot and sticky. She pinned her hair into a knot to cool the back of her neck and padded out to the sitting room. The bungalow was eerie in its silent movement, with shadows cast from windblown trees sliding about the room like lost souls. With a shiver, Devora got a glass of water from the icebox and went to stand by the veranda door to gaze out at the black, wet night. She drank thirstily, feeling the water spill down her throat in an icy stream. The rain didn't appear to have cooled the air off at all. If anything, the moisture intensified the heat.

Devora looked at the dark outlines of the juniper bushes and geranium plants that lined the veranda. Rohan wouldn't have to worry about watering those for at least a week. She started to turn and go back to her bedroom, but then she caught sight of a shadowed figure seated on the veranda. Her heart leaped with fear for a moment before she recognized the man's figure.

Frowning, Devora turned on a light in the sitting room and pushed open the door. As she stepped onto the covered veranda, the sound of rain and a rush of cool air greeted her like an old friend.

"Rohan?" Devora let the door close behind her as she approached him. "What are you doing out here?"

His eyes opened with a start and focused on her. "*Memsahib.*"

"I came out to get a drink of water and saw you sitting here," Devora explained. "What on earth are you doing here?"

"It is cooler out here." Rohan dragged a hand through his hair and sat up. "My room gets very hot."

Devora glanced down at his attire, realizing that this was the first time she had seen him in anything other than his very proper white jacket and trousers. The light from the sitting room spilled onto the veranda, illuminating Rohan's loose cotton trousers and shirt. His feet were even bare. For some odd reason, Devora found him to be very approachable.

"You sleep out here?" she asked.

"Sometimes."

Devora rubbed her arms and glanced out at the inky hole of the garden. "How can you? It's a bit eerie, isn't it?"

Rohan shrugged. "Just rain. There is nothing to be frightened of."

Devora gave him a disdainful look. "Well, of course there isn't. I never said I was frightened of rain."

A smile quirked his mouth. "Of course not, my apologies. Might I ask what *you* are doing out here?"

"I saw you and thought I'd come out," Devora said. She sat

down in one of the wicker chairs, painfully aware that she was clad only in a thin, cotton nightshift. She crossed her arms over her breasts in the hopes of concealing the fact that the cooler air had hardened her nipples.

"You could not sleep?" Rohan asked.

Devora shook her head. "You're right, it does get hot inside. Sometimes the fans barely seem to work. I never knew that rain could be so hot."

"It is Indra at work."

"Indra?"

"The ancient Vedic god of rain. He is like the Zeus of Greek mythology. He splits clouds with a thunderbolt and causes them to open. He is said to be the leader of the waters."

"Well, he certainly is doing his job," Devora said, gazing out at the sheets of shimmering water. "I don't understand how you Indians can remember the names of the Indian gods, let alone what they do. It's all very confusing."

Rohan shrugged. "You have multiple saints, disciples, and historical figures in Christianity, I believe."

Devora nodded as she recalled her own habit of bringing up Western traditions whenever a British colonizer criticized the complexity or strangeness of Indian heritage.

"Yes, that's very true," she agreed. "Christianity is just as complex."

"Father, son, and holy ghost," Rohan murmured.

Devora glanced at him. "What about them?"

"We have a trinity as well, you know," he said. "Shiva, Vishnu, and Brahma."

"Ah, yes, Shiva," Devora replied. "The god associated with the phallus."

"That bothers you?"

"No, not at all," Devora said quickly. "I find it unusual, but then, as I'm sure you know, plenty of ideas in Western religion are unusual."

"Indian gods have very human traits," Rohan said. "I think perhaps that is what makes it so easy for us to worship them.

They inspire awe and fear, but they have also exhibited anger, happiness, jealousy, revenge, and love."

"Those are human traits to you?" Devora asked.

"They are something else to you?"

"No, I agree, they sound very human. I'm merely surprised that you even know what being human is all about." She knew she was goading him, but she couldn't help it. The energy of the rain and wind pounded into her skin, stimulating her blood.

"Have I just been insulted?" Rohan asked.

"Yes."

"Regarding what?"

"The fact that you rarely exhibit any emotions," Devora replied. "I've hardly even seen you smile, do you know that? You never seem happy, never seem to laugh or get angry. Even when I know you're angry, you're not *angry*. Do you understand what I mean?"

"I understand you, but I fail to know why this is of such importance to you."

"It's not important to me," Devora said snappishly. "I just find it to be highly maddening."

"It is not my intention to madden you, *memsahib*."

"Oh, for lord's sake, stop calling me that! I'm tired of being called a *memsahib*. In fact, I'm *not* a *memsahib*. My name is Devora."

"I cannot call you by your Christian name."

"No, of course you can't." Suddenly feeling very peevish, Devora sat back and glowered at the dark garden. "Heaven forbid that the British and Indians actually treat each other as equals."

"You must know by now that equality is not part of the tradition in British-ruled India," Rohan said. His voice was surprisingly kind despite Devora's outburst.

"Yes, I know that, but I don't have to like it."

"Ah, if things were different, you would not be here in India at all," Rohan said. "If equality were a characteristic of life, you would find it to be very intolerable."

"What does that mean?"

"Merely that it is easy to criticize inequality when one is of the ruling class."

Devora sighed. "Oh, don't start with that business, Rohan. All right, I admit that it's easy for me to criticize inequality in India, but that doesn't mean that I shouldn't criticize it at all."

Rohan inclined his head. "Point well taken. And this is another difference between you and the other *memsahibs*. They are very bigoted. They thrive in the inequality of their status."

"Yes, and they think all Indians are uncivilized animals, particularly the men." Devora leaned her head against the back of the chair. "They warned me against the men straight away."

"And what did they warn you of?"

"Mrs. Thompson is convinced that Indian men can't control their sexual urges," Devora replied. "Something to do with spicy food and erotic art, she claims. Those things have adverse effects on Indian men."

"Sexual urges are adverse?" Rohan asked, his voice lined with humor.

"Not all of them." Devora's thoughts went back to the Maharaja, and she shivered slightly. She had been enraptured with the idea of him and of what he could offer her, but now she was just grateful that she discovered his true nature before she became even more involved with him. "According to Mrs. Thompson, sexual urges are adverse if they take place in Indian men."

"But not in Mrs. Thompson herself."

Devora chuckled, remembering when she had encountered Mrs. Thompson getting a thorough fucking from the squat Major Cuthbert. "No, definitely not in Mrs. Thompson."

"Or in you." His suggestive words floated on the damp air.

Devora looked at him and shook her head. Her heart began to pulse a slow, steady rhythm. "No, not in me. Although I don't consider sexual urges in Indian men to be necessarily adverse either."

"Necessarily? Then what is your criteria for determining the adversity of sexual urges?"

"The Indian man himself, of course."

Devora met his gaze, stunned by the attraction that crackled in the air between them. His black eyes watched her through the dim light that spilled onto the veranda. Not five seconds could have possibly passed, but to Devora it felt like an eternity. She pressed a hand against her chest, trying to calm her racing heart.

"Perhaps I should go back inside," she murmured, rising from her chair.

"Perhaps so." Rohan stood in a gesture of respect. "Good night, *memsahib.*"

"Yes." Devora ran her hands down her night shift. She felt hot and cold all at once. "Good night."

She started to turn, but couldn't help pausing and glancing back at him. God, no man had ever looked at her like that, not even Gerald, and certainly not the Maharaja. Rohan's eyes, usually so unreadable, looked at her now the way a man looks at a woman he desires. Devora's heart pounded against her rib cage as she recognized the magnitude of what might happen. And the fact that she wanted it to. A thousand thoughts splashed around in her mind, but a dominant one broke through her momentary confusion. *I want him. I've always wanted him.*

Without pausing to question her thoughts, Devora crossed the veranda to Rohan, meeting him halfway. Their bodies collided with sudden urgency. His arms went around her swiftly, pulling her tight against him as he bent his head to kiss her. Devora clutched at his cotton shirt, sinking against him as if he were the only solid element in the rain-washed world. A moan escaped her when his mouth fitted against hers with clumsy perfection. Warm and slightly rough, his lips felt utterly delicious, sparking the heat of desire in her blood.

Devora returned his kiss with an intensity borne of desperation, unbearably relieved that the sexual tension between them had finally given way to sweet surrender. Rohan urged her lips apart to explore the cavern of her mouth with his tongue, his movements probing and seductive. His hands stroked down her back to clutch her rounded buttocks. Devora gasped when he pulled her lower body against his groin, making her feel the hard bulge of his erection. Her pulse pounded wildly in her throat, her senses fogged with pure need. She thrust her fingers through his hair, stroking the coarse strands as he lifted one hand to the back of her neck. He slanted her head back so that he could deepen their kiss. His tongue slid lusciously over her lips as if he had known all along that an erotic kiss could affect her with such potency.

Heat broke out on Devora's skin. She drew in a sharp breath when Rohan stepped slightly away from her. He clutched the transparent material of her gown in his fists and pulled it off her body, his gaze raking over her nakedness with such thoroughness that Devora couldn't help but be self-conscious. She crossed her arms over her breasts, but Rohan grasped her wrists and pried them apart to expose her to his gaze. His dark eyes seemed to see right through her as he looked at the slender proportions of her body.

Without a word, he bent to capture one of her nipples between his lips, sucking on it so lightly that exquisite sensations rained over Devora's skin. Her self-consciousness slipped away like pieces of torn silk. She watched Rohan with fascination as he clutched her bare hips and went down on his knees in front of her. His lips stroked a path down her abdomen, his tongue dipping into the indention of her navel as he moved toward her mons.

Alarm fluttered briefly through Devora as she realized his intentions. No man had ever touched her so intimately with his mouth, but she knew with an instinct as old as time that she had nothing to fear from Rohan. He urged her thighs apart gently with his hands and pressed his mouth between her legs.

Devora gasped, clutching the veranda railing to steady herself. Rohan's tongue slipped into the damp folds of her sex, teasing her sensitive nerves with such finesse that Devora's entire body went weak. Sheer arousal coursed through her body like fire. She gripped Rohan's hair with her other hand, almost unable to bear the acuteness of his touch.

"Wait," she said breathlessly. "Wait. I want to touch you, too."

Rohan stood, his dark eyes burning into her as he clutched her against him and kissed her. The flavor of her own nectar was a powerful aphrodisiac. With a moan, Devora reached between their bodies to massage the hardness of his erection. Her sex swelled with a rush of moisture at the thought of Rohan burying his cock inside her.

"Take off your clothes," she murmured hoarsely.

Rohan stepped away and pulled off his shirt and trousers to reveal his nakedness. Devora stared at him unashamedly, drinking in the sight of his lean, muscular body. A mat of dark hair covered his chest and arrowed down to his groin, where his deliciously long and thick penis jutted forth from a nest of curls.

"You're beautiful," Devora whispered.

"As are you." Rohan approached her again and gripped her bottom in his hands, kneading and stroking the resilient flesh. His fingers dipped into the crevice between them, causing Devora to start slightly before she gave herself up to the pleasure of his intimate caress.

Urgency lit in the air around them. Rohan's cock pressed insistently against Devora's belly. She grasped the thick stalk in her hand and stroked it from base to tip, thrilled when Rohan gave a low groan of pleasure. His muscles went tight with tension as she rubbed her thumb over the hard tip, massaging a drop of moisture back into his skin.

"Turn around," Rohan ordered, his voice rough with the onslaught of need.

Excitement sparked in Devora's belly at the mere thought of

being in such a position. She turned, allowing Rohan to clutch her hips and position her over the veranda railing. She closed her eyes, drawing in a sharp breath as he pushed her thighs apart and exposed her fully to his hot gaze. Devora knew she had never been so utterly stimulated. Droplets of heavy rain splashed on her face to cool her heated skin. The knob of Rohan's cock pressed against her sex, teasing her clitoris before he started to push himself into her. Devora let out a choked gasp, clutching the railing tightly as he began to fill her body with his stiffness. Her inner flesh clenched around him. He immersed himself in her inch by luscious inch, leaning over her body to stroke his fingers over the ridge of her spine. His breath rasped hotly against her back, and then he began to pump inside her with increasing force.

Arousal surged in Devora's loins as her tension began to ascend. The railing pressed hard against her belly, but she welcomed the abundance of sensations. Rohan's cock thrust in and out of her like pliable iron, his hands gripping her hips. His belly slammed against her buttocks as the wet, delicious sounds of sex filled the air and seemed to drown out even the noise of the rain. Devora's heart pounded so hard she could hear it inside her head as Rohan filled her again and again, his hard testicles slapping against her sex. He slipped one hand underneath her, sliding it over the slick surface of her belly and through the damp curls of her mons. Devora gave a cry of pleasure when his fingers began rubbing her sensitive clit.

"Oh, yes," she moaned. "Harder. Oh, please . . ."

Rohan thrust into her with rapid strokes, his pathway eased by Devora's overflowing fluids. With a groan, he pulled out of her suddenly and pressed the shaft of his cock between her buttocks, sliding it up and down before his semen spurted out onto the round globes. He leaned over her, reaching around to massage her breasts with one hand as his other hand continued working at her clit. Devora couldn't breathe for an instant as her body hovered on the precipice of rapture, and then a final stroke from Rohan sent her over the edge into a swirling mass of color.

Gasping, they both remained locked together for a long moment. Devora straightened slowly, her limbs both shaky and weak from the overflow of such intense carnality. She turned to look at Rohan, whose expression was sated and filled with lingering hints of passion. His chest still heaved as he tried to catch his breath.

He reached out to run his finger down her cheek.

"That is not an adverse sexual urge," he said.

Devora smiled slightly and shook her head.

"No," she agreed. "Not at all."

She bent and picked up her shift, slipping it over her head. She suspected that she would be entirely confused about this tomorrow, but right now she felt nothing but pure contentment.

Rohan tugged on his loose trousers and sank down into a chair. "You will regret this," he remarked.

Devora shook her head again and sat down across from him, pressing her thighs together to urge every last sensation from her body. "Will I? What makes you so certain of that?"

"I am still a servant."

"You're also a man."

"An Indian man."

Devora frowned. "Now, don't you start acting the part of a martyr with me. For all I know, you might be the one to regret it. Either that, or you'll think it's something to be proud of. Screwing a *memsahib*."

Amusement lit in Rohan's eyes. "Proud of or ashamed of?"

Devora couldn't help chuckling. "Well, even I find the idea of screwing a *memsahib* to be rather hideous."

"However, you claim not to be a *memsahib*," Rohan said.

"Yes." Devora wrapped her arms around herself, thinking she had never felt quite so replete. "Do you think I'm a *memsahib* like all the others?"

"No. Not like all the others. Not at all."

Devora knew that his words were a compliment. And for now, they would have to suffice. "Good night, Rohan."

"Good night, *memsahib*."

Devora went back into the stifling bungalow, closing the door against the relieving coolness of rain-drenched air.

chapter eleven

R eally, darling, you must at least take the carriage if you're
going into that god-awful village," Gerald said. He sipped
his lemonade and looked out at the vast expanse of the lawn
where a number of men were engaged in a spirited cricket
match.

"Yes, Devora, you never know when riots are going to break
out," Mrs. Thompson added. "And certainly a tonga *wallah*
couldn't get you out of the mayhem in time."

Devora didn't even bother replying. She poured herself another cup of tea and gazed at the properly dressed British men
and women who roamed about the gardens of the club. A number of tables with large umbrellas had been set up around the
cricket field so that people could sit in the shade, drinking,
gossiping, and watching the game. If it weren't for the turban-
wearing Indian servants and the scorching heat of the sun, one
wouldn't have known that they were even in India.

"Besides, it's not proper for a British woman to simply walk
around the villages like that," Gerald continued.

"Rohan was with me. I thought you didn't worry about me
if he was around as a watchdog."

"Of course I'm glad that he was with you, but even Rohan
couldn't have helped you if something happened. You must
exercise more caution."

"I can't imagine why you'd want to walk around that filthy village anyway," Mrs. Thompson declared. "The smells alone make me feel faint."

"I think it's fascinating," Devora said. "I even had a *paan*."

"Devora, *paan* is for men." Gerald was beginning to look exasperated. "And occasionally for Indian women. Certainly not for the British."

"Gerald, I was only trying something different."

"You're looking well, anyhow," Mrs. Thompson said, her pale eyes glancing over Devora's relaxed figure. "How are you feeling? Adele said that you were ill last week."

Gerald looked at Devora. "You were ill? Why didn't you tell me?"

"Oh, it was just a bit of stomach flu or something." Devora waved her hand dismissingly in the air. "I'm fine, really."

"Adele said that you arrived at the club, only to turn and leave again," Mrs. Thompson went on.

"Yes, it came upon me rather suddenly," Devora replied.

"Darling, I wish you'd told me." Concern darkened Gerald's expression. "Did you go and see Dr. Waterford?"

"No, it wasn't necessary," Devora said. "I was fine by the following morning. Do stop worrying, Gerald."

"I hate leaving you alone in that house," Gerald said. He took out his handkerchief and dabbed at his forehead. "I wish I didn't have to go on tour so often."

"My dear, you'll have to come stay with me and Reginald the next time Gerald leaves." Mrs. Thompson patted Devora's hand. "I won't take no for an answer."

"That's very kind of you, Mrs. Thompson," Gerald said. "I can't help worrying about her."

"As well you should," Mrs. Thompson said. "One never knows what could happen with all this talk of violent gangs running about the countryside."

"And what about that rumor that the Maharaja was involved with them?" Devora asked, purposely shifting the tide of the conversation. She had no intentions whatsoever of staying with the Thompsons at any point in time, but she would wait until Gerald left again before making her feelings clear.

"With the gangs?" Gerald asked. "I dare say he's funding them himself."

"Have you had lunch with him again, Devora?" Mrs. Thompson asked, glancing quickly at Gerald.

Gerald's mouth tightened as he looked at his wife and waited for her response.

Devora shook her head. "Oh, no. We had very pleasant lunches, but I believe he has other matters to attend to."

"Good," Mrs. Thompson said. "As I've told you, it's quite improper to dine alone with an Indian man, even if he is a Maharaja."

Devora stifled a chuckle. She'd done so much more than simply dine alone with an Indian man.

"Quite right," Gerald agreed.

"Oh, you know, there's a polo match this coming Saturday," Mrs. Thompson said, snapping open her fan. "I do hope you'll both attend."

"Of course, we'll be delighted," Gerald said. He gave Devora a smile. "Won't we, darling?"

"Utterly delighted."

A sudden barrage of gunshots broke the air, startling them all.

"What on earth . . ." Mrs. Thompson sat up and clutched her chest as a number of British officers began making their way out of the club grounds.

"That's from the village," Gerald said. "The damned anti-British riots. Bloody hell."

He stood, pushing his chair back. "I'd better go see what's happening. Lord knows we'll probably have to make some arrests." He bent to kiss Devora. "I'll be back as soon as I can."

"Be careful." Devora and Mrs. Thompson watched Gerald stride off with the other men.

"You know, you're very lucky to have him," Mrs. Thompson remarked, working her fan rapidly to stir up some cool air.

"Ambitious fellow, he is, and intent on preserving the British way of life in India. He will become very successful in the civil lines."

"Yes," Devora murmured. "That's what worries me."

"Have a good day, darling." Devora gave Gerald a perfunctory kiss and patted his lapels. "You look quite spiffy."

"I don't think I've told you how pleased I am that you seem to be adapting so well to India," Gerald said, reaching for his hat. "At least, now that you understand the customs. I told you that you would adjust just fine."

"Oh yes, I've adjusted," Devora murmured.

"And what are your plans for the day?"

They walked outside onto the sunbaked steps of the bungalow. Rohan stood at the bottom, holding the reins of Gerald's horse.

"Mostly painting," Devora replied. "I might call on Louise later this afternoon."

"Very good. I'll be back late this evening. As you know, there's been some trouble in the village."

"Is everything all right?" Devora asked. "With the rioting, I mean."

"Well, we had to make a number of arrests," Gerald replied as he descended the steps. "We're expecting a demonstration today at the city jail. Of course, we'll have to make an example out of those we arrested."

"An example how?"

"Why, by keeping them in jail, of course. The magistrate has also ordered several of the rioters to be publicly flogged. That will undoubtedly make a point."

"Publicly flogged? Why, that's barbaric!"

"You forget, darling, that we are dealing with barbarians." Gerald swung up into the saddle of his horse.

Devora watched him go until he was no longer within her sight. Then, she looked at Rohan, who still stood at the bottom of the steps. Even the mere sight of him elicited a rush of desire in her, particularly now that she knew how unbearably passionate he could be. He was wearing his knee-length white jacket, sash, and black trousers again, appearing every inch the proper, Indian servant. If her night with him hadn't been so terribly vivid, Devora might have believed that it hadn't even happened. But vivid it had been. So vivid.

"What are you doing today?" she asked.

"I will go into town to make some purchases," Rohan replied. "Then I must find another stablehand, as the one who has been caring for the horses is returning to his village."

"I see." Devora glanced up at the sun, which hung halfway to the summit of the sky. "You'd better go into town now. It's going to be terribly hot later this afternoon."

"Yes, *memsahib*." Rohan climbed the steps, not glancing at her as he passed to enter the house.

Devora followed him inside. They had reverted back to their roles as mistress and servant, although of course neither one of them could deny what had taken place between them. At least, Devora couldn't.

"Rohan."

He paused on his way toward the back of the house and turned to look at her. His expression had once again taken on that impassivity that Devora so disliked.

"You know, I don't blame you for anything," Devora said. "You don't have to avoid me."

"I apologize. I was not aware that I was doing so."

Devora sighed. "Oh, stop talking to me as if we didn't fuck each other just last week."

"*Memsahib,* that was my mistake. I have dishonored my position in this household by taking advantage of you in such a manner."

"You didn't take advantage of me," Devora snapped. "I was perfectly willing, in case you didn't realize it at the time."

He didn't reply, but an emotion flickered in the depths of his dark eyes that made Devora realize that he wasn't as immune to their attraction as he would have her believe. She crossed the room and stopped right in front of him, folding her arms over her chest.

"You know, I can understand your coldness when it comes to your role as head servant," she said. "You have a job to do, and you do it extremely well. However, given what I recently experienced with you, I know for a fact that you're not a cold man all the time. And it's foolish of you to think that you can treat me the same way as you did before."

"How would you have me treat you differently?" Rohan asked. "I am certain that you do not want your husband to know what has transpired between us. Treating you differently would give him cause for suspicion."

"My husband isn't here right now!" Devora said, feeling frustration start to build inside her again. She closed her eyes and took a deep breath. "Look, I think it's safe to say that we're friends now. At the very least."

"*Memsahib*, you fail to understand the intricacies of British-Indian relations," Rohan replied. "Friendships develop, of this there is no doubt. But not between British women and Indian men. This is not acceptable."

"Since when are you so concerned with what is or isn't acceptable?" Devora asked coldly. "Was it acceptable to do what we did?"

"No. That is why it was a mistake." He turned and started to walk away.

"Funny," Devora called after him. "I was under the impression that mistakes didn't feel quite that good."

Her words caused him to hesitate for the briefest second, but then he disappeared outside, letting the back door close behind him. Irritation swelled in Devora's soul as she realized that not even such intimacy could fully break through Rohan's implacable veneer. With a sigh, she went to the dining table and began to organize her paintings and drawings. She had already done at least fifty drawings of temple art, both erotic sculptures and statues of gods and goddesses. She looked at the sketch she had done of Rohan, thinking that she would love to turn it into a painting.

Well, why couldn't she? Simply because he was choosing to be a right bastard didn't mean she couldn't paint him. His attitude didn't distract from the strong, sculptured planes of his face and the incredible beauty of his eyes. Devora stared at the drawing for a long moment, then placed a small, primed canvas on the easel. Using a charcoal pencil, she copied the drawing onto the canvas with strong, confident strokes that would combine to form the base of Rohan's personality. Strength, confidence, and an almost complete inflexibility.

Almost. Devora smiled. When a person broke through that shield, what treasures she would find. Devora remembered what Kalindi and Lota had told her about Rohan's supposed bride-to-be. What if he really had been in love with her, she mused as she stared at his charcoal likeness. What humanity she could instill in his painted expression if she knew that he had locked himself away over a broken heart.

Intrigued by the possible romanticism of the story, Devora put down her charcoal pencil and hurried outside to the servants' quarters. A small, white-washed building stood some distance away from the main bungalow. Gerald had told her that it consisted of two rooms, one of which was used for storage and the other for Rohan's living quarters. Devora knocked on the door sharply.

"Rohan?"

He opened the door, looking mildly exasperated by her persistence. "Yes, *memsahib?*"

"I want to ask you something. May I come in?"

"That would not be . . ."

"Oh, sod propriety," Devora snapped.

She pushed her way past him and went into the room, her gaze sweeping over the neat, clean furnishings. A large bed sat pushed against the wall, draped by a mosquito net. Toiletry items were arranged with meticulous care on the dressing table, and a small desk held writing paper and pens. Thankfully, the air was not coated with the thick, cloying scent of incense, but instead smelled fresh and clean.

"Do come in," Rohan said dryly.

Devora gave him a cheeky smile. "Why, thank you. What a nice place."

"Please, sit down." Sounding resigned to her presence, Rohan pulled the chair away from the desk and gestured toward it. He then sat down on the bed and fixed his gaze on her. "What is your question then?"

Devora realized rather suddenly that it wasn't exactly polite to start questioning someone about his personal life. Still, she seethed with curiosity to know the truth behind the rumors. She shifted on the chair as she tried to think of a way to voice her thoughts.

"Well," she said. "I don't know if it's a question, really, but perhaps more of a curiosity."

Rohan's eyebrows lifted slightly. "Curiosity about what?"

"You. I mean, your past, to be more specific."

"I've told you about my past."

"Yes, I know, but you haven't told me everything."

Rohan frowned. "How do you know what I *haven't* told you?"

"I've heard rumors of a woman."

His expression darkened suddenly. Devora sensed his emotional withdrawal as if he had closed a door between them. She put out a hand to try and assuage him.

"Wait. Wait. I don't mean to be rude. You must know that people have talked about you."

"What people?" Rohan snapped. "Kalindi?"

"Don't be angry with her. She's simply repeating what others have said."

"As are you, apparently."

"No, I haven't told anyone," Devora protested. "I don't know anything, Rohan. That's why I'm asking you."

"This is not your business."

"I know." Devora could think of no earthly rationale as to why he should tell her anything at all, so she decided to simply ask him. "Did you love her?"

He looked at her for a long moment, his eyes still flashing with anger. The silence stretched between them like a taut rubber band until Devora thought that she had made a serious mistake in coming here. She clutched her hands together and prepared to stand.

"I'm sor—" she began.

"No," Rohan interrupted.

Startled, Devora met his gaze. "No?"

"No, I didn't love her."

"Oh." Devora didn't know what to say, but she was aware of a slight disappointment. For some reason, she was hoping that his stoicism was the result of a bittersweet love story. "I'm sorry."

Rohan shook his head. "There is no need to be sorry. I simply did not love her."

Devora eyed him cautiously. "Yet you were supposed to marry her?"

"Yes. I was working for a British family near Delhi. They knew of another British family who had an entire family of servants working for them. They were seeking a husband for their daughter, and so they asked to meet me."

"And what happened?"

"We met and agreed to marry," Rohan replied. "I wanted a son just like any other man."

A horrific thought struck Devora. "Did she die?"

"No, nothing quite so dramatic," Rohan said. "I heard five years ago that she was living in Delhi."

"Well?" Devora said, unable to keep the impatient note out of her voice. "What happened? Why didn't you marry her?"

"I learned she was pregnant," Rohan replied.

"Oh, my."

"With a British man's child. Unfortunately, the British man happened to be the master of the household in which I worked."

"What did you do?"

Rohan lifted his shoulders in a shrug. "I thought it was best if I terminated my service with them. I could no longer respect the *sahib,* so I decided to leave and seek employment elsewhere. I soon found that it was not so easy."

"Why not?"

"One of the British daughters had developed an attachment to me. She told me that I couldn't possibly leave, and that she would seek revenge on me if I did."

"And did she seek revenge when you left?" Devora asked.

"Yes. She accused me of raping her."

Devora gasped in shock. "No."

"It became a bit of a scandal. I did go to trial, but of course there was no evidence to substantiate the accusation. The city magistrate, who was Indian, dismissed the case, but I had to leave town. All of the British were against me. None would have hired me."

"I expect that was also because of the Indian magistrate."

"Probably."

Devora was quiet for a long moment. So much for romance and love. A nagging thought occurred to her, creating an unsettled feeling in the pit of her stomach. She glanced at Rohan almost hesitantly.

"You don't like the British very much, then," she said.

"I have reason not to," Rohan replied.

"You also have reason to use a British woman for your own type of revenge, don't you?"

"Yes, I suppose that I do."

Devora waited for him to deny her implication, but he didn't. A tremble went through her body with the force of a lightning bolt. She hadn't particularly cared about the motivations behind the Maharaja's interest in her, but Rohan was different. Devora didn't know why, but he was.

"I see," she said stiffly. "I hadn't realized you were capable of that. I've thought you were cold, but I also thought that you had integrity."

"If you want to know if I'm using you for revenge, the answer is no," Rohan said.

"But you just said—"

"I said I have reason to use a British woman," Rohan replied. "That is not, however, what I am doing."

Devora stood slowly. She looked at him for a moment, thinking that she had come here in the hopes of clarifying things. And now she was leaving more confused than ever.

"Well, I guess that's good to know," she said. "Thank you for your time."

"I assume that your own motivations are also less than crystal clear," Rohan said. "Is it for your own revenge? Or the desire to rebel against convention and conformity?"

His words slammed into her like a physical blow. "None of those things," she answered, her voice icy. "But you'd like it if I had those kinds of motivations, wouldn't you? It would confirm all the negative things you think about British *memsahibs*."

"I have told you that you are different."

"You're not exactly doing a wonderful job of convincing me of that," Devora snapped. "If I'm so different, why do you still say that we can't be friends because it's not *acceptable*? Acceptable according to what standards? Some ridiculous convention that allowed an entire community to turn against you on a false charge? Is that the convention you want to live by?"

"These things only serve to remind me that British and Indian relations cannot be successful ones," Rohan said. "There are too many differences of perception."

"God, you are so inflexible!" Devora retorted angrily. "And you're a hypocrite. You hate the fact that all the British turned on you because you were Indian, and yet you can make a sweeping statement like that and expect me to sympathize with you?"

His eyes hardened. "I did not ask for your sympathy or even for your understanding, *memsahib*. If I recall, it was you who came here."

"I came here because I wanted to know the truth behind a rumor!" Devora said. "Why is that so difficult for you to comprehend? *I'm* not going to accuse you of rape, if that's what you're thinking. Simply because one British woman falsely accused you does not mean that you can't be friends with a different British woman."

Rohan stood, leveling a gaze on her. "I would not have told you what I just did if I did not believe that."

His words silenced her. She should have known that. His unyielding nature would prevent him from revealing such a personal matter if he did not, at the very least, trust her. She nodded.

"Yes. I realize that. I apologize." Devora approached him almost hesitantly, afraid that he'd had too much time to think about what they had done. She paused in front of him and reached up to trace her fingers over his sensual mouth.

"You know, even if you think that friendships are difficult between British and Indians," she said. "Lust can obviously be quite easy."

Amusement flashed in Rohan's eyes. "Yes. That I have discovered."

He cupped her chin in his hand and bent to brush his lips against hers. Warmth bloomed in Devora's soul like a fresh rose, spilling over with color and luscious scents. She slipped her arms around his waist and allowed herself to sink against his chest. The urgency of their first time together was replaced by a slow, deliberate pace that seemed to break through so many weeks of restraint.

Devora smoothed her hands over Rohan's back and wondered how anyone could possibly be so narrow-minded as to categorize all Indian men. She parted her lips under his as his hand slid behind her neck. Their tongues danced together, breath mingling in hot rushes. Arousal swept over Devora's skin like a thousand delicious feathers, so soft and sensual that she felt as if she were entering a place she didn't want to leave.

Rohan whispered something in her ear, Hindi words whose meaning escaped her but whose lyricism invaded her blood. She stroked her palm over Rohan's strong jaw, tracing her fingertips over the coarseness of his whiskers. Her breasts pressed against his chest, her nipples already tenting the thin material of her dress as Rohan clutched her hips in his hands and pulled the skirt to her waist. Then he gently insinuated his knee between her thighs. Devora drew in a sharp breath at the sensation of his hard thigh pressing against her sex. She pushed her body downward, her pulse throbbing as her clit rubbed against his leg. The heat of Rohan's skin burned clear through his trousers and the cotton of her panties. Her body seemed to move of its own volition, her hips rotating with increasing frenzy. Sensations spread like fingers from her sex upward through her pelvis, inflaming her need beyond reason. Rohan supported her lower back, bending to kiss the hollow of her throat. His tongue flickered out to taste her damp skin.

"Wait," Devora gasped, tightening her fingers around the front of his jacket. "I want—"

She didn't have to finish her sentence. Rohan pulled her dress and slip over her head, exposing her to his heated gaze. Devora stretched out on the bed and let him remove her panties, her excitement intensified merely by the way that he was looking at her naked body. She had never seen eyes like his, eyes that could smolder with such desire and yet also had the ability to shut him off from the world.

Watching her, Rohan removed his jacket and trousers, then leaned over her and pressed his palm against the apex of her thighs. The tip of his finger slipped into her tight passage, eliciting a rush of moisture in readiness for his complete penetration. With a moan, Devora spread her legs apart and gripped his arms to urge him toward her. She splayed her hands over the muscles of his chest, twining her fingers through his thick mat of hair and toying with the flat, male nipples. She loved the way his skin and muscles felt underneath her palms, and the way the heat emanated from him to slide directly into her. His erection nudged against the fissure of her sex, pressing forward with slow strokes. Devora opened up to him fully, wrapping her arms around him to pull him closer as his body began to intensify their sweet, hot union. As they merged together, all thought dissolved into sensations, and a quiet desperation that neither of them could identify.

Devora woke with slow ease, lifting her arms above her head for a satisfying stretch. She took a deep breath of the clean, fresh air drifting in from the garden and opened her eyes. Rohan stood in front of the cracked mirror, fastening his sash around his waist. Devora rolled onto her side and smoothed her hand over his pillow.

"Have you told anyone about us?" she murmured.

Rohan glanced at her in the mirror. "You think I would?"

Devora shrugged. "I don't know. I was only curious."

"No. I have told no one."

"Neither have I."

"Haven't you? Not even Mrs. Thompson and the gossiping *memsahibs* of the club?"

"Heavens no. Why on earth would I tell them?" Devora propped herself up on one elbow as she watched him finish dressing. He really was a beautiful man. And so noble-looking, as if he had been raised among the regality of court. "Are you going into town now?"

"Yes. You require something?"

"Pick up some desserts, if you would. Perhaps *gulab jamun*. I enjoy that. But make certain that it's fresh."

"Yes, *memsahib*."

Devora wondered if it was customary among Indian men to continue to refer to women by formal titles even after they had been sexually intimate. She reached for her discarded dress and slipped it over her head, then patted her hair back into place.

She thought about going with him into town, but decided that she would much rather work on her painting of him.

"I will return in an hour," Rohan said.

"Fine." Devora put on her shoes and followed him outside. She went toward the veranda, while he went around to the front of the house. Devora's heart jumped slightly as she saw Kalindi standing on the veranda, watching both her and Rohan return from the direction of his quarters.

"Do you want something, Kalindi?" Devora asked, putting an authoritative tone in her voice.

"Yes, *memsahib*. I was wondering what you would like me to prepare for lunch." Kalindi glanced at Rohan as he disappeared around the side of the house.

"Is it lunchtime already?" Devora hadn't realized just how long she had been with Rohan. Nor did she like the curious look on Kalindi's face. "Just some fruit and perhaps a chicken pie."

"Very well." Kalindi turned to go back into the kitchen, but then glanced at Devora again. "Did you discover what you wanted to know about Rohan?"

Devora frowned. "Yes, thank you."

"He is not dismissed, is he?"

"No, of course not. Why on earth would he be dismissed?" Devora moved past Kalindi to go into the house. She hoped that the young woman didn't know that she had been with Rohan for at least four hours. The last thing she needed was Kalindi gossiping. "Kalindi, do get back to work. I dislike idleness."

"Yes, *memsahib*." Kalindi hurried back into the kitchen.

Devora returned to her painting, realizing that she had left her drawings of Rohan in plain view for the servants to see. She sighed, but figured that drawings were not exactly incriminating evidence. All one had to do was look at Rohan to realize that he was a perfect subject for artistic endeavors. Not to mention sexual endeavors.

Devora smiled. A shiver of delight skittered over her skin.

No man had ever satisfied her so thoroughly, both on mental and physical levels, not even her own husband. And then there was the sheer illicitness of their relationship, which gave it a heady kind of beauty.

She picked up her pencil and gazed at the sketch on the canvas. After a moment, she erased the drawing and started over. Within half an hour, she had redrawn Rohan's likeness. As she stepped back to critically examine the result, satisfaction filled her. She hadn't consciously intended this, but she had captured his expression as it was in the moment just before he bent his head to kiss her.

chapter twelve

I thought you liked visiting him." Gerald looked at Devora as he fastened his waistcoat and slipped on his jacket. "Especially with all those lunches you attended."

Devora didn't miss the sarcastic note in his voice, and she gave him a mild glare.

"I *did* enjoy visiting him," she replied. "However, I just don't feel up to socializing tonight."

"Well, darling, I'm sorry, but you're going to have to," Gerald said. "It's just not good form to turn down an invitation from the Maharaja."

"Yes, I know." Devora fastened on her pearl earrings and picked up her pocketbook. "Please, though, let's come home early."

"We'll come home as soon as it's proper."

Proper. Good form. Devora thought that she had never met a group of people who were so rigidly confined by a set of rules as the British "empire-builders" were. She followed Gerald outside to the car they had borrowed to take them to the Maharaja's palace again.

Rohan stood by the car, his hand on the handle of the open door. "Good evening to both of you," he said.

"Good evening, Rohan," Gerald stepped aside and helped Devora into the car. She glanced quickly at Rohan as she climbed in, not surprised by the fact that he didn't exhibit a flicker of emotion toward her. Once she and Gerald were settled in the backseat, Rohan got behind the wheel and headed for the palace. Devora looked out the side window at the reddish-bronze landscape, wondering how anyone could live here for as long as many of the British did and yet still be so ignorant about the country and its people.

The entrance of the palace was lined with lights, making it stand out like a beacon through the late-afternoon air. Rohan left them at the entrance before he went to park the car alongside the other vehicles.

Devora took a deep breath as she and Gerald went into the palace. She hadn't seen the Maharaja since the day he had both frightened and angered her with his disregard for her own feelings. She slipped her arm through Gerald's as they stepped into the reception room that bustled with movement, silk, and voices. Devora's fingers tightened around Gerald's arm when she saw the Maharaja approaching them.

Weeks had passed since their final encounter, but he looked much the same: a plump man elaborately decked out in satin and embroidery. An exotic, colorful feather bloomed from his turban. Devora watched him approach, realizing that he had lost the mystique that had so enraptured her in the beginning. He may have been a prince, but ultimately, he was a manipulative, aging man who did nothing but conspire against the British and exercise control over his court officials and harem. It made perfect sense that he would also attempt to exercise the same control over a British woman.

"Sir, you honor us by inviting us to your home once again." Gerald shook the Maharaja's hand. "Thank you."

"You are most welcome at any time," the Maharaja replied smoothly. His gaze went to Devora, his full lips curling into a semblance of a smile. "Mrs. Hawthorne, I am sorry you have been unable to come for lunch again."

"I've been busy," Devora replied.

"Yes, that is a pity. I did so enjoy our visits."

"Will you gentlemen excuse me?" Devora asked. "I see Louise over there, and there is something I want to ask her."

The men nodded. Devora gratefully escaped the Maharaja's presence and went to join the group of women in the corner.

"Devora, isn't it wonderful to be here again?" Louise kissed Devora's cheek in greeting. "I just love being able to visit a palace!"

"Yes, wonderful," Devora murmured.

Adele eyed Devora with suspicion. "You don't seem very excited. Perhaps that's because you've been here much more often than we have."

"Perhaps," Devora replied absently.

"Now, Adele, don't be rude," Louise said. "I think it's a great honor that the Maharaja invited Devora to lunch with him."

"Provided that's all she did," Adele muttered.

Devora chuckled. "You mean anything more would *not* be a great honor?"

Louise gasped and giggled. "Devora, really!"

"I'm going to find the powder room," Devora said, realizing that being with the *memsahibs* was no more bearable than being with the Maharaja. "Please excuse me."

She went out into the courtyard, hoping that she could remember which direction to turn in. The palace had a number of rooms and corridors, so that her chances of getting lost were sufficiently high. She headed toward the erotic art room and found a powder room several doors down. After using the room and fixing her makeup, Devora went back out onto the mezzanine. She stopped in her tracks at the sight of the Maharaja leaning against the railing, smoking a cigarette.

His eyes, already overly bright from an excess of alcohol, traveled with slow insolence over her body. Devora bristled with anger.

"What do you want?" she asked, her voice cold.

"I thought I would find you here," he replied. "I knew you would seek out my erotic room once again."

"I was doing no such thing," Devora said. "I wanted to use the powder room."

"Of course you did." The Maharaja flicked the cigarette over the railing and approached her. "But you cannot tell me that you do not remember what we did in that room."

Devora backed up a step, only to encounter the wall. She disliked the look in his eyes.

"What we did was a mistake," she snapped. "It might have been exciting at first, but I no longer want anything to do with you. Please leave me alone."

"Ah, my dear Mrs. Hawthorne." The Maharaja reached up and traced the scooped neckline of her dress with his finger. "You have a sensual nature unlike that of any British woman I have known."

"And I'm sure you've known plenty of them," Devora snapped, swatting his hand away. "I'm going back to the reception."

"You mean, you don't want to stay here with me?" Something wicked glinted in the Maharaja's expression as he pressed his large body against hers, pinning her to the wall. His stale breath rasped against her cheek.

Fear lit in Devora like a struck match. She suspected that people did not often refuse the Maharaja anything. She pressed her hands against his chest and tried to push him away. "Get away from me."

"You know that you enjoyed what I did to you," he whispered, skimming his hand up her abdomen to her breast. "Wouldn't you like to do it again?"

"No!" Devora snapped. "Get the hell away from me! If you don't, I swear I will charge you with assault! How do you think the British officers will react to that?"

"Considering that you have willingly given yourself to me at least twice, I suspect that they will consider you to be quite a little whore." The Maharaja grasped her breast in his hand and tried to press a kiss against her lips.

Nausea rose in Devora's stomach like a tidal wave. Without

thinking, she slammed her knee upward and hit him squarely in the groin. He grunted in pain and released her, doubling over to clutch at himself.

"Keep treating me like this, and what little you have down there will be so damaged that it'll no longer work," Devora snapped. While he was down, she slapped him across the face for good measure, then turned and fled.

Devora couldn't return to the reception room in her current state, and so she pushed open the closed door of one of the rooms along the mezzanine and ducked inside. She shut the door behind her and leaned against it, her chest heaving as she tried to catch her breath and collect her senses.

After she had calmed down a bit, she focused on her surroundings. Her eyes widened at the sight of three beautifully made-up women draped in silk saris and an abundance of gold jewelry. They lounged on velvet couches, and one of them was smoking from a hookah pipe. All three of them were staring at her.

"Oh," Devora said. "I'm sorry. I didn't mean to intrude."

None of them replied, and Devora realized that they probably didn't speak English. She couldn't believe the room itself, with its rich furnishings of velvet and gold brocade. A dressing table held lacquer boxes overflowing with gold jewelry and precious gems. Devora suddenly felt almost frumpy in her beaded dress and pearl earrings.

"You are the Maharaja's *memsahib,* are you not?" one of the women asked. Devora recognized her as the woman who had approached her in the lounging room during her first lunch with the Maharaja. What was her name? Channa.

"No, I'm not," Devora said. "I mean, I was . . ." Her voice trailed off.

"He has spoken of you," Channa said. "He has said that you were not good enough for him."

"More that he has been cruel to me," Devora replied. "I discovered that he is not a kind man."

Channa's expression darkened. "No, he is not."

Her voice was so certain that Devora looked at her in surprise. She wondered what odd perversions Channa had suffered at the Maharaja's hands.

"You are lucky," Channa said. "You are free now, yes?"

"I . . . yes."

Channa waved a hand toward the other women. "We are not. Perhaps we never will be."

"I—I'm sorry." The thick scents of smoke and incense made Devora slightly dizzy. What was this woman telling her? "Excuse me."

She hurried back out onto the mezzanine, relieved to discover that the Maharaja was no longer there. She paused by the railing to catch her breath and collect her composure before following the sound of voices back to the reception room.

"Excuse me, Gerald, but may I speak with you?" Devora put her hand on Gerald's arm as he stood talking with a group of British officers.

"Of course, darling." Gerald followed her to a corner of the room. "What is it?"

"I'm feeling rather ill," Devora explained. "Would you mind terribly if we returned home now?"

A crease of concern appeared between Gerald's eyebrows. "What's the matter?"

"I just have a bit of a headache. I'd really like to go home."

"Darling, I have some important business to discuss here," Gerald said, glancing back toward the group of men. "Can't you stay for a little while longer?"

"No, I'm really not well."

"Well, why don't I ask Rohan to drive you home, then? I can return with the Thompsons after dinner."

"Yes, I would appreciate that."

"I'll go and fetch him while you apologize to the Maharaja." Gerald headed for the front entrance.

Devora had no intention of seeking out the Maharaja again, so she quickly told Louise that she would be leaving and asked her to convey her regrets. Then she went outside, breathing in a rush of fresh air as if it could cleanse her of the repulsive incident.

"All right, darling?" Gerald came toward her. "I'm sorry I can't return with you, but this has to do with the Maharaja's politics."

"No, no, it's all right," Devora assured him. "I'll be fine."

Rohan drove the car up to the entrance and opened the door for Devora. Gerald kissed her on the cheek and helped her inside.

"You're not well, *memsahib?*" Rohan asked as he guided the car onto the road.

"I'll be fine," Devora repeated. "Just a little sick to my stomach, that's all."

Rohan glanced at her in the rearview mirror. "Does this have to do with the Maharaja?"

Devora gave him a sharp look. "Why do you ask?"

"I recall that you were quite distraught the last time you left him," Rohan explained. "It would not surprise me if he were the cause."

"Why? What do you know about him?"

"I know that he is very tyrannical," Rohan said. "And as you know, rumors abound."

Devora thought of the harem women. Channa had been right. At least she was able to free herself. Heaven only knew just how intense the Maharaja's tyranny could get.

"Was that the reason you kept trying to prevent me from visiting him?" she asked Rohan.

"Of course. I wanted nothing to happen to you."

Devora considered his words. "Then I'm sorry I didn't listen to you."

Rohan shrugged philosophically. "Often people do not heed words," he said. "They must discover the truth for themselves."

"Well, I certainly did that," Devora replied, turning to look out the window. "He's an unpleasant, greedy man. I think that he is so used to people obeying him that he has completely lost all regard for others."

"Yet, it took you some time to discover that for yourself," Rohan said.

Devora nodded, not finding his words to be particularly offensive.

"It's a very romantic idea, meeting a Maharaja," she admitted. "I suppose I was rather taken by the whole idea. Unfortunately, the man himself quickly destroyed any illusions I might have had."

"Perhaps it is better that he did so sooner rather than later," Rohan suggested.

"Yes, perhaps," Devora agreed. The sun still shimmered over the horizon, coating the plains in crimson. A distant river ran parallel to the road, bordered by trees and tall reeds with a small temple standing on the banks. "Rohan?"

"Yes?"

"Would you pull over to that river, please? I'd like to stop for a moment."

Rohan guided the car off the road and parked underneath a tree near the river. Both he and Devora got out and walked to the river. The air was much cooler now than during the day, creating a refreshing, sweet breeze. They stopped close to the river, whose undulating waters moved swiftly south. The only sounds were those of the river, the rustling trees, and the chirping of birds. The purity of the riverbank and the air easily washed away the garish opulence and noise of the Maharaja's party. Devora took a deep breath, cleansing her lungs of the cloying scents of incense and perfume.

"What river is this?" she asked.

"The Ganges. The holiest of India's rivers. The waters are known as *amrita,* the nectar of immortality."

Devora looked at the temple, which was so close to the river that its steps descended beneath the water's surface. A half-naked man stood on the steps, waist-deep in the river, pouring water on his head with the help of a small pot. Several flowers floated on the water around him.

"It is considered that bathing in the Ganges washes away one's sins," Rohan explained, following her gaze to the worshipping man. "The Ganges is said to have come down from the heavens onto the head of Lord Shiva. For thousands of years, the waters spread through his hair before descending onto the earth. If you look at the Shiva Nataraja statues in which he is performing the cosmic dance of creation, you will see a small female figure in his hair. That is a personification of the Ganges River."

"That's fascinating," Devora said. "Do you know all of this from your studies? You play the piano so beautifully, you know so much about Indian religion and philosophies, and yet . . ." Her voice trailed off.

"Yet I am merely a servant," Rohan finished.

"It does seem a bit strange," Devora admitted.

"There is no shame in servitude," Rohan replied. "There is no shame in any job, no matter how menial. If the duties are carried out properly and the job is done well, then one should take pride in that."

"But haven't you wanted to be something more?" Devora asked. "Haven't you wanted to be a teacher or a doctor or even a . . . a concert pianist?"

"The piano I learned when I was a child, as I told you," Rohan explained. "I play for enjoyment. As for teaching, I teach English to a group of schoolchildren twice a week in the village. I am happy doing what I do. No, I have not wanted for more."

"Well, I think you could be much more than be a servant," Devora said. "What about all of the Indian mythology that you know? Did you learn that in school?

"Ah, India." Rohan shrugged. "One learns through life."

"Are you very religious?"

"I am not as devout as perhaps I should be."

"Do you believe in things like karma and reincarnation?" Devora asked.

"Of course. And destiny."

"I don't believe in destiny. I dislike the idea of assuming that one's path is already set and unchangeable."

"That is not the destiny of Hinduism," Rohan said. "If that were the case, we would all be idle. Destiny is the result of one's actions in previous lives, that is true. However, destiny is insignificant without exertion. One must take action in order to follow one's path."

"Well, that makes more sense," Devora said. "Otherwise, what is the point of karma?"

"Exactly. One must act well in this life in order to secure happiness for the next life. My father always told me that."

"Were you close to your father?"

"My father?" Rohan sounded surprised. "Yes. I loved my father very much." He paused. "And your parents?"

"Yes, I have wonderful parents. They're both alive and living in Tunbridge Wells. My father is a retired professor."

"What did he teach?"

"English literature. Hence, I was brought up with Shakespeare and Chaucer."

"Two decent enough chaps to be brought up with."

Devora smiled. "Yes, that's very true."

"You live in London now?"

"I did before I moved here," Devora said. "I miss it sometimes, especially the coolness and the fog. I do love the fog. It makes everything very mysterious and soft-edged. In India, the sun is so hot and strong. It seems to expose every tiny detail, illuminating things that would perhaps be better left hidden."

Rohan didn't reply, but Devora could sense him looking at her. She wrapped her arms around herself and gazed toward the man standing in the river. He began to chant, his cryptic words rising on the mild breeze. His arms lifted with graceful movements as he bathed in the holy waters. There was a strange beauty in his isolated devotion.

"Would you like to see the temple?" Rohan asked.

Devora looked at the worshipper for a moment longer. "No, I don't think so. I don't wish to disturb him."

"You will not. People worship on the *ghats* all the time."

Devora shook her head. She couldn't imagine intruding upon the man's piety, if only through her presence. "No, it's all right. I'll come back some other time."

She turned and started back to the car. Rohan followed her, reaching out to open the car door for her. Just before she got into the car, Devora glanced at him. He was looking at her so intently that she was surprised.

"What?"

Rohan shook his head, his lips curving into a slight smile. "I find you to be very intriguing."

"Is that a good thing?" Devora asked.

"Yes, I think so."

Swiftly, he bent his head and brushed his lips over hers in the lightest, most delicious movement. A hundred butterflies took flight in Devora's soul. She responded with a rush of affection, enchanted by the silent holiness of their surroundings and the pure spontaneity of his kiss.

She pulled back slightly to look at him. "What was that for?"

Rohan's dark eyes crinkled at the corners as he smiled at her again. Devora's heart swelled. That smile of his affected her like nothing ever had before, perhaps because it was so beautiful and so rare.

"You have an old soul, *memsahib*."

"What does that mean?"

"You have a soul that has been reincarnated many times on earth," Rohan explained. "It means that you possess a deep understanding of many of life's mysteries."

Devora wasn't certain of that at all, but the idea was captivating. "That's lovely," she said. "Thank you."

He put his palm against her cheek for a brief instant before moving away. Devora climbed into the car, realizing that something quite powerful had just happened between them. Rohan closed the door and got into the driver's seat. He started the car and guided it back onto the main road toward the enclave of British-owned bungalows.

They fell silent for the remainder of the ride, but Devora occasionally felt Rohan's enigmatic, mirrored gaze on her as if it were a reflection of herself.

chapter thirteen

G erald will be gone for three days," Devora said. "Please?"
"This is a very bad idea." Rohan picked up a broom
and carefully urged a lizard back out onto the veranda.

Devora noticed that he didn't say no. "Why is it a bad idea?
No one will find out."

"You are naïve to think so," Rohan said. "You know your
fellow British."

"Yes, but they don't come to visit every single day," Devora
replied. "Besides, I just had them over for tea this afternoon,
so they should leave me alone tomorrow."

"It is highly improper for a British woman to travel with an
Indian man."

"We won't be traveling *with* each other," Devora persisted.
"We'll just be in the same car."

He gave her a derisive look. "There is a difference?"

"Yes, if we pretend that you're simply the driver." She approached him and reached out to put her hand on his arm. "If
we leave before dawn, no one will see us go. From what I
understand, it should take us a few hours to reach Agra. We
can spend the day there and return in the evening. We won't
even have to stay there overnight."

"*Memsahib*, I find you to be most maddening."

Devora chuckled. "So I've gathered."

She took the broom out of his hand and tossed it aside, then wrapped her arms around his waist. "Don't you think it would be fun, just the two of us? And I would love to get away from here for awhile."

Rohan shook his head, but reached up to brush a lock of hair from her forehead in a tender gesture that almost surprised her. "You are much too headstrong, do you know that?"

Devora gave him a cheeky smile and let her hands drift down to his buttocks. "But you like me that way."

She tilted her head to look up at him, letting her gaze drift over the sharp planes of his face and the square set of his jaw. And those eyes. How she loved his eyes, coal-black and filled with hidden fire and mystery.

"I've been wanting to see Agra since I first arrived," she continued, pressing her pelvis lightly against his. "Don't make me go with the Thompsons on one of their boring outings."

"There is the matter of Kalindi and Lota."

"Tomorrow is Kalindi's day off," Devora said. "As for Lota, we'll give her the day off as well. I'm sure she and Kalindi will find some way to occupy their time."

"They will become suspicious."

Devora thought of the manner in which the two women were certain to occupy their time off. She smiled. "I don't think they will. Even if they do, they won't say anything for fear of being dismissed. And I do so want to see the Taj Mahal."

Rohan rested his palm against the side of her face. "Your husband can take you."

"When? He's always off on tours or census-taking. Besides, I don't want to go with him. I want to go with you."

Rohan was quiet for a moment. "We are making a mistake."

"Does that mean we're going?"

"All right. I will take you to see the Taj Mahal."

"Oh, thank you!" Devora hugged him tightly and stood on tiptoe to press a kiss against his cheek. "We'll have a lovely time. I just know it."

Thrilled, she hurried into her bedroom to pack a bag for their journey. Finally, she was going to see the famous mausoleum! And not only would she not have to tolerate her compatriots, but she would have Rohan all to herself for an entire day.

After packing a few things, she went into the kitchen where Lota was busy scrubbing laundry in a pot of soapy water.

"Lota, you don't have to come here tomorrow," Devora said. "I'll be going out for the day, so there's no need for you to work."

"Really? Thank you, *memsahib*!" Lota's bright eyes sparkled with pleasure. "Will you be returning to the Maharaja's palace?"

Devora frowned. "Heavens, no. Whatever gave you that idea?"

"Oh, forgive me if I offend you, but you have been spending some time with him."

"Yes, well, I won't be in the future."

Lota nodded. "That is a wise choice. We have heard that he is a wicked man."

"Yes, I've heard that too," Devora muttered. "I'll be going on an outing with a friend tomorrow. You and Kalindi can spend the day together."

A flush rose to color Lota's cheeks as she quickly turned her attention back to the laundry. "Thank you."

Devora thought briefly of telling the younger woman that she had nothing to be embarrassed about, then decided against it. For all she knew, Lota had also been one of Gerald's mistresses in her absence.

That evening, Devora ate a light supper alone and went to bed early, leaving the curtains open so that the sun would wake her. Instead, she woke to the touch of a male hand.

"*Memsahib*, wake up." Rohan's low voice spoke in her ear. "We must leave soon."

"Mmm." Devora hugged the pillow against her, trying to wipe away the threads of sleep. "I'm getting up."

"You have fifteen minutes," Rohan ordered gently.

Devora heard him leave the room. She pulled herself out of

bed and washed quickly before dressing in a green cotton dress and matching shoes. As the rumble of the car engine sounded from outside, she grabbed her hat and hurried out to the front porch.

"Maybe waking up before dawn wasn't the best idea." Devora yawned and patted her lips as she watched Rohan unlock the car door. He looked almost annoyingly good this morning, dressed in black trousers, a tie, and a crisp, white shirt. Devora thought it was rather unfair that he didn't appear the slightest bit rumpled, even at five in the morning.

"Can't we at least have a cup of tea?" she asked as she descended the steps.

"Not if you intend to visit Agra and return this evening," Rohan replied. He held open the back door.

"I don't want to sit in the back," Devora said. "I'll sit in the front with you."

"You know that is not—"

"Oh, stop it," Devora groaned. She climbed into the front seat, hearing Rohan mutter something to himself in Hindi as he went to lock the bungalow door.

"Here. It appears as if you need this." Rohan got behind the wheel and handed Devora a small, silver flask.

Devora's eyes widened slightly. "Rohan, I hope you're not in the habit of drinking at the crack of dawn."

Amusement flashed in his eyes as he started the engine. "Nothing sinful, if that is your concern."

Devora twisted the cap off the flask and sniffed cautiously at the contents. "Tea?"

"It should still be warm." He gestured to a small bag at Devora's feet. "There are cups in the bag and a box of biscuits."

"How thoughtful of you." Devora poured them both cups of tea. "You always surprise me, Rohan."

"For the better or worse?"

"Both," Devora admitted. She settled against the seat, appreciating the fact that for once she could ride in the car and look at his handsome profile rather than the back of his head. "You know, I didn't like you one bit when I first arrived."

"I suspected as much."

"I thought you were arrogant and extremely pompous, not to mention just plain strange."

"Do go on," Rohan said dryly.

"Oh, I've changed my mind about you." Devora gave him a sly smile and reached out to rest her hand on his thigh. "Even Mrs. Thompson would change her mind about Indians if she knew you the way I do."

"Please. It is too early for lascivious thoughts about Mrs. Thompson." Rohan eased the car onto the main road and headed north toward Agra. "Come to think of it, there is never a right time for lascivious thoughts about Mrs. Thompson."

Devora grinned. "So, tell me something, Rohan."

"Yes?"

"Am I the first white woman you've ever had an affair with?"

He glanced at her, his expression unreadable. "And you ask me this for what reason?"

Devora shrugged and began opening the box of biscuits. "Curiosity. If you've been working for the British since you were fifteen, it seems to me that you'd have plenty of opportunities with British women."

"And you think I make a habit of seducing them?"

"Hardly. If I remember correctly, I was the one who came to you." Devora held out a biscuit, aware that he was avoiding the question. She had little doubt that any number of women would be attracted to Rohan's tall, dark masculinity, not to mention the aura of mystery that appeared to surround him.

"I believe ours was a mutual decision," Rohan said.

"So, what about the other women? Was it mutual with them, too?"

Rohan crunched into the biscuit and gave her another glance. "You appear to be very certain that there were others."

"And you appear to be avoiding the question," Devora retorted. She turned away from him and looked out the window at the blossoming dawn.

"One," Rohan said.

Devora looked at him. "One?"

"I have been with one British woman."

"Really? Who was she?"

"You."

"Me? You mean I'm the only one?" Devora couldn't prevent the swell of relief that rose in her.

"Yes. As you can expect, I did not feel particularly magnanimous toward the British after the trial."

"Why did you keep working for them?"

"For several years, I didn't. I taught English and worked at an Indian restaurant, but I had less freedom."

Devora's eyebrows rose. "You have freedom working for the British?"

"More than one would think," Rohan replied. "And I soon realized that by thinking all British are alike, I was doing exactly what so many of them do to Indians."

"Were you ever friends with a British person?"

"Yes, I consider several to have been my friends."

"And me?"

He gave her a slight smile. "Yes. And you."

"And what about Indian women? They've been your lovers, I assume."

"Yes, of course."

"Were you ever in love with one of them?" Devora asked.

"You ask many questions, *memsahib*."

"I'm just curious about you, that's all. Lota told me that Indians marry for convenience and not for love."

"That is often true. However, we are as deeply capable of love as anyone else."

"I suspect you wouldn't have such passionate gods if that wasn't true," Devora murmured.

Rohan smiled slightly. "An excellent point."

"The Maharaja explained a great deal of Indian philosophies to me," Devora said. "It's a pity that the rest of the world doesn't know the reason for such sexual sculptures."

"Did he take you to see them?" Rohan's voice was guarded. Devora shot him a quick look. "Yes. Why do you ask?"

"For the same reason you ask me so many questions. Curiosity."

"He took me to Khajuraho," Devora admitted. "But don't worry. I told you that I was wrong about him. That's the one time I should have actually heeded Mrs. Thompson's words. She warned me that there were rumors about his sexual appetites."

Rohan's entire body tensed suddenly. "He hurt you, did he? The bastard. I will—"

"Wait, Rohan." Devora put out her hand. She couldn't help being warmed by his sudden display of protectiveness. "He scared me, but he didn't hurt me. I promise."

"There are indeed rumors about him," Rohan said. "That is why I was concerned for your safety."

"What are the rumors?" Devora asked.

"His harem is allegedly filled with young women he has taken from the villages against their will. It is said that he prefers virgins, often very young girls. He employs a group of men solely for the purpose of finding women for the harem."

Devora shuddered and hugged her arms around herself. "It's creepy that he seems so kind at first."

"Most Indians in town know better. He has been known to dispose of women if he grows tired of them. And of course he does whatever he wants to them when they are his captives."

"Is it true that his wife committed suicide?"

"I do not know," Rohan said. "She died under mysterious circumstances. Poison, I believe. Heaven only knows what actually happened to her."

"Well, I think he's a horribly manipulative man," Devora muttered. "I'm just sorry I didn't realize it sooner."

"As I said to you, learning this before you were truly hurt is soon enough," Rohan replied. "I suspect you're not the first woman to have fallen under his spell."

"I imagine that the Maharaja isn't the only one with some sort of sexual power," Devora said. She was immensely grateful that Rohan didn't chastise her for her experience with the Maharaja. "For example, I think Indian women are very beautiful. It seems as if men would have a very easy time falling in love with them. They have a great deal of grace."

"As do you."

Devora stared at him. "Did you just pay me a compliment?"

"Contrary to your perception of me, I do have occasional bouts of human warmth." He glanced at her with a smile tugging at the corners of his lips. "Believe it or not."

Devora laughed, unable to resist leaning over and kissing him. Then she stroked her fingertips gently over his lips. She'd never met a man with such a sensual mouth.

"I'm glad there was never another British woman," she murmured.

He kissed her fingertips. "I am as well."

The red sandstone gate to the Taj Mahal grounds loomed at the end of the road like the tower of a medieval castle. Vendors selling everything from rugs to brass curio objects lined the front of the gate, along with a number of beggars. Several British tourists roamed about, but it was still early and the hoards hadn't yet descended on the site.

Devora put on her hat as she and Rohan walked down the road to the gate. A glimmer of excitement rose in her as she realized she was about to see one of the most famous sites in the world.

"Have you been here before?" she asked Rohan.

"Yes, many times. When I worked in Delhi, one of my duties was to accompany the family and their friends on outings. They often came here."

"Then it must seem quite ordinary to you now."

"No, the Taj never becomes ordinary."

They went through the gate and into a square of lovely gardens and fountains. A long, rectangular fountain stretched toward the mausoleum, whose reflection glimmered in the water. Made of pure, white marble, the surface glowed in the early morning light. A gentle, curving onion dome rested with precision upon the sturdy, square base, which was flanked by a surrounding terrace. The verticality of four, graceful minarets at the corners of the terrace provided a striking visual contrast to the dome. The grounds were an magnificent oasis amidst the heat and dust of India.

Devora drew in a breath as they started toward the building. "It's incredible."

"Yes, it is." Rohan reached out as if to take her arm, then pulled back. "The gardens and the mausoleum itself are all in perfect proportion to each other."

"It looks like something out of a fairy tale."

"In a way, I suppose it is. Shah Jehan built it for the wife he loved very deeply. He was so grieved by her death that he wanted to create for her the most beautiful monument ever built."

"I dare say he succeeded," Devora murmured.

They walked up the steps to the mausoleum's courtyard. The steps had been trod on for so many centuries that gentle curves were worn into the marble. A fine, lattice-work screen stood at the entrance. Devora paused and placed her hand on the side of the structure. Pink and green marble carved into flowers and leaves lay embedded delicately in the stone.

"Do you know how many people were used to build it?" she asked.

"I believe it was twenty thousand. Shah Jehan had also intended to built a black, marble mausoleum for himself and to link the two structures with a silver bridge. He died before the second one could be built."

"How sad."

"Yes, it makes a nice love story."

Devora glanced at him, surprised by the cynical note in his voice. "You don't think it was?"

"He loved his wife, yes. But to build such a monument at the cost of slavery and human lives." Rohan shrugged. "One must wonder about the true reason."

"What do you think it was?"

"He wanted immortality for himself."

"Then it seems as if he succeeded again."

He tilted his head in acknowledgement. "That is true."

Devora continued walking around the mausoleum, enraptured by the craftsmanship and the incredible attention to detail. She and Rohan spent several hours wandering around the complex. The tombs lay in a dark vault beneath the building, and Devora was surprised by their simplicity in contrast to the grandeur of the exterior architecture. After they had thoroughly explored the mausoleum and the grounds, they sat on a marble bench near the fountain.

"Thank you so much for bringing me here," Devora said. "I've been wanting to see this ever since Gerald and I talked about me joining him in India."

She felt Rohan's dark gaze on her, and she wondered what he saw.

"You love your husband," he stated.

Startled at the sudden remark, Devora met his gaze. "Is that a question?"

"Perhaps."

"I love Gerald. He's a good man." Devora was painfully aware that her words sounded feeble. She looked back at the Taj Mahal and thought of the intensity of love required for a man to build such a monument to his wife.

"Is that all?" Rohan asked. "The reason you love him is because he is a good man?"

"Isn't that enough?"

"For some women, maybe it is. For you, I think not."

Devora didn't answer. His perceptiveness cut her to the quick, bringing to light all the doubts and confusions she had about Gerald and their marriage. Doubts that had become even more sharp-edged since she became involved with Rohan.

"You never answered my question about being in love," she said. "Were you ever deeply in love?"

"Yes. I loved the daughter of the restaurant owner where I worked."

"Why didn't you marry her?"

"Her parents sold the restaurant and returned to their village. They brought her with them. At the time, I had little money and could not afford to marry her."

Devora looked at him for a long time. He had thick eyelashes that made shadows on his cheekbones when he blinked.

"Didn't it hurt you?" she murmured.

"Of course. But we do not always get what we desire in life."

A sudden irritation swept through Devora. She picked up her pocketbook and stood. "I think you're too complacent, Rohan. Sometimes it's worth it to fight for what you want."

She turned and headed toward the exit of the grounds, not glancing back to see if he was following her. He fell into step beside her as they went through the front gate.

"What makes you think I didn't?" he asked.

Devora stopped. For some reason, her heart was beating with increasing rapidity. "You mean you did?"

"As I said, *memsahib,* I am not the statue you think I am."

"I know that. I just don't understand you sometimes." She eyed him curiously. "So, what did you do?"

"I went to her village and tried to convince her to return to Calipore with me. She almost did, but her father stopped us both and threatened to disown her."

"Why did he dislike you so much?"

"He didn't dislike me at all. He just knew I couldn't provide for his daughter in the way he wanted. In the end, I had to respect that."

"Well, I think that's terrible. If two people love each other, then they should be together."

"It is never that simple," Rohan said gently.

"Well, it should be." Devora took off her hat and patted her damp forehead. She suddenly felt mildly overwhelmed by all this talk of deep love and sacrifice. Her own marriage seemed decidedly boring by comparison.

"If you are hungry, I can leave you at a teahouse that is close by," Rohan said. "They serve British tourists frequently. Then this afternoon we will have time to visit the Red Fort before returning home."

"I don't want to eat at a teahouse," Devora said. "Why don't we go on a picnic?"

"A picnic?"

"Yes. Maybe near the river." Devora climbed into the car next to him and settled against the seat. "And don't tell me it's not proper. There's no one here to see us anyway."

She soon realized the naiveté of her statement when she and Rohan went into a grocery shop to pick up some things for lunch. The road in front of the shop was covered with dust and stones, and Devora's shoe caught on the edge of a particularly large rock. With a gasp, she tripped and felt herself start to pitch forward before Rohan grabbed her around the waist and hauled her upright.

"You are all right, *memsahib?*" he asked.

Devora grasped his arm to steady herself. "Yes, thank you. Just a bit startled, that's all."

"Miss! Miss, are you all right?"

Devora and Rohan looked up at the sound of the British, male voice. A group of tourists stood near a carriage across the street, and two young men broke away and began running toward Devora.

Devora sensed Rohan stiffen as he released her immediately and stepped back.

"Miss, we saw the coolie grab you." Panting, the man stopped in front of them. His face was reddened from sunburn, his eyes flashing with dislike as he looked from Devora to Rohan. "Is he bothering you?"

"No, of course not," Devora said. "I tripped on a stone, that's all. There's nothing to be concerned about."

"We're not so sure of that." The other man glowered at Rohan, adopting what he seemed to think was a belligerent stance. "These coolies will take every opportunity to grope a white woman."

"You don't have to be frightened of him, miss," the first man said. "We can take care of him for you."

"I'm not frightened of him," Devora replied sharply. "He's my servant. As I said, there's nothing to be concerned about. Thank you for your interest, but we're in a bit of a hurry."

"You shouldn't be out alone with an Indian," the man continued. "They can't control themselves, you know."

"I've heard the same about the British. Good day to you both."

The men looked at Rohan again with their eyes narrowed in suspicion, but began backing slowly away. Devora spun on her heel and stalked into the shop, her entire body trembling with anger. She turned to look at Rohan, but he wasn't behind her.

"Rohan?" Devora stepped back outside and saw that he hadn't moved, his gaze fixed warily on the two men. Only after the two men turned away did he approach Devora.

"I'm sorry," she said. "I hate men like that."

"I'm used to them. I will wait here while you make some purchases."

Worried that the unpleasant men would come back, Devora quickly bought some fruit and mutton pies before she and Rohan returned to the car.

"I guess it's not really possible to escape, is it?" she asked.

Rohan shrugged and pulled onto the road. "It depends entirely on your definition of escape."

"Have you had many encounters like that?"

"Some."

"Rohan, don't you ever just want to leave here?" Devora

asked. "I mean, move to another country or something? It must get unbearable at times."

"I have a much better life than most. I am not complaining."

He pulled the car over to the side of the road and parked near a grove of trees by the river. For moment, they watched the flow of the water as it drifted south, then got out and spread a blanket underneath a tree. The sun had become increasingly warm over the course of the morning, but the leafy tree branches provided a lovely coolness.

"There, now, isn't this better than a teahouse?" Devora asked. She handed him a mutton pie and uncapped a bottle of soda water. "I imagine those places are a great deal like the British clubs."

She unstrapped her shoes and took them off, wriggling her toes with pleasure as a rush of air swept over them. They ate lunch in companionable silence while listening to the rhythm of the river and the twittering of birds.

Devora popped a slice of orange in her mouth and glanced at Rohan.

"Why don't you relax?" she asked.

"I am very relaxed."

"No, I mean, unbutton your jacket." Devora leaned over and unfastened the buttons of his suit. "And loosen your tie, for heaven's sake. Don't worry about looking rumpled, because there's no one to see you."

"Now, why do I think you find that fact particularly inviting?" Rohan asked, a teasing look in his eyes.

"You can't possibly think I'm going to seduce you right here and now."

"I think you are capable of almost anything, *memsahib*."

Devora gave him a mock frown. "You think I'm a complete tart, don't you?"

"Complete," Rohan agreed. His dark eyes grew warm as he slipped his hand around the back of her neck and pulled her gently toward him. "A tart of the most delicious flavor."

His lips brushed lightly over hers in a kiss that caused a little quiver to run down her spine. Thoughts of their unorthodox situation slipped into oblivion as she parted her lips under Rohan's and allowed him to explore her mouth with his tongue. He kissed with a rich sensuality that belied his reserved persona. Slowly, his hands slipped around to cup Devora's face as he deepened their kiss. The gesture made her feel almost cherished, as if he were holding something precious within his grasp. She moved closer to him and wrapped her arms around his neck, letting her body sink against his.

"This is perhaps not wise," Rohan murmured, his lips moving over hers.

"Nothing about our situation is wise," Devora reminded him breathlessly as she drove her hands into the thick coarseness of his hair. "We're a couple of fools, you and I."

She slipped his jacket off his shoulders and began to unbutton his shirt, exposing the hair-roughened skin of his chest inch by tantalizing inch. Lowering her head, Devora followed the pathway with her lips. Her hands stroked down over his chest to his groin. Rohan's breathing increased as Devora slipped her hand into his trousers and closed her fingers around the length of his penis. She pulled it out and murmured a husky sound of admiration, rubbing her thumb lightly over the bulbous tip before taking him in her mouth. Rohan's hips jerked upward with a suggestive movement when Devora's tongue swirled lightly over him. Her own sex grew heavy with the thick blood of lust. She slid Rohan's sleek phallus in and out of the warm cavern of her mouth, murmuring lewd little noises in the back of her throat designed to incite him further.

"Wait." The word emerged from Rohan's throat on a chocked gasp. His hand twined into her hair to still her movements. "Stop."

Devora pulled away, flashing him a wicked smile as she reached underneath her dress to unclasp her garters and remove her stockings. Then she eased closer to Rohan and straddled him, brushing the head of his shaft against the moist folds of her sex. His body tensed with pleasure as Devora enclosed the tip of his penis in her body. She clutched her dress and pulled the material over her hips as she lowered herself onto him.

Clenching her inner muscles around Rohan's shaft, she leaned forward and began to ride him, watching with satisfaction the painful contortion of his expression as he fought to retain control over himself. His hands lifted toward her swaying breasts, their hard nipples pressing enticingly against the fabric of her dress. He undid the buttons quickly to expose her breasts and palm them in his hands.

Devora splayed her body over his, crushing her breasts against his chest and delighting in the sensation of his crisp chest hairs scraping the bare v-neckline of her cleavage. The heat of his body burned into her, his skin damp with sweat. Twisting her hips, she found a particular angle that created the most pressure in her sex. Tightness gathered in her loins, coiling around her body until her breath came in rapid pants and her skin prickled with heat. The tense control of Rohan's body under her, his muscles straining, his hot breath against her forehead, swayed Devora's senses like a potent aphrodisiac.

"Say something," she whispered, her tongue flickering out to capture a bead of sweat trickling into the scorched hollow of his throat.

Stilling her writhing movements, she tightened her satin depths around his shaft and reached up to grip his hair again. Rohan opened his eyes, which were filled with heat and desperation over being poised on the brink of rapture.

"Something wicked," Devora urged.

Rohan grabbed the back of her head, forcing her mouth down on his again.

"Fuck me," he hissed. The words sounds deliciously salacious and musical in his accented English. "Fuck me good and hard."

Devora's blood seethed as his words spilled into her. She curled her hands around the hard biceps of his arms, digging her fingernails into his flesh as urgency stretched to the breaking point. This was the moment she craved the most, the precipice so fraught with tension and pain. She let it build before forcing herself to quell the threatening waves, heightening her anticipation until she could stand it no longer and plunged her body down on Rohan's cock with a moan of ecstasy. His hips bucked upward as he groaned and thrust into her with an almost violent release.

Devora stretched over her lover, relishing the endless shudders that rippled outward from her sex as her inner walls convulsed around him. She lifted her head and smiled at him, reaching to run her hand through his dark, damp hair.

"Let's try and do this more often," she suggested languidly.

"Make love, you mean?"

Devora rested her head on his chest as she gazed out at the gently undulating waves of the river. "And simply be together."

chapter fourteen

Gerald stomped the dust off his boots before entering the bungalow. The damned hot season seemed to be arriving early, and everyone, both British and Indian, was getting irritable and belligerent. Gerald hoped that Devora wouldn't argue too much about going up to Simla in a month or so when the temperature would be truly unbearable. She'd find it to be much cooler in the hill station. Gerald was also convinced that a long separation would be good for both of them. He was beginning to find her constant nonconformity rather tiresome. A couple of months spent in the company of the *memsahibs* would surely straighten her out.

"Devora?" Gerald called out her name as he shed his jacket. He did like it when he arrived home after a long day and she greeted him with a drink. She always looked cool and lovely, and she'd learned how to make his gin and tonics just right. "Devora, are you home?"

Kalindi poked her head out of the kitchen. "*Sahib*, you are home early."

"Yes, I know. Where's my wife?"

"She has gone for tea at the club," Kalindi informed him.

"Right, well, bring me a drink, would you?"

"Yes, *sahib*. You wish tea?"

"No. A gin and tonic."

"Gin and tonic?"

Gerald sighed. "Oh, never mind." He waved his hand dismissingly. "Go draw me a bath."

"Yes, *sahib.*" Kalindi hurried out of the kitchen and went down the hallway toward the bathroom.

Gerald strode to the sideboard and poured himself a drink. He took a long draught and closed his eyes with relief. The dust from this bloody country seemed to have permanently settled in his throat.

He went into the bathroom, his gaze going to the rounded curves of Kalindi's buttocks as she leaned over the bathtub. His penis twitched in his trousers as he remembered what it felt like to grasp those buttocks in his hands while plunging deep inside of her.

Kalindi straightened and turned, starting as she saw him standing there. "Oh, *sahib,* I did not know you were there."

"When is my wife returning?"

"Before supper. I do not know the exact time."

"Well, then, you'll just have to wash my back, won't you?" Gerald set his glass down and stripped off his tie and shirt.

Kalindi let out a small giggle and perched on the edge of the tub. "If I must."

"What about Rohan?"

"He has gone into town."

"Good." Gerald shed his trousers and climbed into the warm water, letting it soothe away the aches and tensions of the day.

With a contented sigh, he leaned his head against the side of the tub. Kalindi picked up the sponge and lathered it with soap, then began to rub it over his chest. She had a nice, soothing touch. She stroked the sponge downward toward his belly in slow circles before reaching his groin. Gerald's prick was half-hard already, and it thickened within Kalindi's grasp as she reached below the water's surface to touch him.

Gerald let out a groan and closed his eyes. "Oh yes. That feels good."

Kalindi giggled again and began to slowly stroke his cock

from base to tip, rubbing her thumb over the hard glans. The sensation of her touch and the water combined to create a wealth of sensations over his sensitive flesh. Kalindi's fingers drifted down to his tight testicles and massaged them gently. She stroked her forefinger against the tender skin between his genitals and his anus, causing Gerald to buck his hips upward.

"That hurts you?" Kalindi asked.

"No, darling, that feels wonderful."

Kalindi continued the delicious caress, even going so far as to trace the tight ring of his anus. Gerald's penis hardened further as the young woman stimulated every single nerve ending. He opened his eyes to look at her, feeling desire heat his blood at the sight of her flushed face and full breasts. He reached out and rubbed his fingers over her nipple through the cotton of her sari. The bud hardened underneath his touch and tented the thin fabric. An unbidden thought occurred to Gerald, causing a rush of excitement unlike any he had known before.

"Who is that girl that works in the kitchen with you?"

"You speak of Lota?"

"Yes. Where is she now?"

"In the kitchen."

"Go fetch her and bring her into the bedroom. I think I'm in the mood for two women right now."

Kalindi stared at him. "Oh, *sahib*, I—"

"Do it!" Gerald snapped.

"You are certain this is a good idea?" A spark flashed in Kalindi's eyes.

"Oh, I'm certain."

Kalindi giggled, dropped the sponge, and rushed out of the bathroom. Gerald climbed out of the tub and let the water drip in rivulets off his body. He grabbed a towel and dried himself, rubbing his hard cock. The rough towel felt exquisite against his erection. After wrapping the towel around his waist, he went into the bedroom and stretched out on the bed.

The two women entered the bedroom together. Kalindi's eyes were bright with excitement as she stopped by the bed. Gerald let his gaze roam over Lota, thinking that she wasn't as pretty as Kalindi, but that she had a nice, voluptuous body. She looked at him with a hint of trepidation.

Gerald reached out and cupped one of Kalindi's breasts in his hand, flicking his thumb over her nipple.

"Take off your clothes," he said, his voice thick with lust.

Kalindi moved away and stripped off her sari to reveal the voluptuous curves of her body. Her black hair fell in sweeping waves over her shoulders and breasts, providing tantalizing glimpses of her nudity. Gerald pressed his hand between her legs to feel the heat of her cunt. She could never hide her own arousal, as copious fluids always trickled down to give her away. Gerald toyed with the thick curls concealing her labia, then pressed a finger into her wet channel. Kalindi gasped with pleasure and steadied herself on the bedpost.

"Like that, do you?" Gerald murmured, thrusting his finger back and forth.

"Oh, yes, *sahib,* that is good."

Gerald glanced at Lota, who was watching them with increasing hunger. He grasped his penis in his hand and stroked the shaft suggestively.

"Come here," he invited. "I think you can do something with this."

Fascination appeared in the Indian woman's eyes as she approached him. She stripped off her sari to reveal her curvaceous body, then climbed on the bed next to him and reached out to touch his cock. She and Kalindi exchanged glances as the air around them thickened with lust. Gerald drew in a breath, unable to believe that he actually had two women devoted to his pleasure. Lota began to stroke his cock, squeezing the shaft with just the right amount of pressure. Gerald leaned back and let himself enjoy the carnal pleasure.

He urged Kalindi onto the bed so that she straddled his neck, then he lifted her enough so that he could plunge his tongue into her overflowing cunt. Kalindi cried out with pleasure, her body swaying over his as Gerald licked up the salty droplets of her arousal and encouraged her pleasure. The scent of her filled his nostrils with a potent stimulation that went straight to his cock, engorging his flesh even more. He swirled his tongue around Kalindi's clit until she bucked her hips and shrieked, her body vibrating so violently that Gerald had to clutch her waist to hold her still.

"Oh, *sahib,* how wonderful," Kalindi gasped as she rolled off him. She looked at Lota, reaching out to kiss the woman with hot affection. The sight of them, their breasts pressing together, nipples touching, almost made Gerald come right then and there. Only the thought of even more acute pleasures reined in his control.

He grasped his cock and gave Lota a meaningful look. "Well?"

She straddled his waist, her chest heaving with the force of her breath. Gerald clutched her hips and guided her over him. Slowly, he eased her down until the head of his cock pressed against her sex. The mere sensation of her hot dampness against his glans sent a jolt of pure need through him. With a groan, he pushed her down harder, sliding into her cunt as her inner walls clenched around him. Lota gasped as he filled her. Her fingernails dug into his shoulders. Sweat broke out on Gerald's chest as he tried to prevent himself from losing control too quickly.

"Now," Gerald gritted. "Move."

Lota moaned and started to move her body so that his cock slid in and out of her with increasing frenzy. Her breasts swayed in front of him so enticingly that Gerald pulled her forward and captured one nipple between his teeth. Pressure built in his loins and the base of his penis as Lota continued her writhing movements. Wet, slapping noises filled the air in tandem with their panting breaths. Kalindi insinuated herself between Gerald's legs, bending to lick his tight testicles with her tongue as his cock slipped in and out of Lota's cunt. Unbelievable sensations built in Gerald's lower body with the combined tight warmth of Lota and the moist licks of Kalindi's tongue. Lota let out a cry suddenly, her body convulsing around him. The feeling of her vibrations and Kalindi's ministrations sent Gerald over the edge. His body exploded with a rush of pleasure as he spilled himself into her.

Lota sank down onto the bed with harsh breaths. Kalindi draped herself over her friend, her hands moving with familiar ease over Lota's body. Gerald closed his eyes as the last of the sensations ebbed away, thinking that this was an experience he would have to try again. Just imagine the possibilities of two women.

Turning his head, he looked at them and rubbed his hand over Kalindi's back.

"Thank you both," he said. "But my wife is due home, and I don't think she would appreciate finding you both here."

Giggling, Kalindi and Lota dressed quickly in their saris and hurried back to the kitchen. Gerald went back to finish his bath in the tepid water, feeling very satisfied. He dressed in a clean pair of trousers and a shirt, then went back to the sitting room and refilled his glass with gin and tonic. He felt good now, incredibly sated thanks to the two women, and loose from the effects of the alcohol.

He added more gin to the glass and caught sight of the dining table. One end of it was covered with Devora's drawings and sketchpads, not to mention a number of paints and pencils. Gerald went to the table and opened one of the sketchpads. Devora certainly had been busy with her hobby, he thought, as he examined the numerous drawings. She did have an eye for detail, though. Perhaps too much detail. Some of the erotic drawings were very explicitly erotic.

Gerald frowned. Where on earth had she seen sculptures like these? As far as he knew, the only temples with that kind of pornography were the Khajuraho temples. And he had expressly forbade her from going there.

Setting his glass down, Gerald began to look at the drawings and paintings more closely. Devora never shared her work with him, and he'd never asked to see it. He had always considered her art to be her own little, distracting hobby. As a result, he hadn't paid much attention to it. He realized now that she was quite talented, although he couldn't believe some of the subjects she had chosen. Sculptures of men and women fucking in all manner of positions, even upside down. Where in the love of God had Devora been exposed to this? It was one thing for him to engage in rather outrageous carnal activities, but it certainly wasn't appropriate for a British woman to even be aware of them.

Gerald flipped over the thick page of a sketchpad, only to be met with an image of Rohan's face. Gerald frowned. Now Devora was sketching the servants? He lifted the drawing to the light and examined it closely. She was undoubtedly talented. She had captured Rohan's likeness perfectly, right down to the man's completely enigmatic expression. He put the pad down and went to the dozen canvases that sat stacked against the wall. The first was a finished painting of a local Hindu temple, and the second was a half-finished painting of one of those voluptuous female statues.

The third painting gave Gerald pause. He looked at the painted likeness of Rohan's face, thinking that it was quite different from the inexpressive drawing. The painting showed the man with a passionate, almost hot countenance, one edged with more than a hint of lust.

When in the love of God had Rohan ever looked like that? Could Devora simply be creating such a look out of her imagination? It didn't make much sense, particularly given Rohan's stolidity. Gerald let the other canvases fall back into place. Something wasn't right. He knew it as surely as he knew that his relationship with Devora had endured several cracks since she had arrived in India.

"Kalindi!" Gerald barked.

She scurried out of the kitchen and came to him. "Yes, *sahib*?"

Gerald was in no mood to phrase his question delicately. "What do you know about the *memsahib* and Rohan?"

Kalindi looked startled. "I am begging your pardon?"

"I said, what do you know about them?" Gerald repeated.

"Oh, they have argued frequently. Rohan did not want the *memsahib* to go with the Maharaja, but she went anyway. He found her to be most uncooperative."

"I know that. What else?"

An uncomfortable expression crossed Kalindi's face. Gerald smiled grimly. Just as she could never hide her physical arousal, Kalindi had always had a difficult time concealing what she was thinking.

"Go on, Kalindi. What else?"

Kalindi twisted her hands together. Dismay lit in her brown eyes. "Oh, *sahib,* I do not know anything."

Gerald swallowed some gin and took a breath. "Kalindi, do you like working here?"

"Oh, yes! I like it very much. You and the *memsahib* are very kind."

"Good. Then, if you want to continue working here, you'll answer my question. What has gone on between Rohan and my wife?"

"I do not know for certain," Kalindi said, dismay flashing in her brown eyes. "I do not know."

"Then what do you think?"

"I did see the *memsahib* enter Rohan's quarters one day last week," Kalindi reported. "I do not know, I think she was there to ask him about his previous marriage."

"Why on earth would she want to know about his previous marriage?"

Kalindi shook her head. "No, not a marriage. He was intended to be married, but he was not. She wanted to know why. I think that is why she was there."

"Well, how long was she there?"

Kalindi looked almost terrified now. She grabbed an end of her sari and twisted it frantically between her fingers. "I think . . . I do not know . . . but I think she was there for several hours."

Shock reverberated through Gerald like a gunshot. He stared at Kalindi. "You're lying."

Kalindi shook her head. "No, *sahib*. It was a long time before they both came out."

"You little bitch!" Gerald smacked his hand hard against the side of the woman's head, sending her to the ground. Kalindi gave a cry as she banged against the edge of a side table. "You're lying!"

"No, I am not!" Kalindi begged. Tears filled her eyes. "She was there for hours, I do know that! I am not lying to you! She went after you left in the morning, and then they did not emerge until lunch!"

Rage boiled in Gerald's blood. He couldn't possibly believe that Devora had spent all that time asking Rohan about his fiancée. He knew that something had been brewing between Devora and Rohan ever since they set eyes on each other, only Gerald had attributed that to animosity and a conflict over who was really in charge of the household.

He looked at Kalindi, who was curled up on the floor, still sniffling and whimpering. "Get up," he snapped. "And get back to work!"

Relief flashed on Kalindi's face as she realized that she wasn't fired and that he wasn't going to hit her again. She scrambled up and hurried back to the kitchen, clutching her hurt head.

Gerald grabbed his gin and swallowed half of it in one gulp. Damn Devora. If his suspicions turned out to be true, then this marriage was over. He had a reputation to maintain in this community, and he couldn't do so if his wife became known for fucking a goddamn Indian servant.

Devora climbed out of the carriage and went up the steps of the bungalow. She hadn't intended to stay at the club for the entire afternoon, but she had been rather intrigued by the gossip about the Maharaja. According to rumor, he was being officially investigated for giving funding and protection to the gangs who were responsible for starting so many riots in neighboring towns. Devora couldn't help but wonder what would happen if he were found guilty. She had every intention of asking Gerald about it, but the minute she stepped into the bungalow, she knew that something was wrong.

All the windows were open. Gerald sat in a chair by the veranda, his feet up on a table and a drink in his hand. He was also holding a small canvas in the other hand and looking at the painting with a scowl.

Devora paused by the door, her heart plummeting. She knew without even having to look at the canvas who the subject of the painting was. "Gerald."

He looked up, peering at her with bleary eyes. "Oh, hello, darling. I was just admiring this lovely painting of yours. I hadn't realized that you'd taken to depicting the servants."

Devora approached him cautiously. "It's only a painting. Rohan has an interesting face."

Gerald lifted an eyebrow. "Oh, so you know which painting this is." He looked at the canvas again, putting on a mockingly critical expression. "Yes, he does, doesn't he? Very noble. Rather like one of those Michelangelo statues or perhaps even the Greek gods themselves. Of course, our Rohan is no Greek god, is he? Why, he's just a bloody coolie."

Devora frowned. "Don't talk like that, Gerald."

"What, you mean 'bloody coolie'?" Gerald asked innocently. "That's what he is, isn't he? And just why do you find it necessary to defend him?"

"I'm not defending him," Devora said. "And you're drunk."

"Yes, I am!" Gerald reached for the bottle of gin next to him and took a long swig. "Bloody good thing, too, considering I just discovered that my wife is fucking a servant."

"Gerald, stop it." Devora went to take the canvas away from him, but Gerald glared at her with such fury that she stopped in her tracks. "Listen to me, it's not what you think."

"What the hell do I think, then, huh?" Gerald looked at the

painting again and put it, face up, on the floor. "You've never done a portrait of me, have you? Why is that? Haven't I got a face that's interesting enough for you?"

"Gerald, I'm not going to talk to you when you're in this condition," Devora said icily. "When you're sober, we'll have a conversation like adults."

"Oh, like adults, will we?" Gerald spat, his voice dripping with contempt. "Is that how you've been acting lately? Have you been so stimulated by all that pornography that you've been drawing? Is that why you spread your legs for a goddamn coolie?"

"Stop it!" Devora snapped. "I said that we'll discuss this when you're sober."

"You're a whore, Devora. Did you know that?" Gerald looked at the painting again and then tilted the bottle of gin over it. He let the gin spill onto the canvas, causing the paints to run together and blur the image of Rohan's face. Devora watched him silently.

"There!" Gerald said with satisfaction. "Now, what do you think of that?"

"I think I'm going to lock myself in the bedroom until you're sober," Devora replied coldly. "You're in no condition to even think rationally, let alone talk."

She strode into the bedroom and slammed the door, ignoring Gerald's rantings behind her. She locked the door and pressed a hand to her chest, feeling her heart beating wildly. She had never honestly considered what would happen if someone, particularly Gerald, found out the truth about her and Rohan. It was ridiculous really that she wouldn't have been concerned with such a thing, but she had been living by an entirely different set of rules ever since she set foot on Indian soil. A set of rules that not only insulted the rigid, British conventions, but created completely new ones. Her own.

Devora wondered if Gerald had spoken to Rohan yet. She went to the window and pushed aside the curtain, wondering where the servant had gone. He went into the village at least once a day to purchase supplies and fresh vegetables, but usually he returned by late afternoon. Nerves clenched in Devora's stomach suddenly. She knew that Gerald hadn't physically fought with Rohan since Gerald appeared unhurt, but that didn't mean they hadn't had an altercation.

Devora didn't dare go outside via the sitting room and have to face Gerald again, so she grasped the edges of the window screen. After three hard yanks, the screen gave way. Devora put it aside and climbed out of the window, tearing her dress on a jagged piece of wood. She hurried through the garden and toward the servants' quarters.

Please, please be there, she thought. She knocked on Rohan's door.

"Rohan? It's Devora. Please open the door."

No answer. She knocked harder. "Please! It's an emergency."

To her infinite relief, the door opened. Rohan stood there, his jacket half-unbuttoned and his feet bare. He frowned at the sight of her.

"*Memsahib,* something has happened?"

"Hasn't Gerald spoken with you yet?"

Rohan's expression darkened. He shook his head. "No. Should he have?"

"Yes. I think he knows about us."

Rohan pulled the door open wider and let her inside. Devora clenched her hands together, trying not to start shaking. She sat down on the bed as Rohan closed and locked the door.

"How do you know this?" he asked.

"He's drunk and furious. He found a painting I had done of you."

"And that is how he knows?"

"No, that can't be all." A realization suddenly broke through Devora's fogged mind. "Kalindi."

Rohan's eyebrows lifted. "Kalindi?"

"She saw us that day I came here," Devora said. "She saw us both come out and return to the house. She was on the veranda. I had hoped that she didn't know how long I had been here, but I assume that she did. She must have told Gerald."

"You think that she volunteered the information?"

"I don't know. I'm fairly certain that she is Gerald's mistress, so maybe she had other designs on him. She must have told him, and then he assumed that the painting confirmed her words."

Rohan buttoned his jacket and picked up his sash. "I will go and speak with him."

"No, don't. He's drunk and violent. He could hurt you."

"As I told you, I have dishonored my position in this household," Rohan replied. He fastened the sash around his waist. "He has been a good master, and I must apologize."

"He'll dismiss you, of course."

"Yes, I know." Rohan headed for the door.

Devora stood and went after him. "Wait. I'll go with you."

"No, *memsahib*. This is not for a woman to witness. Please wait here."

Devora bit her bottom lip, feeling sick to her stomach. "Rohan, he could really hurt you."

"Please wait here. I will return." With that, he left the room, closing the door behind him.

Devora went to the window and watched him walking toward the house, his stride long and certain. A tight knot curled inside her at the thought of what might happen. Oddly enough, however, she couldn't find it within her to berate either herself or Rohan for having succumbed to lust. It was as if the entire course of their relationship had been leading to the inevitable end of carnality and affection. They had simply worked to follow a path that had already been laid out for them. Destiny and exertion.

And, oh, how they had exerted themselves. While Devora was sickened by the thought of the damage that would surely be caused by the discovery of their affair, she could not regret the affair itself.

She sat on Rohan's bed, hugging her knees to her chest as

she waited for him to return. She wanted to ignore his request and go to the house anyway, but just as she was about to do so, the doorknob turned. Devora scrambled off the bed as Rohan entered the room.

"What?" Devora asked, her heart suddenly racing frantically. "What happened?"

A bruise darkened Rohan's left cheek, but other than that, he appeared to be physically unharmed.

"He was too drunk to attack me with much force," Rohan replied. "Although I suspect that he might attempt to find me again once his head has cleared. Of course, he is furious and dismissed me."

Devora stared at him. "That's it?"

"I'm not saying it was pleasant," Rohan said. "I will not repeat his words to me, but he wanted to rip me to shreds. He would have, too, if I hadn't stopped him."

"Did you hurt him?"

"No. He hit me once, but as I said, he was too drunk. He is asleep on the sofa now."

"I see." Devora watched as he removed a suitcase from the closet. "You're leaving now?"

"You suggest I wait until he wakes up?"

"No, of course not. Where will you go?"

"I will find a temporary room in the village," Rohan replied. "After that, I do not know."

Devora wanted to ask him if she would ever see him again, but she knew that such a question would be foolish. They may have had an intense physical attraction toward each other, but ultimately, Rohan was right. British-Indian relations would never reach a point in which a relationship between a British woman and an Indian man would be acceptable.

Rohan started to fold his clothes and put them in the suitcase. Devora stood and moved toward the door.

"I'd better check on Gerald." She looked at him for a moment, wishing that she could touch him. "I'm sorry, Rohan. You know I never wanted this to happen."

"There is no need for an apology," Rohan replied. "I am as much at fault. As I said, I have disgraced my position and your husband's employment."

"Yes, well, I've been a bit of a disgrace myself." Devora opened the door. She paused and glanced back at him, unable to help herself from asking a burning question.

"Do you regret it?" she asked.

He straightened and returned her gaze, his expression as enigmatic as it had ever been. And then, his eyes softened ever so slightly.

"No, *memsahib,* I regret nothing."

Devora smiled. "Neither do I. Must have something to do with that old soul you said I possess."

"Having an old soul also means that the karma of your many previous lives conspired to create your destiny," Rohan said. "Do not forget that."

"No, I won't. Good-bye, Rohan."

Aware of a growing ache in her heart, Devora left the room and went back to the house. She entered the sitting room from the veranda and was greeting with the noisy sound of snoring. With a sigh, Devora approached her husband, who lay on the sofa with one arm hanging to the floor and the empty gin bottle beside him. The room itself also bore signs of altercation, as two tables and a chair had been tipped over and the shards of a broken vase lay scattered on the floor.

Devora retrieved a broom and swept up the porcelain pieces, then righted the tables and chair. She threw the damaged painting of Rohan in the rubbish bin and arranged the rest of her drawings and sketches into a portfolio. She was grateful that Gerald hadn't seen fit to tear up her other work, as he might well have done in his rage.

A loud snort from Gerald split the air like thunder. Devora glanced at him, noticing that his forehead was bleeding from a small cut. She found some antiseptic and dabbed the wound. Luckily, Gerald was so gone that he didn't awaken and only muttered some unintelligible words of protest. After bandaging the cut, Devora went into the bedroom and began to pack her things. She didn't know what Gerald had in mind, but she had realized that their marriage was stifling her. That *he* was stifling her. Or else why would she have sought excitement and stimulation elsewhere?

She thought about staying to talk things out with him. She didn't even know where to go, let alone what to do next. In the end, she locked up two valises, picked up her portfolio, and headed out the door. Gerald would need time to recover and collect his own thoughts, and it was better that he do so without her there.

Devora walked out to the road and hailed a tonga. She climbed into the back, thinking that there was really only one place she could go.

"The Thompsons at the end of the road," she told the tonga *wallah*.

He nodded and began to peddle. Devora knew she was in for serious punishment, but she didn't think that the Thompsons would deny her request to temporarily stay with them. As it turned out, they didn't, although they made no attempt to hide their shock and disapproval.

"Really, Devora, this is a disgrace!" Mrs. Thompson gasped, pressing a hand to her abundant chest as if the news alone were a strain on her heart. "You and Gerald, separated? Does this have to do with the Maharaja?"

Devora sank down into a chair and sighed. She suddenly felt very tired. "No, Mrs. Thompson. I'd rather not discuss it, but I expect that the news will be all around town by tomorrow. It has to do with our head servant, Rohan."

Mrs. Thompson's eyes widened. "No."

"Yes, I'm afraid so."

"My dear girl, you must be joking!" Mrs. Thompson's eyebrows went up so high that they nearly touched her hairline. "And Gerald is throwing you out of the house for that?"

Devora gave her a confused look. "Shouldn't he?"

"Because a servant took advantage of you?" Mrs. Thompson replied. "Certainly not!"

Comprehension dawned. "Oh, Mrs. Thompson, you misunderstand me. Rohan didn't take advantage of me. Not at all."

"Then I'm afraid I don't understand."

"We had an affair," Devora explained, "Rohan and I."

Mrs. Thompson gasped in horror. "No!"

Devora nodded. "Yes. If you'd rather I leave now, I'll understand."

"My god, Devora! What on earth were you thinking?"

"I really don't want to discuss it," Devora said. "Suffice it to say that Gerald found out. I expect that he'll want a divorce. Right now, he's passed out drunk in the sitting room."

Mrs. Thompson's mouth hung open in a perfect *O*. She sat rooted to her spot in shock, as if Devora's revelation was more than she could take.

"Devora, this is scandalous! I've always known that you were a bit odd, but I never dreamed you would be capable of something like this! You'll be the disgrace of the entire community! How could you do something like that? And with an Indian man, no less!"

"That's the problem, isn't it?" Devora said, her voice tight. "He's an Indian man. If I'd been having an affair with . . . with John Fielding, then everyone would simply turn a blind eye, is that it?"

"Well, for heaven's sake, Devora, of course it's disgusting that he's an Indian man. I mean, how could you? They're so dirty!"

Devora fought back a wave of anger. "Rohan is not dirty."

"Well, whether he was Indian or not, women are simply not to be unfaithful to their husbands."

"Oh no? You'd better start practicing what you preach, Mrs. Thompson."

"What on earth are you talking about?"

"I know you're having an affair with Major Cuthbert." Devora stood and reached for her bags. "You know, I think I should find another place to stay."

Mrs. Thompson stared at her in shock for about the fourth time in the last hour. "Wh . . . how did . . . I'm not having an affair!"

"Oh, stuff it, Mrs. Thompson. I saw him screwing you against a wall the day I first met you at your garden party."

Mrs. Thompson gasped. Her face turned red with outrage as she sputtered, "How dare you speak to me like that, you little slut! You'll be cast out of town with this scandal, you know that, don't you?"

"Well, good," Devora retorted. "I'm tired of living here anyway. I love Calipore, but the British make me sick."

She started toward the door, only to be stopped by Mrs. Thompson's voice.

"Wait! Wait, Devora."

Devora turned to look at Mrs. Thompson. Regret fluttered through her as she realized that she had truly shocked the older woman beyond all reason. Mrs. Thompson's chest heaved as she began to hyperventilate, and her skin had taken on an odd bluish tint. Devora set her bags down and went to pour a glass of water from the decanter on the sideboard.

"Here, drink this," she said.

Mrs. Thompson took the glass with trembling hands and drank down half the water. She leaned back in her chair and patted her damp neck with a handkerchief as she tried to breathe.

"Better?" Devora asked.

Mrs. Thompson took a deep breath and nodded.

"I apologize," Devora said. "I spoke without thinking, and I was very rude."

"Devora, I just can't believe what you're telling me," Mrs. Thompson said. "You're having an affair with an Indian man even after all the warnings we've given you!"

"I'm not having an affair with him any longer," Devora said.

Tears pricked the backs of her eyes, but she forced them away. "Gerald dismissed him, of course. I believe he's left already."

"My god." Mrs. Thompson pressed the handkerchief against her forehead and closed her eyes. "This is all too much. What a disgrace."

"I'm sorry for having burdened you with it," Devora said. "As I said, I'll find another place to stay."

"No, no." Mrs. Thompson took another drink of water and shook her head. "No one else will take you in once the news gets around, and you can't possibly take a room in the village. Heaven knows what other Indian men will try to do once they hear that you willingly gave yourself to one Indian man. For your own safety, you'll have to stay here."

"That's very kind of you, but I don't want to cause problems for you. You have your own reputation to consider."

"My husband is the chief officer in this district and has been for ten years," Mrs. Thompson said. "I dare say that our reputation can withstand an illicit affair, even if it is such a reprehensible one. Really, Devora, the whole thing is so utterly disgusting."

She stood and walked toward the back of the bungalow. "You can stay in our guest bedroom until you and Gerald work things out."

Devora couldn't deny the fact that in spite of Mrs. Thompson's horror and contempt, she was being decent about allowing Devora to stay.

"Thank you. I do appreciate this." She followed Mrs. Thompson into the bedroom and placed her valises next to the dressing table.

"Yes, well, we don't have much of a choice. I certainly can't turn you out onto the streets." Mrs. Thompson waved toward the chiffarobe. "You can hang your dresses in there. You'd better stay in here until I explain the situation to my husband. He is not going to be happy about this."

"No, I expect he won't."

"I'll bring you some tea and biscuits, but I don't want you

to come out until I tell you that you can." Mrs. Thompson headed for the door, but then stopped and turned. "And, Devora?"

Devora looked up from opening a valise. "Yes?"

"Please don't bring up Major General Cuthbert in front of my husband. He will not understand."

"Of course not."

Mrs. Thompson nodded, pursing her lips slightly as she left the room. Devora unpacked her dresses and hung them up, then sank down onto the bed with a sigh. Her entire life had changed in the course of a few hours, although for better or worse she could not say.

chapter fifteen

Devora sat next to Mrs. Thompson on the sofa. Gerald sat across from her, his elbows resting on his knees and his hands clasped between them. He was staring intently at the floor, as if it would help him formulate his sentences. Devora gazed at him for a long moment. He looked horrible, as if he hadn't slept or shaved in two days since his discovery of her betrayal.

"I'm sorry," Devora finally said, aware of distinct pangs of regret. "I know that means nothing to you, but I am. I didn't want you to find out like that."

"Oh, but you did want me to find out," Gerald replied bitterly. "Goddamn it, Devora. I thought you loved me."

Mr. Thompson, who sat in an overstuffed chair puffing on his pipe, reached out and put his hand on Gerald's shoulder. "There's no doubt, my boy, that she's deceived you. But cursing her out will solve nothing."

"I did love you," Devora said. "I wouldn't have married you if I hadn't."

"Then why in the hell did you have to go off and fuck . . . sorry, Mrs. Thompson . . . have an affair with a damn Indian?"

"You did as well, I believe."

Mrs. Thompson set her teacup down on the table and stood. "I think it would be best if Reginald and I left you to your discussion," she said. "This is between you. Come along, dear."

"We'll just be out on the veranda," Mr. Thompson said, as he followed his wife outside.

Gerald ran a hand through his hair and gave a tired sigh. "All right, Devora, look. It's common enough for British men to have Indian mistresses. The number of schools for Eurasian children is proof enough of that. But you know that things are different for women! My god, Devora, everyone is already talking about you! They're calling you a whore and a slut, not to mention a traitor."

"They can say what they like," Devora said, realizing that she wasn't particularly disturbed by his words. She had never really cared what the British community thought of her. That, no doubt, would be her undoing.

"All right, look," Gerald said. "I've given this some thought. I think we can work this out. If we claim that Rohan attacked you and that you didn't consent to an affair with him, we might be able to get through this. The only people that know the true story are the Thompsons. I'm sure they will help us cover it up."

"Oh, Gerald." A rush of sadness swept over Devora. "I'm not going to claim that Rohan attacked me. He did nothing of the kind."

"Dammit, Devora, you have your reputation to consider!" Gerald snapped. "Not to mention mine! You'll at least have a chance of salvaging it if you claim that you were a victim. Everyone will believe you over an Indian man, regardless of how rebellious you are."

"Gerald, I'm not going to concoct a lie to cover up the truth," Devora said. The mere idea of Rohan's previous experience with a false rape accusation still made her nauseous whenever she thought of it. "I had a consensual affair with him. I refuse to accuse him of such a hideous act."

Gerald leveled a long look on her. "You realize that this is the only chance you have of saving our marriage," he informed her. "If you agree to do this, I will stick by you and let everyone know that you have my support. If not, I have no choice but to divorce you."

"Then you have no choice," Devora replied. "I'm sorry. I won't lie like that."

With a mutter of frustration, Gerald stood up and began pacing furiously across the room.

"What the hell are you going to do without me?" he snapped. "What, Devora? Where are you going to go? You're nothing without me, you know that, don't you? You can't stay in Calipore, and you certainly don't have the money for passage back to England."

"I don't know what I'll do," Devora admitted.

"Devora, I think you need to seriously consider my offer," Gerald said, his voice cold. "If you do, then you have a slight chance of salvaging both your reputation and our marriage. But if you let the truth get out, then everything will be in shambles."

"Gerald, don't ask me this again," Devora said. "I'm not going to accuse Rohan of anything, least of all rape."

Gerald eyed her suspiciously. "Are you trying to hide something?" he asked. "I can't even believe that you would willingly have an affair with an Indian. He hasn't threatened you or anything, has he?"

"Of course not. I simply won't lie about the fact that I had an affair with him. If that makes me the disgrace of the British community, then so be it."

"You, hell," Gerald said bitterly. "What about me? What happens to my reputation when people realize that you decided to fuck a bloody servant?"

"I'm sure that everyone will be very sympathetic toward you," Devora told him. "As you said, I'm the one who is considered the whore and the slut. The British *memsahibs* will pity you greatly for having married me in the first place."

Gerald shoved his hands into his pockets, his shoulders sagging as he appeared to realize that this was the end.

"Devora, you know I love you," he said. His voice cracked slightly. "If you'd just cooperate, I think we can get through this."

Guilt lanced through Devora like a thousand needles. She shook her head. "I'm sorry, Gerald. There's nothing else I can do. I betrayed you, and I admit it."

"But, we had a good marriage!"

To Devora's surprise, Gerald approached her and went down on his knees in front of her chair. He stared at her with blood-shot, tired eyes that nearly broke her heart.

"Didn't we?" he asked plaintively.

"Yes, of course we did."

"Then what happened?"

"It's not you, Gerald," Devora said. She wrapped her hands around his and clutched them tightly. "It's completely my fault. You've always been good to me."

"Was it Kalindi? Was that when you decided to get revenge, after you'd realized the truth about her?"

"No, it wasn't for revenge. Kalindi had nothing to do with it."

"Devora, please, let's work this out," Gerald begged. He gripped her hands hard, looking completely defeated. "We'll think of a story and call in the police commissioner right away. What does it matter if Rohan is arrested? He's nothing, Devora. He's just a servant. India has thousands of servants."

Devora pulled her hands away from his and shook her head again. She knew that she was hardly a model of morality, but the thought of falsely accusing a man of assault was abhorrent to her. Particularly when that man was Rohan. "No, Gerald. I won't do that. And I dislike you for even suggesting that I accuse an innocent man of a crime simply to save our reputations."

"Devora, it's the only way to fix this mess!"

"Then, *this mess* will have to remain broken, I'm afraid."

Gerald stared at her for a long minute. His mouth tightened

into a thin, hard line as he pulled away from her. He nodded, standing up and brushing off his trousers.

"All right, then," he said. "This is your last chance, Devora. I will file for a divorce as soon as possible unless you change your mind."

"I won't change my mind."

"Then our relationship is over." Gerald picked up his hat, giving her one long, final look. And then he turned and strode out the door.

"I simply don't understand you." Mrs. Thompson shook her head and began to butter a piece of toast. "You're a very odd girl, Devora."

"Very odd, indeed," Mr. Thompson agreed. "You're what my mother would call a bad seed."

Devora bit her tongue to prevent herself from retorting. The Thompsons were being very decent about allowing her to stay with them, even if she did have to tolerate their constant contempt. She cracked open her soft-boiled egg and focused her attention on picking at the shell.

"He's just an Indian man," Mrs. Thompson went on. "I mean, really, Devora, they *are* dispensable. It isn't as if this country doesn't have a million of them."

"You're ruined now, you know that, don't you?" Mr. Thompson sipped his tea and patted his mustache. "Corrupted. No decent British man will want you now."

"Good," Devora replied, unable to help herself. "I don't want a British man anyhow."

"Well, what on earth do you intend to do?" Mrs. Thompson asked. "I'm sorry, but you can't stay here forever."

"I don't know yet." Over the past few days, Devora had begun to realize that her tenuous situation was cause for unease. She honestly had no idea what to do.

However, a thought had been brewing in her mind since the previous night. She suspected that it wouldn't work, but she wanted to at least try. "Would you mind terribly if I borrowed your carriage for the morning? I need to run an errand."

"You shouldn't go out, Devora," Mr. Thompson said. "Everyone is utterly appalled by what you have done."

"This will only take a few hours," Devora said. "I want to visit a friend who might be able to help me."

"Not that horrible servant, surely?"

"No, not Rohan."

Mr. and Mrs. Thompson exchanged exasperated looks. Then, Mr. Thompson threw his napkin on the table and pushed his chair back.

"Oh, all right, Devora. I expect there's little else you can do that will damage your reputation any more than it already is."

Devora murmured her thanks and excused herself from the breakfast table. She went back to her room and fixed her hair, then powdered her nose and applied lipstick. After donning a flowered hat and gloves, she picked up her pocketbook and went outside.

A servant waited at the carriage for her. He helped her inside, then swung up to the driver's seat. "Where, *memsahib*?"

"To the Maharaja's palace, please."

He gave her a strange look, but shrugged and urged the horse forward. Devora sat back and watched the British bungalows pass by. She did regret the way things had turned out, but she was also glad that she would no longer have to define herself by proprieties constructed by a group of very narrow-minded individuals. She passed several British women, who were either walking or riding in their own carriages. In each case, their expressions changed to shocked horror as they recognized her. Then they would turn away and whisper to one another behind their hands.

Devora let her thoughts drift to Rohan. She wondered what had happened to him in the few days since his encounter with Gerald. Had he found a place to stay, or was he being shunned by the Indian community for his intimacy with a British woman? Perhaps such an association was considered to be consorting with the enemy.

The carriage driver passed through the village and onto the road leading toward the palace. Devora looked at the flowing Ganges River parallel to the road, remembering when Rohan had told her that she possessed an old soul. If that were indeed the case, then her soul was not cooperating to reveal her understanding of life's mysteries. Instead, she was beginning to feel both nervous and very alone.

The driver pulled up to the entrance of the palace and glanced back at Devora. "You wish me to announce you, *memsahib?*"

"Yes, please. My name is Devora Hawthorne."

The driver hopped off the carriage and went to talk to one of the palace guards. He looked at Devora, nodded, and then disappeared into the palace. After a moment, he returned.

"The Maharaja says you may enter."

"Thank you." Devora followed him inside, her nervousness increasing as she realized that she was willingly entering the lion's den. She had no escape here, but she also had no other choice than to talk to the Maharaja.

The guard led her into the dining room, where the Maharaja was seated at the head of the table with an array of dishes spread out before him. A pretty young woman lavishly dressed in silk and gold sat in a corner of the room. Devora recognized her as Channa, the woman who had hinted that Devora was lucky to escape the Maharaja's cruelty. Channa eyed Devora curiously, but made no comment.

The Maharaja glanced up from his plate of curry and rice, but did not bother to stand. "Well, Mrs. Hawthorne. To what do I owe this honor?"

The guard pulled a chair away from the table. Devora sat down, clutching her hands together as she tried to think of a way to phrase her question.

"Thank you for agreeing to see me. I have a small problem."

The Maharaja swallowed some water and chuckled. "Yes, I have heard. I would call it a big problem, wouldn't you?"

"Perhaps."

"You find a servant to be more satisfying than a prince, do you?"

Devora winced slightly. The last thing she wanted was contempt from the Maharaja, although she should have expected it. He knew everything that went on in the district, so it stood to reason that he would have been one of the first to hear of the scandal.

"As you know, I've left my husband," she said, ignoring the question. "I've come to ask for your help."

The Maharaja's eyes widened slightly as he stared at her. Then, he started to laugh, his belly shaking. "My dear Mrs. Hawthorne, you must be joking. You want me to help you? After you abused me so?"

Devora's fingernails dug into her palms as she tightened her hands into fists. "I didn't abuse you. Both times, you were forcing yourself on me."

The Maharaja spread his curry-stained hands out in a gesture of supplication. "Now how is that possible after we had been so intimate? You are terribly mistaken."

Devora fought the urge to argue with him. She couldn't afford to insult him right now. "Well, regardless of what happened then, I need your help now. I want to return to England, but I don't have enough money for passage back."

"And you want me to fund your return to England? Why should I help you escape this hornet's nest that you are responsible for stirring up?"

Good question, Devora thought.

"What about a train ticket to Bombay?" she asked. "No one knows me in Bombay. I can at least start a new life there."

The Maharaja shoveled rice into his mouth and shook his head. "You cannot start a new life. You are ruined, you know. A tainted woman."

He seemed to enjoy telling her this.

"Yes, so I've been informed," Devora said. "Look, I haven't asked any of the British because I know that most of them would refuse my request. I think the Thompsons would loan me the money, but I don't want to be indebted to them any more than I already am."

"Hence, you have come to me, thinking that you can sweet-talk me into helping you."

"I'm not trying to sweet-talk you. I'm simply asking for your help. I'll pay you back once I'm settled again and making money. I know that a return ticket to England would hardly make a dent in your fortune."

"I dare say that money is hardly the element in question."

"Then what is in question?" Devora asked.

"What you are willing to give me in return."

"If you're asking me to have sex with you again, I won't," Devora said, pushing back her chair. "I can see that coming here was a waste of time. I'll be leaving now."

She headed for the door, but the Maharaja's voice stopped her. "Wait, Mrs. Hawthorne. I will pay for your return ticket to England."

Devora turned and eyed him suspiciously. "What do you want from me?"

The Maharaja picked up a piece of nan bread and swirled it around on his plate to soak up the curry juices. "I believe you are aware that a number of Indians have been arrested for rioting."

"Yes, I've heard that."

"I want a list of their names," the Maharaja said. "As well as the names of people who are under suspicion."

Devora's eyes narrowed. "Why? So that you can help release them, and then offer them protection?"

The Maharaja ripped off a piece of bread with his teeth. "You see, Mrs. Hawthorne, the anti-British movement is increasing daily. If we can accumulate enough manpower on our side, it will not be long before the British are compelled to leave."

"So you're saying that you want me to help you build forces against the British."

The Maharaja shrugged. "Call it what you will, Mrs. Hawthorne. You can get the lists for me, I'm sure. After all, you are staying with one of the senior British officers."

Devora hesitated, but she knew that she had no other choice. She nodded. "All right, I'll try. I want the money first."

"Oh, no. How do I know that you won't leave without fulfilling your end of the bargain?"

Another good question, Devora thought.

"I'll bring you the information by the end of the week, then," she said. "And you are to tell no one."

"Do not worry. I would not admit to an association with you."

"Nor I with you," Devora retorted. "May I use the powder room before I leave?"

"Yes, you know where it is."

Devora left the dining room and walked out onto the mezzanine of the inner courtyard. She went into the bathroom and pressed a damp cloth against her neck. Nerves stretched like rubber bands in her stomach. Would she be considered a traitor if the British discovered her subversion?

Devora looked at herself in the mirror, wondering if she even recognized the woman who returned her gaze. She wouldn't falsely accuse an Indian man of assault, but she was willing to help strengthen anti-British forces? She was almost becoming a stranger to herself.

She left the bathroom, closing the door behind her. Her startled gaze met the dark eyes of Channa, who stood outside next to the railing. She appeared to be waiting for Devora.

Devora looked at her for a moment, not knowing what to say, then turned to leave.

"Wait, *memsahib*." Channa approached Devora cautiously, pulling a fold of her sari over the lower half of her face.

"Yes?" Devora asked.

"Take this." Channa thrust a small silk purse at her.
"Quickly!"

"What—"

"Take it!" Channa peered frantically down the mezzanine,
as if expecting someone to appear at any second.

Devora closed her fingers around the purse. The Indian
woman turned and rushed off, disappearing behind an open
door.

Confused, Devora looked at the purse and started to open
it.

"Mrs. Hawthorne, are you ready to leave?"

Devora looked up at the approaching Maharaja. She quickly
opened her pocketbook and hid the silk purse inside. "Yes,
thank you."

He walked her outside and waited while she climbed into the
waiting carriage. "I will expect to hear from you at the end of
the week."

"I'll return on Friday."

The Maharaja snapped a few words of Hindi at the carriage
driver, who guided the horse back out to the road. When they
were a good distance away from the palace, Devora opened her
pocketbook and removed the silk purse. She unfastened the
button and peered inside. Her heart leaped into her throat at
the sight of the glittering jewels that lay within.

What on earth? Stunned, Devora spilled the contents out
onto her lap and found herself staring at a gold necklace embedded with precious gems, several gold bracelets, and a pair
of diamond earrings. She pressed a hand to her chest in sheer
shock. Why would Channa have given her all of this? This was
worth a fortune.

Devora turned and looked back at the fading oasis of the
palace. She remembered seeing Channa not only during her first
lunch with the Maharaja, but also during her last visit to the
palace when she had entered the woman's room by mistake.
Devora remembered the overflowing boxes of jewelry and gems
that she had seen on the dressing table. If that cache was any-

thing to judge by, what she held in her lap now was a minuscule part of the Maharaja's fortune. And of his harem's ornamentations.

Her heart pounded as if she had run a mile. She carefully replaced the jewelry in the purse and put the purse back into her pocketbook. Channa must have realized that the Maharaja would never miss these few riches. But why would she give them to Devora?

Devora clutched her pocketbook tightly and tried to reason out such an extraordinary gesture. Innately, however, she knew that she would never be able to. Perhaps Channa's firsthand experience with the Maharaja's cruelty had caused her to sympathize with Devora's plight. Or perhaps she didn't want to see him manipulate women anymore. What had Channa told her that night? *You are lucky. You are free.*

Devora held the fortune against her chest and realized that indeed she was.

chapter sixteen

I'll be leaving tomorrow," Devora said. She swallowed the last of the wine, feeling more relaxed and secure than she had felt in weeks. She knew that she had to at least leave the district of Calipore as soon as possible, lest the Maharaja discover what had transpired between her and Channa. The sooner she left, the better.

Mrs. Thompson frowned. "Where will you go?"

"I have enough money for a train ticket back to Bombay," Devora explained. "From there, I'll obtain passage back to England."

"How do you possibly have enough money for that?" Mr. Thompson asked.

"I have just enough," Devora said, thinking that was quite an understatement. She had managed to sell two of the gold bracelets to a merchant in the village, and he had given her a far greater amount of money than she had expected. "You've been very kind to me, but I really must leave."

"Yes, it's a bit difficult, being the center of a scandal," Mrs. Thompson said. She patted her forehead with her napkin. "Well, I suppose it's best that you leave soon. Then Gerald can get on with his life. I expect people will still be talking about you, but the gossip will die down more quickly if you're not here."

"Yes, my thoughts exactly. If you'll excuse me, I'm going to go and pack my things. My train leaves at ten tomorrow morning."

Devora stood and returned to her room. She finished packing her things, then changed into a dark blue dress and a pair of flat-soled shoes. She took a blue silk scarf and wrapped it loosely around her head, then sat on the bed and waited for dusk to melt into pure darkness. After an hour, she heard the Thompsons retire to their room.

Slowly, Devora made her way into the sitting room and went out the front door. She closed the door quietly behind her and hurried down the steps of the bungalow. Her heart beat with silent fierceness as she walked out to the road. She knew the dangers involved in a woman walking alone at night, but she had no choice. Trying to ignore the stares of passing men, she flagged down a tonga *wallah* and told him to take her into the village.

Even at night, people wandered around the village purchasing goods from the few stalls that remained open. Goats and cows wandered aimlessly about, oblivious to everything but the possibility of food. Devora directed the tonga *wallah* to Kalindi's room and told him to wait.

She knocked loudly on the front door, relieved to see a light on in the window. "Kalindi! Open the door."

The door opened. Kalindi stared at Devora in shock for a moment, taking a step backward. *"Memsahib!"*

"Kalindi, do you know where Rohan is?"

"Oh, *memsahib,* I am so sorry!" Tears filled Kalindi's eyes suddenly, and she pressed a hand against her mouth. "The *sahib* forced me to tell what I knew! I did not want to hurt you."

"Never mind, Kalindi. It's over and done with."

"Please, please forgive me," Kalindi begged as the tears spilled over.

"Yes, I forgive you," Devora said, glancing behind her with fear that someone would recognize her. "Kalindi, I need your help now. Do you know where Rohan is?"

"This is all my fault!" Kalindi wailed.

Devora stepped forward and grasped the young woman by the shoulders, giving her a gentle shake. "Kalindi, please! I forgive you. This isn't your fault. I was the one who had an affair with Rohan. You had no choice when you told my husband. I know that. But I need your help now. Where is Rohan?"

Kalindi hiccuped and swiped at her tears. "Rohan?"

"Yes. He was dismissed, and he said he would find a room here in the village. Do you know where he is?"

"Oh, wait. I think he informed Lota." Kalindi went back into her room, then returned with a happy expression. "Yes, Lota knows where Rohan is."

"Wonderful! Where?"

"Oh, you want to know *where*. Wait, I will ask." Kalindi hurried back to ask Lota. "Okay, *memsahib,* he is here in the village. You want to see him?"

"Yes, I do."

"I tell the tonga *wallah* where to go, yes?"

"Yes, please." Relieved, Devora climbed back into the tonga as Kalindi conversed with the *wallah*. Then, Kalindi came around and looked at Devora with her wide eyes and tear-streaked face.

"You are leaving forever?"

"Yes, Kalindi, I'm afraid so."

"I am very distressed by this."

Devora smiled and reached out to put her hand on the younger woman's cheek. "Don't be. I think I'm going to be quite happy. None of this is your fault, Kalindi. Please remember that."

Kalindi sniffed and nodded. "Good-bye, *memsahib*."

"Good-bye."

Kalindi said something to the *wallah* again. He began peddling toward the center of the village. After about fifteen minutes, he stopped in front of a small whitewashed bungalow next to a spice shop. Devora paid the *wallah* and went to the front door. Her heart raced wildly, but she forced herself to knock. No answer.

"Come on," Devora muttered, knocking again with more force.

After an infinite moment, the door opened to reveal Rohan clad in loose cotton trousers and a white shirt. An overwhelming relief flooded through Devora like an ocean wave.

Shock flashed in Rohan's expression at the sight of her. *"Memsahib."*

"Hello, Rohan. May I come in?"

"Yes. Yes, of course." He pulled the door open wider to let her pass, then closed it. "What are you doing here? How did you find me?"

"Kalindi told me." Devora entered his room, which was about the size of the Thompson's bathroom. There was room only for a bed and a small desk. Rohan's clothes hung neatly on hooks from the walls, and his shoes were lined up underneath the bed. "Did you have a difficult time finding a room to rent?"

"No, *memsahib*. This belongs to the father of a good friend. He has kept the rent low for me." Rohan gestured to the desk chair. "Please, sit down."

"That's kind of him." Devora sat, her eyes drinking in the sight of him. He looked good, at least, if a little tired. "Have you found work elsewhere yet?"

"No, I am still looking."

Devora sighed. "I'm sorry."

"I have told you that there is no need for apology. I am as much at fault. The time for regrets has passed anyhow."

"Yes, I believe you're right." Devora clenched her hands together, wishing she could touch him, that he would take her in his arms and make the unpleasantness disappear.

"Where have you been staying this past week?" Rohan asked.

"With the Thompsons."

"Good Lord. Now, for that, I am indeed sorry."

Devora smiled for what seemed like the first time in years. "At least they've been good enough to let me stay. I doubt any of the other British would, not with the scandal I've created."

Rohan sat down on the bed and gave her an amused look. "I suppose you have finally let the world know that you are different."

"*Corrupted* is the word I've been hearing," Devora replied. "And *scandalous*."

"Does it bother you very much?" Rohan asked.

Devora shrugged. "Not as much as it should, I think. I'm sorry for having hurt Gerald, but I suspect our marriage wouldn't have lasted anyway. He's well entrenched in the British civil lines. He would have realized sooner or later that I wouldn't fit in."

"As you would have as well."

Devora smiled again and nodded.

"And what will you do now?" Rohan asked.

"I have a ticket for Bombay," Devora explained. "I leave tomorrow, and I wanted to say good-bye to you before I left."

"I see. And from there you will return to England?"

"I expect I will. Although I might stay in Bombay for a while. I don't know. I haven't made up my mind yet."

"You appear to have a great deal of freedom."

"I've had a nice surprise." Devora explained what happened with the Maharaja's harem woman and the jewelry.

Rohan's eyebrows lifted as he listened. "That is indeed good fortune. You have positive karma then."

"I don't know why," Devora said. "I haven't exactly been a moral person."

"Remember that karma and destiny also come from previous lives," Rohan replied. "And you have been honest to yourself."

Devora considered his words. "Yes, I guess I have."

"I will miss you."

Devora looked at him in surprise. "You will?"

He nodded. "I have always found you very intriguing. I will miss our conversations."

"And here I thought you just found me frustrating and head-strong."

"Well, that, too," Rohan agreed.

Devora chuckled. "I'll miss you, too, Rohan. You're the truest person I've met in India. Even in my entire life. I'm sorry that we . . ." Her voice trailed off, and she shook her head. "Never mind. I should be getting back before the Thompsons realize I'm gone."

"I am glad you came to see me."

"So am I." Devora stood and approached him, clasping his hands in hers. "Thank you for everything."

They looked at each other for a moment, and then Rohan reached up to curl his hand around the back of her neck. His palm felt warm and strong against her skin. He drew her head down toward him slowly as his dark eyes began to burn with heat. Devora loved that flare of passion, knowing the sensualities promised by his gaze. Heart pulsing, she moved easily into the kiss. An intense contentment overcame her, as if she had known all along that by coming to see him, she was returning to a place of security and peace. With a moan, she pressed her mouth against his and slid her hands into the coarseness of his hair.

Rohan's lips parted slightly, his tongue flickering out to caress her mouth with deliberate ease. He tugged Devora down onto his lap, sinking onto the bed until he was lying on his back and she hovered over him. Her knees pressed against his hips, her sex brushing tantalizingly against the increasing bulge in his trousers. Bracing her hands on either side of his head, Devora deepened their kiss. She stroked her tongue over his lips, loving the slightly rough sensation and the faint taste of spices.

She lifted her head to look down at him, stunned by the inflamed darkness of his eyes. Such unfathomable depths. There had been a time when she thought that she would never break through his shield, that he would forever be inaccessible to her. And now, looking into those eyes of his, she realized that no one had been *as* accessible to her as Rohan. The disconcerting part was that so many mysteries lay uncovered within him, layers that she had never unfolded. And yet she had never felt so close to another person in her entire life.

"My god," she whispered in amazement. "It's inconceivable."

Rohan stroked his hands up her back, his fingers tracing her spine. "What is, *memsahib?*"

"You and I. Isn't it?"

"Of course. That is what makes it so good."

He pulled her down toward him again to plunder her mouth with his. Devora shoved her hands into his hair, delighting in the way the thick strands felt against her palms. She drew her tongue over his lower lip and pressed her body downward to rub her sex over his throbbing erection. The intimate sensation of his cock pushing against her through the confines of their clothing sent a rainfall of pleasure through her.

With a moan, Devora tugged Rohan's shirt off his body and sat back to look at the gorgeous expanse of his chest. She stroked her hands over him, loving the texture of his hair-roughened skin and wanting to memorize everything about him. Her fingertips traced the structure of his rib cage as she bent to capture one of his flat nipples between her lips. Rohan groaned and clutched the back of her neck, pushing his hips upward against the apex of her thighs. Devora rotated her hips slowly and rubbed their sexes together. Moisture flowed from her vulva, flowing down to dampen the fabric of his trousers.

Devora gave Rohan a wicked grin as she moved down to hook her fingers underneath his waistband. She pulled the trousers off his legs, her pulse surging at the sight of his freed erection. Grasping the shaft in her hand, she stroked up to the tip. A sheen of sweat broke out on Rohan's forehead as he watched her touching him. Devora bent to take him in her mouth, wanting to please him as she had never wanted to please a man before. His cock throbbed against the surface of her tongue, the tangy taste of him filling her mouth deliciously. Devora closed her eyes and took him in fully. Rohan's breath came in harsh pants as she slid her lips over his shaft and traced the veins with her tongue. His fingers twined through her hair.

Devora pulled back with a slow, luscious movement, flicking her tongue into the little indentation of the glans.

"Your dress," Rohan whispered, his voice hoarse. "Take it off."

Devora unbuttoned her dress and pushed it off her shoulders, then removed her slip. She straddled Rohan's hips again, grasping his cock and guiding it to the opening of her body. He reached up to touch her swaying breasts, skimming his fingers over her areolae until sublime tension wrapped itself leisurely around her body. Devora moaned with pleasure at the feeling of his cock pressing against her, and she eased herself down onto him with a desperation borne of need.

"Oh yes . . ." She braced her hands on either side of his head and lifted her hips, allowing him to thrust in and out of her with increasing movements. Her clitoris rubbed lusciously against him, expanding her ache to infinite depths.

"Turn over." Rohan clutched her hips, rolling them both over so that he was above her. He pushed her legs farther apart and sank into her with a hoarse groan. The slick, juicy length of his cock pounded into her as he began to work his hips back and forth. Pure sensation wiped out all reason and thought, leaving them submerged in the rough carnality of their union.

Whimpers spilled from Devora's throat as she writhed heatedly underneath him, never wanting them to separate, never wanting this to end. She wrapped her legs around his thighs and clutched his buttocks to urge him even closer. His testicles slapped against her sex with every thrust, his mouth open against her neck. Devora pushed her hips up to increase the sensation on her clit, digging her fingers into his buttocks when the pressure began to mount. His mouth covered hers, his lips muffling her cries. An orgasm broke with powerful sweetness over her, washing her in the scent, taste, and feel of both ecstasy and her lover. Rohan's cock stroked in and out of her with intense movements, filling her repeatedly before he groaned low in his throat and succumbed to his own rapture.

Devora clutched him to her, their chests heaving as they tried to catch their breath. She skimmed her hands over Rohan's muscled back, suddenly wishing that she didn't have to leave so soon. Rohan pressed his lips against her neck and moved to roll away from her.

Devora tightened her arms around him, murmuring a sound of protest. "Don't go."

"I am crushing you." Rohan moved onto his back and pulled her on top of him. "Better."

With a contented sigh, Devora rested her head against his chest. She let her leg slide between his in a position that felt eternally natural.

"What time must you leave tomorrow?" Rohan asked.

"My train leaves at ten," Devora replied. "But I have to go back and pick up my belongings from the Thompsons."

She looked at him, propping her head on her hand. "I wish you could come to Bombay with me. You probably shouldn't stay in Calipore either. I suspect that no British family will hire you." She grinned. "Well, the women might."

Rohan gave her a slight frown. "You know I did not do this regularly."

"Oh, no. I didn't mean to imply that. I was only joking." Devora reached out with her finger to trace the lines of his mouth. A thought occurred to her that was both thrilling and terrifying. "Why don't you?"

"Why don't I what?"

"Come to Bombay with me. I have more than enough money to buy you a ticket."

"I have enough of my own money. I do not need you to pay for me."

"Does that mean you'll come with me?" Devora asked.

Rohan looked at her for a long minute, brushing her hair away from her face. The touch of his fingers was light and soothing. "I do not think that is wise. An Indian man and a British woman cannot travel together."

"We won't be traveling together," Devora pointed out. "I'll have to ride in a separate car with the other British women anyway. We'll just be on the same train, and we can meet at Victoria station in Bombay."

"And then what?" Rohan asked.

Devora shrugged. "I don't know. You'd have an easier time finding a job there. I know that much."

"True enough," Rohan allowed. "But, I could just as easily return to Delhi."

Devora sighed, disappointed that he didn't seem more enthused about the idea. "You know, you can be annoyingly practical when you want to be," she said. "It was only a suggestion. If you don't want to go, then don't."

Rohan splayed his hands over her moist back, rubbing her skin with gentle strokes. "And a good suggestion."

Devora looked at him as hope sparked in her. "Really?"

"You should not travel completely alone, anyhow. It is not safe for a British woman to do so."

"Great, you can be my bodyguard," Devora said dryly.

"I would like to guard your body." Amusement flashed in Rohan's expression.

"It's yours to guard if you want to." Devora kissed him again, sliding her tongue over the smooth surface of his teeth. "And do other things with," she murmured.

"You are indeed a wicked woman, *memsahib*."

"Yes, I know. A wicked woman with an old soul. What on earth are you going to do with me?"

Rohan's hands curved over the globes of Devora's bottom and pressed her pelvis against him.

"Ah, Devora. I will think of something."

Devora lifted her head and stared at him, stunned by the sound of his deep voice saying her name. "What did you just call me?"

"You have a lovely name."

"Say it again."

"Devora."

Warmth broke open inside Devora spilling a sudden, incredible peace to every corner of her soul.

"That's nice," she murmured. "I like that."

"As do I, my Devora."

epilogue

London, 15 years later

Devora set the old scrapbook aside and turned on the light above her desk. The approach of winter had begun to result in shorter days. Darkness invaded her workroom much sooner than it had before, but she didn't mind since the windows overlooked the sky and her garden. There was a sublime pleasure in watching the sky and earth become submerged by the twilight. Devora gazed out the window for a moment at the sky painted with red and gold cloud ribbons. Her garden below still bore remnants of blossoms and flourishing greenery, but soon a cloak of white snow would cover the grass and plants. How lovely it would be.

Reluctantly breaking out of her reverie, Devora returned her attention to her latest array of drawings illustrating different aspects of Indian mythology. Her publisher had requested that she turn out at least ten watercolor paintings to include in her next book, and Devora was only too happy to comply. She couldn't wait to see what color plates of her work would look like. Her last four books had been enormously successful, although the first one about the Khajuraho temples had to be published by an underground British publisher because of the sexual content. Still, that hadn't prevented it from becoming a success.

"Tea, *memsahib*?"

Devora turned at the sound of the teasing male voice. She smiled as Rohan entered the room with a tea tray in his hands and a package tucked under his arm.

"Thank you," Devora said. "You didn't have to bring it up here. I could have come down."

"I know you are working hard." Rohan set the tray down and poured two cups of tea. "Is it going well?"

"Yes, very well. What's in the package?"

Rohan handed her the package. "From your publisher, I think."

Devora picked up a pair of scissors and cut open the package. Eagerly, she reached inside and pulled out an advance copy of her next book.

"Oh, look! The cover is beautiful." Devora ran her hand over the glossy cover, admiring the gold lettering that read *Parvati's Wish: The Goddesses of India.*

"Yes, it is attractive," Rohan agreed. He touched her hair gently. "I am very proud of you."

Devora smiled at him. His black hair was shot through with threads of gray now, and his abdomen had thickened slightly over the years, but Devora had never considered him to be more handsome than she did now. Fifteen years ago, she had stayed in Bombay for an entire year before booking passage to England. She hadn't even considered the notion of Rohan returning with her until he casually mentioned something about always having wanted to see Westminster Abbey. He refused to take her money for a ticket, choosing instead to remain in Bombay and work until he had enough. Eight long months later, he had arrived in England. Devora soon realized that she couldn't have imagined what her life would be like without him.

"The publisher is going to find out about distributing it in India," Devora said. "I hope they do. Then, perhaps we'll have an excuse to take a trip back there."

Rohan shook his head. "There is much unrest in India now,"

he said. "I do not know what will happen, but the Indians are determined to free themselves from British control."

"As well they should," Devora muttered. "I heard that Gerald is still there, only he's in Calcutta now. Apparently, he's a top official in the freedom negotiations, only of course on the British side."

Rohan shrugged. "We all live according to a certain destiny."

"Really? And what was mine?"

"To go to India and discover the true nature of your old soul," Rohan replied. "You needed to find the place of its birth."

Devora lifted an eyebrow skeptically. "You mean I was a withered Indian woman in a previous life?"

Rohan chuckled. "Honestly, Devora, I would not be surprised."

"And you? What was your destiny?"

He smiled at her. "To find you, of course."